RIVER OF MY
BLOOD

Selina Hossain is a prolific writer and has so far published thirty novels, eleven volumes of short fiction, twenty children's books and seven articles. Her stories and novels have been translated into many languages, such as English, French, Korean, Russian, Hindi and Finnish. She has also edited fifteen books on gender and women's issues. Selina has won national and international awards, amongst them the National Award for Best Story. She also received the Rabindra Memorial Award for her novel *Gaitry Sandhya* in 2010, and was made Premchand fellow at Sahitya Akademi, New Delhi in 2011 for her contribution to South Asian literature.

*

Dr Pascal Zinck is an associate professor of postcolonial literature at the University of Paris Sorbonne Cité with a PhD in English literature from the Sorbonne. He has published extensively on Kazuo Ishiguro and postcolonial Sri Lankan fiction with a more recent focus on terror studies in South Asian literature and film, as well as Pakistani anglophone literature. He is currently engaged in research for a book on Pakistani fiction.

Jackie Kabir is a Bangladeshi writer and translator. She obtained her MA in English Literature from the University of Dhaka. Many of her translations have been anthologized, among them are *Contemporary Short Stories from Bangladesh*, Selina Hossain's *Fugitive Colours*, Jharna Rahman's *The Dawn of a Waning Moon*, Papree Rahman's *Lilies, Lanterns and Lullabies*. A translation of one of her short stories: 'A Flash of Lightning' was anthologized in Ganthagolpo and in the online magazine Write.this. Jackie Kabir also contributed to the translation of Kazi Nazrul Islam's 'Badhon Hara' as Unfettered.

RIVER OF MY
BLOOD

Selina Hossain

Edited by Dr Pascal Zinck
& translated by Jackie Kabir

RUPA

Published by
Rupa Publications India Pvt. Ltd 2016
7/16, Ansari Road, Daryaganj
New Delhi 110002

Sales centres:
Allahabad Bengaluru Chennai
Hyderabad Jaipur Kathmandu
Kolkata Mumbai

Copyright © Selina Hossain 2016
Translation copyright © Dr Pascal Zinck 2016

This is a work of fiction. Names, characters, places and incidents are either the product of the author's imagination or are used fictitiously, and any resemblance to any actual persons, living or dead, events or locales is entirely coincidental.

ISBN: 978-81-291-3734-0

10 9 8 7 6 5 4 3 2 1

First impression 2016

The moral right of the author has been asserted.

Typeset by SÜRYA, New Delhi
Printed at HT Media Ltd. Noida

For Satyajit Ray

O friend, when you come to my gate
At dusk
What is it you ask?

Rabindranath Tagore

কার্তিক

Kartik

Red is blood is birth is life is…Or is it the other way round? Some rock-hard betel nut to crack that was. Red were her bandaged hands or the name tag that was strapped to her wrist, as she lay drugged and delirious in a hospital bed.

Light was bleeding from the outside, picking out snake shapes of her drip feed or an elusive shoal of silver fish.

Red were the riots, the pro and anti-death penalty pitchfork battles that had torched Dhaka* for days on end, in the wake of the Supreme Court ruling against the perpetrators of the '71 genocide. There was a time when she sought justice. That was then. Now, she wasn't so sure with her life ebbing away. She was confused. Thoughts swam in her head. Words remained anchored in her mouth. Only the past remained.

Red was the colour of her earliest memories, the seeds that burst and rooted in the shallows where the cranes stalked fish. She didn't remember much else from her first dawns. Maybe the lush green smells that tickled her nostrils or tingled her tongue. She was the youngest of the twelve children. Her parents named her Boori. Allah knows if they gave her that name because they liked her or disliked her. All she knew was that she had been Boori for as long as she could remember. Hoot! How she resented the name. It made her feel fractious. She felt everyone should have pretty names. Names like Noori, Nargis or Yasmeen. They should feel good on hearing their name.

---

*The modern spelling is used here, but the pre-independent spelling of Dacca has been retained elsewhere.

'Boori! Boori!'

But where was she? She was nowhere to be found. Her mother's squawk didn't even reach her as she was lost in her own thoughts. The village, Haldi, and its surroundings were her little world. Halima Khatoon would call out her name. At times, she got tired of calling her. Her mother thought about Boori as she gazed at the fire burning in the stove.

'That girl with a head of hair like a *kaak's* nest, she is not so young anymore. Will she ever realize that she must act sensibly? Or maybe she won't come to her senses until she is really old and grey, and all her teeth have fallen out.'

Her mother was worried about her. She wasn't as worried about her other children though. All of them were brought up quite liberally. But Boori was incorrigible. Either she was climbing up a tree looking for a *babui's* nest here, or a mango to lick there. Or she would be idling at Akali's grandmother's house, asking her if she would like a betel leaf or *moori*.

Akali's *nanee* would laugh and say, 'Just sit next to me and keep me company. That will make me happy. Only you can quench my thirst. It gives me such joy to have you around.'

It was Saleha who told Boori about trees. Their names, shapes, leaves and fruit. Not only was she soon able to tell one from the other, but she picked up tips from the old woman on which herbs to use to chase mosquitoes; which root, bark, leaves or sap to rub on bites from red ants and snakes; how to get rid of a leech that has stuck to your feet in the paddy fields. She also learned a range of voices and birdsongs.

Her mother knew she was different from her other children. So she let her be most of the time. She let her grow up with her own ideas as long as it suited her. The villagers were silenced. No one ever complained about her. She was content with that.

Just then Boori returned home with a bunch of *helencha*.

'I know you love *helencha*, Maa, so I got you some. I will clean them for you. Then I will get some baby prawns from the brook near our house. Then you can cook *helencha* with prawns. Baba will be so proud of me. He will say "Boori, you are a sweetie!"'

She laughed her heart out before running across the yard. Her mother just stared after her and thought, 'Allah alone knows how much longer it will be before she matures. May she be safe from the evil eye!' She prayed for her well-being.

Her father had named her Boori, meaning 'the old lady'. Of course Ramjan Ali was fond of her, despite coming up with that mouthful of a name. But with a brood of twelve children, how could her parents love her just the same? Was she just another baby for whom they didn't really care? She had hated her name ever since she was a child. Every time someone called her by that name, she felt as though they were addressing an old lady and simply ignored them. She also did that on purpose to wind her mother up. So her mother would scold her.

'You do as you are told, Boori or I'll drag you down by the hair. And if you think you can just come and go as you please, you've got another thing coming!'

'Am I really an old lady that I should respond when you call me Boori?' she answered back when she was told off. 'You can't be proud of a daughter with such a horrid name!'

'You talk as though you are an adult, not a child!' Her mother would then give her another earful, which made her laugh out loud.

She couldn't understand how anyone could be given such an awful name. She wished she could rename herself. She cried and asked her father one day, 'How can I get rid of this curse? Baba, please change my name!'

Her father ignored her. Boori begged her friends, 'Please stop calling me Boori.'

'But you are Boori! So we will call you Boori.'

'What kind of a name is that?' one brute of a boy jibed.

'What a rotten name!' another one slammed.

'Boori, Boori, you old hag!' chorused a gaggle of children.

They thought it was fun to get under her skin with that name. And so it came to be that, for the rest of her life, Boori was saddled with a name she hated so much. At night, she would wake up with the staccato of the train calling out, 'Boori! Boori! Boori!'

Even though Boori was a very strong-minded girl, she was as tender as a drop of water on a *maankochu* leaf. Like the small fly which flew about the short grass that grew in the swamps. She felt serene as she dipped her feet into the water. She tried to see her reflection in the muddy water but couldn't. She learned to accept the fact that one can't have everything exactly as they want. But then one shouldn't hold a grudge for not getting something. Life became easier when people learned to let go of their anger.

One day, Boori was very upset. She wanted to run away and said to herself, 'I will go! Definitely! I'll go away one of these days! No one will be able to find me then. What will happen if I go? Will anyone miss me? If Jalil can, then so can I. Am I any less than him? We are the same.'

But then she knew that in reality they were not the same. Jalil was a boy and that made all the difference!

Boori collected some pebbles from the rail tracks. She hummed the rhyme:

A train passes with *jhom jhom* noise,
If you slip then you get squashed.

Jalil came to her and asked, 'What are you doing Boori?'

'I am playing the train game. It's quite fun actually, playing the train all by yourself.'

'*Wah*! *Wah*! That's nice! You are curious, you know! Just like a mouse!'

'What? Are you comparing me to a mouse?'

Jalil laughed at that.

'Get this, you devil! You dog!' Boori pretended to throw stones at his face.

'I quite like it when you call me names! Here, have some sugar cane.'

He offered her a piece of sugar cane that was half eaten.

'I don't want the sugar cane which you have eaten. You have it.'

She walked past him at a quick pace. She carried the sack of pebbles in her dress by holding up the edges of her frock. She collected some more on her way. Jalil loitered around the station for a while. He actually wanted to jump on a train and leave this damn village. On the other hand, Boori was stuck. Hopelessly stuck. She blended into village life like an insect camouflaged against bark or foliage. She wanted so many things, but they were beyond her reach. Her dreams faded like the mail train into a faraway land. She would never be able to see what the world was like outside Haldi.

On her way back she threw away all the pebbles. The touch-me-nots shrank as the pebbles rained on them. She really liked the clatter of the train passing by; it kept her in a trance. She would rise from her sleep with the noise. She would stay awake for the rest of the night. She couldn't help it. She had this insatiable desire to find out what lay at the end of the road. She felt a pang in her heart which overwhelmed her.

Boori was not brought up like the other girls in Haldi. She built a world of her own. She dreamed she had wings to fly, and she flew and flew fearlessly. No one could match her indomitable spirit. She built a world of her own. Sometimes, she would meander along the dusty tracks leading away from Haldi. She would give those paths strange names and conjure up encounters with wild animals or mythical creatures. Now and then, she and

Jalil would chase snakes with bamboo sticks or raid mango groves. The pair of them had heaps of fun with climbing games. They scrambled up all kinds of trees, the higher the better, regardless of bruises and cuts.

'*Shabash! Shabash!*' Jalil would cheer her on, as she hoisted herself up into a tree crown.

'Come on up, sleepy-head!' Boori teased him.

'Just let me catch my breath!' Jalil pleaded from a crook in the branches.

'Chicken!' she clucked.

Jalil's fingers itched to cuff her ears. The two of them peeked at nests through the foliage. Down below, people were dwarfed to bug size. Once, Boori challenged Jalil to clamber up a palm tree. She meant it as a joke, but it fell flat. Luckily, Jalil hadn't taken her at her word.

At other times, the wild girl invited one or two villagers to sit with her. She listened to them. Boori was far ahead of anyone else in the village. Children of her own age failed to understand her. None of her school friends wanted to play with her. The adults were scared to talk to her. Her best friend Pushporani once told her, 'I tell you this, Boori! Awful things are in store for you!'

'Really? I will swallow all of those awful things or burn them down,' Boori replied as she laughed out loud.

'Are you sure you can do that?' Pushporani asked her in amazement.

Boori snapped her fingers, 'Oh yes, I can! I don't care about sorrow!'

All the village children cowered in front of her.

'You scare the wits out of us. You are worse than Kana Bhoot, the troll!'

'Let's have a race,' Boori said, unfazed, eyes locked on these wiggling minnows. 'When you run you forget all about your fears and sorrows. We will outrun our sadness!'

'We'll outrun sadness!' All the children clapped and cheered in unison, and off they ran.

They went quite far and came to the river ghat. Then they went back to the railway tracks, only to realize that Boori had left the group and walked on the other way. She jumped on the rail tracks. She didn't look back even when they called out her name. They knew that Boori wanted to be alone at that moment. She was upset for some reason. Even then, she would say that she would kick her sorrows.

'Poor Boori!' They said with one voice.

Boori hated this word. She would answer back, 'Get lost! Go and play *ekka dokka*!'

One day at school, the children were busy drawing tree leaves when Shimu Begum, their teacher, had to rush home to look after her ailing mother. Boori took charge of the class. Munir, a big boy in her class, would have none of it. He told her that she was getting his goat with her airs and graces. Grabbing her by the arm, Munir said he would sort her out. She fended him off with a flurry of slaps. He backed off, then started to mess with his neighbours' drawings and cuffed the little ones in class. To take the wind out of his sails, Boori said she was *Nodi*, a river spirit, and she had cast a spell on him. He was no longer Munir; she said all the children were to call him *kumeer*, or they would share the same fate. Other potential bullies like squat, sweaty Salman and lanky Ashik were turned into *bhaluk* and *hash*, while *makorsha* had claimed the soul of Shoma, a creepy girl and a pest.

Now that she had the entire class's attention, Boori began to tell them which birds nestled in which trees, what they pecked, how they sang and built their nests. Then she flew away to her magic kingdom and spun tales about the mythical *moyoor*. Her stock of yarns and stories was running out fast when Shimu Begum returned. The teacher commended Boori in front of the whole class. She was so pleased with her she forgot to have the class sing, 'This flag of the crescent and the star, leads the way to progress and perfection'. For the rest of the time she let the children play a few games of shadow tag and *borof pani*. Initially, the bullies didn't want to have the young ones stepping on their shadows. They eventually gave in, as they didn't want to be left out either. The catch-me-if-you-can games went down well amid wild screams for *borof pani*.

Sometimes, Boori even ignored her mother. Halima Khatoon was always in the kitchen, busy with her household chores. Boori would bolt from the house. She would rather spend time under the *jamrool* tree alongside the little brook that passed by.

At times she felt that she was the most carefree person in the whole world. There was not a single bond that could hold her. She called out to her mother, 'Maa! Maa!'

There was no response. She wanted to call her mother by her name.

'Do you want to play cooking games, Halima Khatoon?' she called out again as she walked along the tracks. 'We will cook *paijam* rice and fish and then we will serve Ramjan Ali. We could fry the fish and make sour stew with *begun*. Then we will go to Ramjan Ali and say, "Please eat the food, Ramjan! You are an old friend of mine. I love giving you a platter of rice. We are mates, right?"'

This earned the girl a glare and a good hiding. Time and again, Boori was told to bite her tongue. Sometimes, she would throw pebbles at the sky out of sheer frustration. She would look at the sky and see the *sonali* eagle which soared high up in the air. She thought, 'Why can't people be like birds?'

Halima Khatoon was sitting in her kitchen, grumbling.

'That girl is a wild one! It goes in one ear and out of the other!'

When her mother called her for lunch, Boori didn't pay any heed. She turned her gaze towards the *jamrool* tree. Her mother fumed with rage.

'I have never seen such a troublemaker! Allah alone knows what will happen to her.'

Boori stretched out on the wet shrubs, licking *tetool* peel. She forgot about lunch. She enjoyed her solitude. She wondered why people had to talk so much. She loved the trees because they were quiet.

'Why do people love to talk?' she asked.

Pushporani was mad.

'The trees can't speak, so they don't speak,' she retorted. 'You stupid girl! Don't you have any brains?'

'Of course I understand. Why wouldn't I? So, you think you know it all?'

'I have never seen such an idiot.'

'Good for you. Now leave me alone! I don't want to play with you anymore.'

Boori loved having guests at her house. Guests meant *puli pitha*, which Halima Khatoon cooked all year round. Her greedy eyes would follow her mother as she kneaded the soft dough into lemon-sized balls, stuffed the pastry with the coconut shreds and jaggery, and then cut them in the shape of halfmoons or crescents. Boori couldn't wait to dip her fingers into the sticky, cardamom-flavoured coconut and date paste. Besides, no one noticed her when guests were around. Everyone was busy with their own work. Halima Khatoon managed both her kitchen and guests. At times she looked very happy while at other times she looked worn out. Boori learned to observe all this at a very young age. She lived in a world of her own. She felt more emotionally mature than any of her friends. Pushporani was no match for her.

After she finished her primary education, there was no chance of her going to high school. Only boys went to the village high school. There were hardly any girls studying there because no one cared about educating them. Boori knew it would be the same for her. But she wasn't bothered. So what if she couldn't continue her studies? She knew enough to read books, write letters. What else did she need? She loved to listen to the chants of Vishnu's worshippers; their songs filled her with happiness. She could live her life with just that. It shouldn't be so difficult.

One day, Jalil stopped her on the way.

'How are you, Boori? You don't have to go to school, do you?'

'Mm-hmm! I have lots of freedom these days!'

'Doesn't it make you feel sad?'

Boori pursed her lips.

'Not at all! Why should I be sad? My job is to husk the rice and work the *dheki* pounder. I know I won't have the chance to become a teacher. What is it to you anyway, Jalil?'

'I just wanted to know if you were sad for not being able to go to school. You said so many things about that. You have a glib tongue too! Allah has blessed you with a ball of knowledge. It just unwinds and unwinds.'

Boori laughed.

'Haha! Didn't you just ask me if I was sad or not?'

'What if I did?'

'Shall I tell you the truth?'

'Yes! Of course you should tell me the truth!'

'I only feel sad for you, Jalil! And nothing else.'

'For me? Really? Why?'

Jalil jumped down and stood beside her. He put his hand on her shoulder and said, 'There is not a single person like you, Boori. You are very beautiful. No one in this village comes anywhere near you.'

'Will you remember me, Jalil?'

'Yes, I will. I will remember you for as long as I live.'

'Will you still remember me once you are married?'

'Why? Yes, of course!'

Boori's smile couldn't hide her embarrassment. Jalil's heart was on fire. He kept staring at Boori. Her face looked like the sky at that moment. He felt as though the sky shone with a full moon, the moon beamed like the sun and there were thousands of stars twinkling away.

Jalil just hugged her tight and said, 'I love you, Boori!'

Later, Boori heard that Jalil was going to Dacca, but she didn't see him before he left.

*

Boori lost her father when she was only in her pre-teens. The whole house was in mourning. A lot of relatives came to stay with them and take part in the *kulkhani*.

All Boori knew was that her father was no longer there. But she didn't understand the full depth of the situation. She was in a daze as she had not faced anyone's death before. She huddled against her mother while she wailed. She tried to make sense of the things her mother was saying as she cried. But the words were muffled by her wailing. She stood next to Ramjan Ali's body which was lying on the makeshift cot for the dead and said, 'You were my mother's best friend! So why did you leave her so soon? Don't you feel bad just leaving like that? Where are you right now, Ramjan Ali?'

She couldn't think any further than that. Someone came forward and asked, 'Would you like to see your father? Come with me.'

She stood still. Since she knew nothing about death, her father's passing away didn't bother her too much. They uncovered his face before taking him for burial. Boori went to see him one last time like everyone else. He looked the same to her. It was as if he was asleep. She cried because everyone else cried, but she didn't feel too sad.

Not much changed in her life after her father's death. She didn't miss his presence. She roamed around the fields with pebbles or paddy stalks in the folds of her frock just as before.

Her days ebbed and flowed as she swam in the *pukur* near the village. Sometimes, she did feel as if she had been forgotten by her family. But she would rather go outside and have fun in the sun than think of these things. She loved the fields, the bushes and the paths in the village which seemed to beckon to her all the time. Somehow, a centrifugal force pulled her away from the orbit of her house.

Days merged into weeks. Boori's routine didn't change. One day, Boori noticed blood trickling down her inner thighs. She ran to her mother, screaming, 'Maa! What's wrong with me?'

Halima Khatoon hugged her.

'It's nothing, you are just growing up! Come with me.'

Boori thought to herself that she had grown up a long time ago. How come she was growing up all over again? She asked her mother all sorts of questions. Would she have to go through this every month? But what on earth for?

No one answered her questions. Even Halima Khatoon couldn't. Boori got upset. Her mother forbade her to leave the house that day. She thought of Jalil, maybe he would be able to answer her questions, but she stopped herself from thinking about him. Her mother warned her.

'It's not safe for girls when the red river flows. It's like a burning fire!'

Boori pulled a face.

'What rubbish! What burning fire? How can one put the fire out if that is so?'

Halima Khatoon smiled.

'By marrying off their daughters!'

'What are you talking about? What *bie*? I already have a problem and now you want to add marriage to the list? Hoot!' Boori screamed out.

Boori came round to the idea of getting married even though she wasn't that keen. As she grew into a young woman, she was married off to her cousin Gafoor. Her mother was in two minds about hitching her up with Gafoor as he was much older. But Boori's elder brother, Nasir, was their *griho korta* after Ramjan Ali's death; it was his decision and they had no say in the matter.

'Who will rein in your wild daughter if not an older man, Mother?' Nasir huffed irritably. 'It was a different matter when she was a child, but now that she is all grown up, she is bound to land us in trouble.'

Halima Khatoon tried to make sense of his words. Boori just stared at her vacantly. Her mother too looked lost. Nasir spoke in a softer tone, 'It wouldn't be so bad after all to hook her up with Gafoor, you know. She will live near us, which would be a whole different kettle of fish if she married someone else we don't even know or trust. You would go crazy then and she would bring shame to our family's izzat. Besides, Gafoor has his feet on the ground. He doesn't poke his nose in household matters. Didn't you see how happy he was with his previous wife? It was his kismet that she died just like that.'

'Shh! You shouldn't say all these things in front of Boori!' Halima Khatoon chipped in.

She was hurt, but she knew things wouldn't change one bit, even if she talked to her son. So Nasir went on with the wedding preparations. He was eager to get her off his back and marry her off as soon as possible. He didn't like Boori and the way she behaved. Boori just listened to what was said about her. She couldn't beg anything from anyone. Especially her brother, of all people! She didn't think a husband would make a jot of difference. But she felt that her nikah could mean some kind of freedom as she would have a different home in a different village.

She was bored to death in her own village. At long last, she would be free to venture beyond the borders of Haldi. She longed to get on a boat and see the world. The feel of a man's hand would steer her life in a new direction, she thought. Yet she would be left with nothing but a grin of betel-leaf-stained teeth. None of her wishes were fulfilled. Everything was the same: the red field of leafy vegetables; the movement of a *doel's* tail; the slim stalk of *shapla*; the purple flowers of the marsh weeds; everything, except the fact that Boori was now deprived of sharing these with someone special.

Her marriage to her cousin only changed her bedroom from the northern room to the southern one. Gafoor had two sons aged six and four. She was quite friendly with them. She had roamed the fields giving them a piggy back. However, after she became their mother, following the wedding, she was a bit dumbfounded; she even found her new role embarrassing. '*Uff!*' she thought. At one point, she felt like throwing the two boys into the *pukur*. At other times, she loved playing with them, and admired their innocent faces. It made her skittish. The rest was all too familiar. She already knew her in-laws, her husband and her household, so she didn't get to meet anyone new. Only when she woke up in the dead of the night did she feel a hairy hand holding her. That was when she realized that something in her life had changed.

Time and again she removed the hand and turned to her side. Sometimes, she got up and sat out on the veranda for a long time. She felt she had missed out on a lot in life. Fireflies flitted about the bamboo grove. The moonlight lit the veranda. Boori felt like crying but couldn't. The owl hooted and she went back to bed. She lay with her back to Gafoor. She couldn't do anything else. Even though her mind wandered all over the world, her physical borders kept her rooted.

Boori would often feel really scared and helpless. She wanted to grow up, for she knew only then would she be able to keep her boat level. How long would she live? When would everything gather around her like the bees on a beehive? She knew she didn't have the answer. That only time could tell.

On some nights, Gafoor would ask, 'Where did you go?'

'I went out.'

'What for?'

'Never you mind! I couldn't sleep.'

Gafoor didn't keep the conversation going, he went back to sleep. Snapping out of her dreams was not plain sailing for Boori. She would just toss and turn in her bed for the rest of the night. She felt at ease when she managed to keep Gafoor at arms' length, but he begged her to let him come close. His pleas sounded like a locomotive's *jhik jhik*. She snuggled against his chest like a kitten. When Gafoor got really aroused, she would lie absolutely still. She didn't have the strength to respond to his muffled calls. Her thoughts and the train's clatter blended together. Boori was beyond anyone's reach. She would be lost in infinite space. That gave her immense pleasure, a kind of thrill that couldn't be shared with anyone.

Sometimes, Gafoor watched his young wife with amazement. He didn't think in his wildest dreams that this girl would ever be his wife. He didn't realize that she was all grown up. It was as if she had tiptoed into his house while playing in the yard. He felt embarrassed at the very thought. He looked away. Boori laughed heartily, 'What are you staring at?'

'Are you happy, Boori?'

'Happy? What does that mean?'

Boori asked a question that Gafoor had no answer to. He didn't know what to say. He couldn't compete with Boori's inquisitive mind. He couldn't figure out how Boori could come up with these kinds of questions living in a village like Haldi. As he wanted to shrug the question off, he said, 'Bring me my hookah. I feel empty inside.'

Gafoor was a chain smoker. He felt bad if he missed his smoke and she knew this. What she didn't know though was what happiness meant. Did it mean cooking, eating, sleeping with your husband? If happy meant all those things, then yes, she was happy. There was a fresh stream flowing in her veins. But maybe it wasn't that. Maybe it was like collecting pebbles on one's way—no, that didn't sound right either. It would be something like finding an egg while picking up paddy sheaves and the way one would scream out loud at this sight. That scream would be akin to being hitched to Gafoor. It was not a scream of surprise or happiness. Boori didn't read too much significance into it. Anyone else would have taken a nikah as their life's turning point. But she didn't see things that way. She could easily erase things that didn't match her expectations.

The Haldi swamps didn't soften Boori's resolve. She could feel the hot summer wind inside her womb. The day she cried the whole family sensed that something terrible must have happened, because she would never cry for simple reasons. Her sadness resonated and spread all around her.

When Boori watched the rainbow-coloured birds, Halima Khatoon's orders would fall on deaf ears. It would drive her mother mad, 'What will become of you, girl? Boori, mark my words, you are in for a lot of sorrow! Come back at once!'

Boori recalled paying no heed to her mother then.

*

Boori's husband was a very simple man. He would never do anything to Boori against her will. Nor did he scold her. He couldn't even pick a quarrel. He was far too keen to keep Boori happy. It seemed as though he was bent on worshipping her as a goddess. So their domestic life did not hit troubled waters. Gafoor listened to everything Boori said. She made no undue demands nor was she jealous of anyone. There was no question of her wrangling with anyone else either. Gafoor was very grateful for all this. But sometimes he froze with Boori in his arms; he pulled her close and said, 'Maybe it wasn't right to marry you, Boori!'

'Why?'

'I am way too old for you!'

'Never you mind! You feed me!'

'Hai Allah! The things you say!'

'I didn't say anything bad! There is a saying which goes like this: if you keep my tummy full, then we'll do just fine.'

Gafoor fell silent. It was difficult to know if Boori was complaining or just being her usual self. Whenever she was asked about big or small things, she would lose track of her thoughts in mid-sentence. If pestered, she would answer in monosyllables. Gafoor would lose his cool.

'Boori, bring me my hookah. I feel a lump in my throat.'

Boori would chuckle and disappear.

Boori wasn't bothered about Gafoor's age. She didn't have time to enjoy her youth; she lived under the shadow of her elderly husband. What was there to complain about? This was all for the best, she was at peace with herself. At times, however, Gafoor's presence was unbearable and she could sense a storm shatter the inside of her heart. She longed for solitude then. She sat outside in the cold wind of Kartik, at the onset of winter. The warmth in Gafoor's arms seemed uninviting. Theirs had become a routine relationship, she thought.

The birds chirped, as the cold wind blew over the tree tops; the branches of the *sojna* swayed in the air. Boori sat with her legs stretched out. The cool breeze caressed her skin. It was as if her childhood playmate was playing hide and seek with her. She felt intoxicated. She could almost feel Jalil's presence now. How did he slip away through her fingers, she wondered. Could he have fulfilled all her dreams? If Jalil and his wife kept fighting, would he remarry? She would have to live with his other wives then. Maybe he wouldn't turn out to be a good man, who knows! No one could read the future. Even then, Jalil was her happiest childhood memory. She couldn't let that go. She let him stay inside her.

Gafoor opened the door leading to the veranda and called her back to bed. He was always a bit overprotective. But he never used force to make her do something unwillingly. Boori was smart enough to yield to his requests. Sometimes, they even went out fishing in the dead of the night.

The village looked mysterious to her on such nights. She felt that the trees, the houses and the fields were all immersed in water. Boori's heart was touched by the softness of the wind at night. In the same way, her easily recognizable cousin in broad daylight turned into her unknown husband by night. To her, Gafoor seemed far away. He looked unfamiliar. In fact, all the folks she knew seemed strange now. At home, she would shrink into her shell. But when she went out, it was as if the shell broke open. Her face flushed, her eyes shone in the dark. She loved being outside the house at this time. This is when her beautiful young self blossomed. Boori took on a new identity; she grew closer to her husband.

One time, Gafoor snatched her by the arm and pulled her into the boat. Then he pushed the small boat before getting on it. The boat bobbed on the river. Gafoor rocked it with his legs deliberately. Boori was more excited than afraid. She loved living on the edge. She couldn't care less if the boat capsized. At least then she wouldn't have to go back to her dull life.

'Are you scared, Boori?'

'You are with me, aren't you? Why should I be scared?'

Boori hugged his knees. She squatted down in the boat and burst out laughing. He asked, 'How come you are like this when you are out in the open? You seem so sad when you are at home. I seem to be a stranger to you then. You hardly talk to me.'

'You see, this is my home, the open space. My heart dances with joy out in the open.'

Gafoor smiled contentedly. She didn't shy away this time. She gave him a proper answer.

The boat floated on the still river. Gafoor dropped his oar and pulled Boori closer to him. Her lips invited him. He tried to find the sweetness of her mouth. He was almost beside himself with passion. She was warm and welcoming to him. 'Ah! Why isn't she like this all the time?' he mused. The boat was heading in the wrong direction; Gafoor picked up his oar again. As he rowed the boat back to shore, she sat quietly and calmed herself down.

Boori's brother, Nasir, complained that Gafoor was spoiling her rotten.

'She's always up on her feet, ready to dance and your *dhol* strikes the tune.'

Boori refrained from answering back as it would cause more trouble. Halima Khatoon said, 'Let them do whatever they like. She accepted her marriage without a fuss, that's the main thing. I am happy if she is happy, insha'allah.'

Halima Khatoon was ageing. Her eyesight was weaker now and she started to become forgetful. Yet, she would always rail against her wayward daughter.

'The girl's always putting her foot in her mouth,' she spat, 'and we can't have other villagers gossiping.'

Outwardly immune to her mother's venomous tongue, Boori was always attentive, polite and could never be faulted. She resented the lectures on how to be 'a good wife', although she smiled and acted as if it didn't bother her at all.

Gafoor had paddled along a long stretch of the dark river. Sitting in a dark corner, Boori brooded with her chin resting on her knees. She kept thinking about her mother, her brother and the neighbours. The pitch black darkness drifted off. She felt the magical caress of the breeze at dawn. Would the villagers ever understand what it meant to be touched by the cool morning air? They couldn't get close enough to the things she loved by a long chalk! She felt the boat surge towards infinity, leaving life's toils behind.

If only she could hear the roar of the Shomeswari, she would be able to discover all her country's treasures. When relatives arrived from their faraway homes, she was all ears to their tales of places she knew nothing about. She didn't know anything about Dacca, its people and their lives—so many things that tested the boundaries of her little world. Boori peered into the distant darkness with boundless appetite. She kept staring at the horizon with parched eyes.

The boat glided on swiftly.

'What are you thinking about, Boori?'

'Nothing. There is nothing to think about.' She laughed and the peals of laughter bounced off and shattered the silence.

Gafoor kept quiet for a while. Then he sighed.

'Marrying you was a mistake, Boori.'

'Why?' she asked, with a hint of surprise.

Catok bance kemone
Suddh megher borison bine
Tumi hey hobo jolodhor
Catokini mole ebar
Tomar songe sokol somoy
*Rekho vubane**

Gafoor stopped singing.

'I can't read you. Can't guess what you're feeling. If I were your age...' Gafoor heaved another sigh, 'it would be easier for me to know what's going through your mind.'

'What will you gain by figuring out everything? Everybody has a mind of their own. If you see through me,' Boori went on to say, 'I'll feel cornered. On top of that, the more you think about me, the more it peeves me.' Boori laughed frantically as she made a face.

---

*Translation of all the songs is provided at the end of the novel.

Her unbridled joy knew no bounds today. Even she couldn't control it. The boat rocked as her body shook with laughter. Gafoor just kept staring at her. He could never understand her. He seldom saw her laughing this hard. It swayed him too and he had half a mind to laugh himself.

'Oh-oh! Don't laugh so much!' Gafoor snapped.

'Why not? Hahaha! If I feel like it!' she replied, still in stitches.

'"The more you laugh, the more you will cry." Someone called Ram Shonna said that.'

'Pah! That's all nonsense! You've just made it up. I will laugh when I feel like it.'

Gafoor began to grin too, albeit somewhat reluctantly. The boat slithered on the water, carrying two thirsty souls. He picked up the song again.

Karo robe na e dhon jibonjoubon
Tobe keno mon eto basha
Ekbar soburer deshe
Boi dekhi dom kose
Uthis na re vese peye jontrona.

If only he could be as young as Boori. He wouldn't wish for anything else for all the world. He would happily give up his house, his land, his boat, his fishing net, his rice and what not. He never was the calculating type. He was another man in Boori's company. His greatest joy lay in making her happy. Gafoor felt responsible for her mood swings; he did think he was somehow holding her back, especially when she remained silent and melancholy, or failed to respond to other people's calls. He muddled through his days, tugging incessantly at the bamboo pipe of his hookah.

He didn't have a good rapport with his first wife. But back then both of them were much younger. Their physical desire was powerful and they felt a warm tingling in each other's touch. His wife, however, could not keep up with his desire. So, Gafoor spent long hours in the paddy, went to musical get-togethers and often stayed out the whole night. His wife never complained. She was afraid of him. Gafoor did not lose sleep over it though. After the two sons were born, their relationship frayed.

Gafoor was in a different mood now. Boori and he shared a strong bond, the kind that he had never experienced before. This bond could carry him a long way. Boori was a green shoot, full of life, albeit not so good at domestic chores. But he liked her. She was something special. She radiated youth and innocence. She was both sweet and sour, and sometimes bitter too. Fearing he might fall short of her fantasies puzzled Gafoor. One day the magnetic pull could drag him under.

Paddling the boat, Gafoor said, 'Today, I will not go back home.'

'Where shall we go?'

'Wherever my mind takes us.'

'Well, paddle on, I'll close my eyes.'

'What if the boat tips over?'

'Never you mind. You're with me.' Boori dabbed her cheek with the back of her hand and gazed into the distance. She seemed to have put her mind at rest.

'What if I can't save you?'

'Then we'll drown while hugging each other,' Boori replied with a chuckle.

Gafoor remained silent. He had no answer to that. He dug into a deeper memory, trying to dredge up something he had blotted out. A long time ago, he had travelled that stretch of the canal and now, years later, Boori helped retrieve those shards of memory.

'What are you gawping at?' she asked.

'I'm just looking at you.'

'I'm a simple girl.'

'Still, I can't figure you out.'

Boori sniggered.

'Why are you so different, Boori,'

'What do you mean "different"?'

'I have no idea.'

'Then how can you feel it?'

'Er…I just feel it in my bones.'

Gafoor combed his fingers through his hair. He could not find a channel to translate his thoughts.

'You think I'm a crazy mess, don't you?' Boori said in a different tone.

'Says who?' Gafoor was taken aback. 'Sometimes you talk wild.'

'You say it at times!'

Gafoor roared, 'I could happily die for you, Boori!'

He tethered the boat at the foot of the *tetool* tree swaying over the water and sank the iron rod into the mud. A wall of foliage and branches secluded them from view. The bushy spot appealed to Boori.

'Why did you stop here?'

'For you.' Gafoor drew her to him.

'This place is really beautiful, almost like home.'

'I'm glad you like it.'

'Hey! What are you doing? There are folks around!'

'Where? It's still dark.'

Gafoor ignored her reticence and gripped her hands. They could feel the caress of the early morning breeze over their bodies. The *tetool* was whispering in their ears. They were tantalized. Everything around was a blur. Boori had her head in the clouds and was completely engrossed in herself. She was unaware that physical contact could open up a source of immense bliss. She wondered how love could change its hue so frequently. Boori smiled to herself.

'Let go of me,' Boori whispered.

'No! You said you wanted to drown in my arms. Now I'll drown in yours.'

'Hmpf! What a silly idea!' she said. 'Will you die in the canal?'

'Sure I will.'

'Okay, then you drown. I'll close my eyes.'

Gafoor took a deep breath as he spoke, 'I feel like biting your lips off.'

Boori laughed at the words. 'You're fishing, in case you didn't notice! You won't want to swallow the hook!'

'Oh, Boori, Boori, Boori!'

Gafoor's voice was muffled by the wind. There was a deep silence.

The fishing was disrupted whenever Boori joined Gafoor. They babbled more than they fished and fooled around even more. The fish basket remained almost empty. It rolled on the bed of the boat. There were days when they wouldn't even throw the fishing net. Gafoor would not go home. He would drop Boori at the ghat and go to the bazaar to buy some fish. The neighbours would poke fun at the empty basket. They would tease Boori too.

On such days she lay down beside Salim and Kalim, pretending to have no clue as to her husband's whereabouts. For his part, Gafoor didn't mind if he didn't catch any fish and was made to look like a chump. He enjoyed riding in his boat with Boori more than anything. They would leave in the dead of night and come home just before dawn. If they happened to be the butt of another fisherman's jokes on the way back, he would shrug it off.

Never in his wildest dreams did he imagine that his life would be brimming over with such joy. He welcomed the change. His sense of fulfilment made up for the empty catch. He wished Boori could get this close to him every day.

A while later Boori would recoil into her shell after coming home. Gafoor would coax her out of it. But she would try to get away from his clutches to go and play with the two boys. Gafoor got emotional, 'I am thankful to almighty Allah for giving you to me. Oh, merciful Allah!'

He joined his palms in prayer. His eyes welled with tears. Boori was busy with Kalim and Salim.

'I think the boys love you much more than they love me!' Gafoor huffed. 'I have almost become a stranger to them.'

'Are you jealous?' Boori teased him.

'Of course I am!' Gafoor felt goaded. 'Sometimes I can't take it. You cast magic spells!'

'Hmph! Magic my foot! If you love your boys, they will love you back.'

'That's a lie!' he shouted. 'Who said you get loved back if you love someone? Why do I crave to be loved back then?'

Gafoor dropped his gaze and voice.

'Pfft! I don't understand what you say! I have work to do!'

Boori left the house. If she stayed in, she knew that she would be trapped against her will. Even if she wanted to, she could not quell the fire in his blood. She went to bathe Salim and Kalim.

Her household chores kept her busy. The days flowed quietly. Gafoor would plough the field, throw his fishing net and go to the bazaar, while Boori took care of the family.

Sometimes she did a good job; sometimes she made a complete mess, inviting a volley of curses from her relatives and neighbours. Her brother would scold her. Her mother would nag. Far from it all, Boori's mind built its own nest where she could be free from her day's dirt and toil.

Boori felt cursed. Her restless, outgoing spirit made her more than ready to welcome motherhood. The first three years of her married life went by quite happily. From the fourth year she started yearning for a baby. Sometimes she felt sorry for herself. She hated her body for not being able to give birth. She wondered why she had never felt any physical change. She was dying to feel the excitement of a baby inside her womb; it drove her to the brink. She didn't want to show it, though. Gafoor was content with his sons and didn't say much.

'Why are you so down? We have two sons. Why do we need more? Don't they make you happy? We are almost free. We can do whatever we want!'

That was partly true; he could make love to her whenever he wanted. He didn't want her to get distracted by anything else. A baby meant a lot of hassle. Besides, Boori only belonged to him. Gafoor hated the idea of sharing his wife with anyone else.

Boori, on the other hand, was desperate to have her first child. It was too much to bear. Days dragged on. She no longer felt like visiting neighbours, yet she could not stand being cooped up within the four walls of her bedroom. She longed for something new, something different. It was difficult for her to concentrate on her household chores. She needed something new now. The past four years of her life seemed such a waste. Gafoor tried to reason her, 'Why are you so restless to have a baby? Don't our sons fulfil your desire for motherhood?'

'Of course they do, but it's not like having my own baby! Sometimes I feel that they are not mine. I want to have my own flesh and blood, a baby from my own womb and the river of my blood. Mine!'

She couldn't continue. She didn't know how to convey to Gafoor how much she wanted a baby from his seed. After all he was a man. He wouldn't be able to understand her ache, her emptiness. So she kept quiet.

As time went by, Boori began to look pale and weary. She would laugh a wild shrill laugh and stop abruptly. All the light faded from her face and a kohl line ringed her innocent eyes. She had changed for the worse and Gafoor couldn't ignore it. Late at night when he left to go fishing, he didn't feel any stir or spark that could give sense to his middle-age life.

'You have to go through a lot of pains if you want a son, you know, Boori,' he said, stroking her hair.

'I know. If I don't feel the pain, how would I know what it means to be a mother? I cook, husk rice, feed the chickens. I want more out of life. If I can't have a child, I'll jump into the river and kill myself,' Boori said, quivering.

She smiled weakly. Gafoor just sat silently by his wife's side. Boori wanted to feel the pain of motherhood. She wanted her pain to bloom like a flower, otherwise her life would go to waste. All her hopes and dreams were pinned on that shred of hope. She even kept Gafoor outside her cocoon. All Boori wanted right now was to have a baby.

'She can't have a child if she keeps running around the village like an overgrown kid herself,' the neighbours would gossip. 'It's something *kharap*. Women should not move so freely.'

She started taking herbal medicine to conceive. She tried everything. She listened to everything anyone said and painstakingly tried to follow it to the letter.

Boori clammed up within herself, swinging in a cradle of doubts. What would her going out have anything to do with having a baby? A few months back, she could laugh off the curses of her elderly relatives. Now every little thing made her anxious. What if her wavering faith affected her chances of bearing a child? So she abided by her elders meticulously.

Two more years passed. Time seemed endless. Boori could not give up hope, but at times it was difficult to carry on. Whenever Kalim and Salim called her, she looked confused and kept staring at them. The very sound of 'Maa' spooked her now. Sometimes, she would hug them tight and stroke them frantically. There were days when she just ignored them and went to sit on the banks of the *pukur*. She stared at the ripples made by the fish in the pond, trying to calm her frayed mind. Then she felt ashamed thinking of the boys' sad faces. She tried to cling to a semblance of peace, yet her desire for a baby was gnawing a hole into her.

During those agonizing days, her childhood friend Namita came to visit the neighbouring village of Dakkin Para. Boori had rarely met her since she was married off in another village and was happy to see her after such a long spell. They began to chat, chewing on betel nut. After a little while, Namita sensed that something wasn't right.

'What's the matter with you, Boori?' she asked.

'Nothing.'

'My, you've changed a lot.'

'I'm growing old.' Boori fell silent. Namita too remained quiet for a while.

'How many children have you got, Namita?'

'Eight. I don't get a minute's rest with that army of toddlers. Count yourself lucky to be free from such hassle.'

'I don't want to remain free from that kind of trouble, Namita.'

Namita was puzzled. She looked at her friend's wan face. She told her to visit the ashram of Holy Kesa Baba in Srinile. Namita's advice rang in Boori's head all day. Dusk fell. Boori didn't kindle the lamp. Salim and Kalim came back from the playground. Gafoor had not yet returned. Boori sat brooding, with the echoes of her conversation with Namita playing in her head. Namita's voice rippled against her roof, her walls, reaching into the recesses of her small world, her rice pots, betel box and even the folds of her sari. It kept ringing in her ears long into the twilight.

There was a Poush mela every winter at the Srinile shrine. Thousands of pilgrims converged to the holy spot seeking an answer to their prayers. Devotees would lie under the old neem tree, tie threads to its branches, rub holy dust on their faces, necks and chests to have their wishes fulfilled. Sterile women became pregnant, sick people were cured, barren lands made fertile and free from insects, farmers harvested bumper crops. The saint's fame spread for miles around the village. To help with the fulfilment of your wish, you had to hang a pouch containing five *annas* on the tree.

Namita's husband, Akshay Das, was critically ill and doctors couldn't cure him. She sold her land in order to pay for her husband's treatment, but to no avail. The hospital authorities released him suggesting he be fed what he liked, for his days were numbered.

Namita had given up hope. She saw a bleak future ahead of her, a dark tunnel to widowhood and poverty. Bewildered and confused, Namita could not believe her ears that her husband was simply to wither away. She wasn't about to flinch and give up. She went to the shrine in Srinile. Miraculously, Akshay Das began to get better slowly. Now he was fully recovered. Talking about the saint, Namita became effusive with gratitude, kneeling humbly before the invisible holy man, with *sindoor* on her forehead and *shakha* round her wrists.

Wiping her tears absent-mindedly with her *anchol*, Namita muttered to herself, 'Why has *Bhagoban* cursed me with a flock of children I can hardly feed?'

Boori shuddered at her friend's talk.

'We are really hard up and have run out of food, Boori. My husband can't earn enough money to feed the children,' she went on to say. 'I pray not to have any more. Yet, I am with child once again and well into my third month.'

Boori mused long after her friend had left. Everything swirled round and round in her head. Akshay Das was better, and so was Namita. And though Boori did not really believe in such superstitions, she could not ignore what had happened to the man. Her mind vacillated between despair and hope. What if this simple belief made her dreams come true? That settled it. She would pay her respects at the Srinile shrine. She felt that the proverb 'faith will move monsoons', that she had been hearing since childhood, had gained a new meaning.

'I understand you, Namita,' Boori whispered to herself. 'I want to be like you.'

Perhaps there really was something supernatural which could make flowers bloom in a barren land. She found courage by looking at Namita's happy face. She made herself strong. But then, Boori remembered her distress. She recalled her friend's sad admission, 'I can't even feed them well, and still *Bhagoban* curses me with more children.'

Poush mela was to be held in eight months' time, Boori calculated, as she gazed at the straw stack in the darkness. All around it grew dark.

'Oh, Salim's Maa! Why haven't you lit up the house yet?' she heard herself being called. 'Allah! Why would you do such an inauspicious thing? The evening light has faded. It's pitch dark but you still haven't lit the candle.'

Boori got up with her betel leaf platter. Salim and Kalim ran up to her and kissed her.

'Maa, Maa, Maa!'

'Shoo! I can't stand on my two feet with you two crawling all over me. You'll knock me down.'

'I am starving,' Kalim shouted.

'I could eat a buffalo,' Salim added.

'Whoa, whoa, whoa! Come on inside, I'll get you something to eat.'

Boori lit the lamp. She kept gazing at the flame. There were eight months to go before the Poush mela, she counted, and eight months was a long time.

অগ্রহায়ণ
Ôgrôhayôn

A few weeks later, Nita Bairagi, the Baul minstrel, came to the village playing her two-stringed *dotara*. Boori and Nita had been friends for a long time, since before Boori's marriage with Gafoor. Whenever Boori saw Nita around, she would tail the singer's shadow. After they had walked some distance, Nita would send her back.

'Now get yourself home!'

'No, please take me with you.'

Nita would laugh at the thought and put her hands on Boori's head.

'Where to? You have a family and home of your own,' she said, 'and I am a homeless wanderer.'

Boori could not fathom Nita. Why didn't she have a home? Nita would let her walk up to the *shimul* tree but no further. Instead of walking on the road, Nita would trudge along the dusty path across the fields towards the next village. Boori watched her figure recede into the distance. Nita reminded Boori of Jalil. He was a free man too. He had never looked back, not even at Boori. As Nita disappeared from sight, Boori would sit down under the *shimul* gazing at the spot where the singer had been. She could not leave right away. What if Nita came back the same way and Boori missed her? Theirs was a special friendship despite their age difference. Today, Nita sang plucking her *dotara*:

Aami tor piriter mora
Tui chaiya dekhna ek nazor,
Bondhu re!
Oporadhi hoileo aami tor

Aami jodi jai moria
Ke korbe tore aador?
Oporadhi hoileo aami tor.

Recognizing Nita's voice, Boori took the curry pot off the stove and ran to the yard. However, she was dumbstruck at the sight of the dusty, frazzled face of the woman singing under the *sojna* tree. Nita looked worn out with her uncombed, raven hair all matted. It seemed as though she had walked a thousand miles. But then the roads were home to Nita. Boori had never seen her friend look so devastated. 'Give me a drink, *soi*,' she croaked as she spotted Boori.

Boori brought her an earthen jar of water that she drank in one gulp.

'I have walked a long way,' she said, and felt a parching thirst. 'I didn't stop anywhere on my way, so I thought I might get a glass of water from you. The others couldn't quench one third of my thirst!'

Boori watched her drink. Allah! The thirst that people have! She knew that Nita's thirst was not for water alone. Nita's heart was ablaze. It was for something else, something other than a mere drink. Boori's heart felt heavy.

'You were right,' Boori answered, 'at least it made you come to me. You've been on my mind for a while. Now let's go inside. You can put your feet up.'

'It's fine here under this tree. It's cool and quiet in the shade. There's no breeze inside. I'm happy to stay here.'

Nita took a tobacco leaf that was tucked inside the fold of her sari at her waist and began to chew. She looked slightly less tired now. Resting in the shade, she seemed at least momentarily at peace. She felt as though Boori was her younger sister and her smile took away all her pain.

'You haven't been around for a while,' Boori pointed out.

'Has it been that long? But the last time I saw you seems like yesterday. I feel really happy when I am with you,' Nita said.

Boori smiled at the older woman, then leaned her head against the *sojna* trunk. She felt that the tree removed all traces of sadness from her life. It was like a friend who soothed her pain. Like flowers in autumn or spring. Nita once said that the shade of a tree or the colour of a flower could make one forget one's pain.

'Where have you been all this time?' Boori asked her friend.

'I've been looking for a new *moner manush.*'

'Why?' Boori asked, 'What happened to Ramdas?'

'He's dead.'

'Dead? Don't say that.'

'Yes, really, he *is* dead,' Nita sighed. She then added more sharply, 'Talking doesn't get your vegetables cooked.'

Boori forgot about her curry pot and hunkered down before Nita, her chin resting on her knees. She listened to her friend stroking the strings of her *dotara.*

'Put your *dotara* down and tell me what happened,' Boori asked.

'I couldn't really figure out what the matter was. He'd been suffering from a fever for seven days. That was the last day of Asharh. It had been raining all day. One of his *shissay,* Shubol, was staying with us. A lamp was lit. Ramdas was lying on the cot with his eyes closed. My ears were filled with the sound of rain dripping off the *devdaru* leaves. Ramdas was lying quietly. He had a high fever. My mind was as restless as a palm tree during monsoon. Every now and then I shot a glance at his face, his eyes. He threw the *dotara* down and peered silently through the window.

Shubol asked me, "Why are you fidgeting so much?"

I couldn't say anything. I kept watching him, hoping he would turn around and look back. I saw a darkness creep onto his face. His cheeks were sunken. His cheekbones stuck out. Looking at his face, I knew his days were numbered. I never knew a human face could get so dark. Ramdas suddenly asked me to play the *dotara*. It caught me by surprise as he was not responding to my words. I called him again. But still, there was no response. So I played the *dotara*. I was shaking like a leaf. I couldn't play. It felt as though I didn't know how to play, not even to pluck one string. It was Ramdas who taught me to play the *dotara*.'

Nita wiped her tears. Feeling a lump in her throat, Boori was tongue-tied. She conjured up a small hut on the bank of the Shomeswari. She knew about the hut from Nita's previous stories. She felt as though she knew everything there was to know about the hut. All she had to do was just close her eyes. She had also heard of Ramdas, who was Nita's soulmate. The two had decided not to get married. They spurned the institution and saw their relationship as the only celestial truth in the world.

Sometimes, they would rest under the shadow of a *devdaru* tree or dip their feet into the Shomeswari, playing the *dotara*. Neither would talk. No bird would sing, no leaf rustle to stop their singing. Only the clattering notes of the *dotara* could be heard. Banks of clouds loomed on the horizon over the Meghaloy Mountains.

As Boori mulled over Nita's story, a wave of happiness overwhelmed her. She saw herself as Nita, wandering along the road with her soulmate, unmarried by choice, obeying no social code and going only where fancy took them. Boori lost herself in her daydream. Drinking a glass of water, Nita asked, 'Are you fed up with my story?'

'No, not at all. Please, carry on. I'm so happy you shared it with me.'

'I couldn't play the *dotara* properly at all that day,' Nita continued, 'my brain was dull. I played out of tune. I have never played it like that before. Suddenly, Ramdas lifted his eyes and reached out to take the instrument, handing it to Shubol. Ashen-faced, he looked at me and said, "You'll never play my *dotara* again."

'My eyes were filled with tears. I clasped his hands to my chest, asking for his forgiveness. I was heartbroken. I leaned close to his face and whispered, "Why did it have to happen to me, Ramdas?"

'"Find a new *moner manush*, my time is up."

'He kept silent. After a while, he opened his eyes and told me to seek a new companion. He motioned me to sit beside him and wheezed, "Don't cry. I can't stand tears. If you want to see me happy, then wipe the tears off your face. The days we have spent together gave us great pleasure, but somebody has to leave this world first. You shouldn't have gone to so much trouble. No one can overstay his time on this earth."

'His words couldn't stop my tears welling up. I wept all night, resting my head on his lap. He didn't say anything else and I could sense his heartbeat was getting fainter. Shubol was lying on a mat by the door. I was alone, watching a dying man. It was still pouring outside. The heaviest rainfall of the season. The lamp flickered with the wind. Shadows flew in all directions. I dreaded the slow march of death. I felt as though I was dying too.

'Ramdas passed away late that night.'

Nita paused for a moment, her eyes bright and clear. She took another sip. Boori couldn't break her gaze. Nita went on thumbing through the pages of her memory.

'You know, that whole night I sat outside under the pouring rain. The pitter-patter sounded like Ramdas' singing. His voice used to make me mad. Shubol once teased me, "Have you washed Ramdas away with the rain?"

'I didn't respond. How could I? The following morning, Shubol and I offered his body to the Shomeswari and watched it drift away. Then I packed up and set off with my things over my shoulder. Shubol began to pluck the *dotara*. I said, "Shubol, you can stay here. I will never come back."

"'I am pretty sure of that," he replied. He didn't even raise his head.

"'You know a thing or two, Shubol," I said.

'He didn't say anything; he didn't even look at me. I could not figure out why he disliked me. He remained silent even as I left. I have never set foot back there. Now the roads are my home. I have travelled far and wide since I took up a Baul minstrel's life. But I've never had any peace of mind. Some people come into this life unwanted like the roadside dust, but some are like the clouds drifting in the sky, never breaking into rain, even when we will them. So, I wend my way through the hours. Sometimes, I don't feel like going on, yet I have to.'

Nita turned the peg of the *dotara* clockwise to loosen the string. She began to sing again.

> *Age ke jane gou emon hobe*
> *Gaur prem kore amar kulman iabe*
> *Chilam kuler kulbala*
> *Prem fandhe badhlo gola*
> *Tanle to aar na jai khola*
> *Bolle ke bojhe*

Nita sang in a low voice without playing. Boori sat quietly, enjoying the song. She would get restless when Nita talked. Nita lingered on the song, exposing her raw pain. All of a sudden, Boori felt lonely, like the victim of an unfulfilled life. Gafoor couldn't become her *moner manush*. Their life was so routine-like and caught up in the wheels of religion and tradition. Nita could do as she liked. Boori couldn't. It was as simple as that. Nita's life could be as carefree as a southern breeze, while Boori was cooped up in her little room. Her marriage and her husband, supposedly her life's light and meaning rang hollow. If only she could break free.

Nita stopped her singing abruptly and looked at Boori.

'I wish I could be like you!' exclaimed Boori.

'What are you talking about?' She asked gently. 'Nobody in his right mind would choose this roving life. You're happy. Why should you take up the life of a minstrel? I would ask for nothing more than a roof over my head, with a husband and a son.'

'A son?' Boori's voice quivered.

Nita was puzzled. She knew one thing or two, and though she wasn't sure what was wrong, she pretty much hit the nail on the head. Boori wiped her tears with her sari. Nita tried to cheer her up.

'I'll take you to the next Poush mela in Srinile. You can pay your respect there and you shall be blessed with a son if you make a vow in the name of Kesa Baba. Kesa Baba is a holy man. You will find some peace of mind when you see him. You would not believe the crowds he attracts! Souls are renewed at this holy place.'

Boori was reminded of Namita who was full of praise and respect for Kesa Baba as well. Boori felt the urge to go and see him right away. Namita's little ray of hope just shone through the clouds. She felt lighter. Soon her hope welled up inside her and the pain stopped gnawing her mind.

'You wash your hands and face,' Boori ordered. 'I'll get you something to eat.'

Boori put her curry pot on the stove again and hurriedly cooked the meal. She cut a piece of banana leaf to serve on as her friend didn't use plates. There was boiled *paijam* rice, *magoor* fish, fried sabzi and *peyajkoli*, all cooked with great care. Nita enjoyed her meal. She usually didn't have enough to eat, not even the measly rice she scraped from alms. It all went soft and gooey when cooked. But she would laugh it off. She couldn't care less about proper food. Many a day went by during which she had to keep going on an empty stomach. Boori treated her heartily, going out of her way to keep her friend happy and well-fed. The old woman shovelled it in, and then licked her fingers clean.

When the meal was over, Nita put some betel nut leaf in her mouth and got up, ready to go with her bag and *dotara*.

'I will take my leave now, *soi!*'

'Where are you off to?'

'To look for a *moner manush*,' Nita replied, tongue-in-cheek. 'I'll leave no stone unturned until I find one. It's hard to struggle and beg all on your own. I tell you, you don't want this life hanging by a thread.'

Nita chuckled heartily. Walking off, she broke into song:

Milon hobe kotodine
Amar moner manuser sone
Chatok prai ohornishi
Ceye ache kaloshashi
Hobo bole carandasi
O ta hoina kopal gune

A puff of dust rose in the singer's wake. Her song kept playing on and on to haunt Boori all day. While going down to the *pukur* for a bath, Boori would pause, suddenly recalling words Nita had said. While combing her hair in the shade of the *tetool* tree, or stirring *chochchori* on the stove, her hands would freeze mechanically for no reason. Sitting in the veranda, she mused. Every cell, every nerve in her body was worn out. Her mind was weary. Gafoor had gone to the bazaar, and would be back in the evening. Salim and Kalim went out to play after lunch. All was quiet, but Boori was on pins and needles. She tried to embroider a quilt, but her dreams got tangled up with the coloured threads.

Salim and Kalim ran home, hollering, 'Maa, Maa, listen, Sakhina bubu has just brought a baby from somewhere. Look, he's a shrimp!' Kalim made hand gestures indicating how tiny the baby was. He was more excited as he was the younger one. Salim, the elder, was more reserved. Kalim hugged Boori and said, 'Maa, why don't you give us a baby sister?'

'Er...I'll get you one someday. Now let go of me.'

'Maa, you know, the baby was going "Waaa! Waaa!"'

Kalim mimicked the baby's mewling. Boori laughed at his clowning.

'When will you give us a baby sister? Please?'

'Hm! Let me think about it. I can't get you one just now. We have to set up a lucky day and then we'll get one. Okay?'

Boori touched his chin affectionately.

'Really, you'll get us one? Then promise three times.'

'Well, you have my word. Now you go and play. That's a good boy.'

Kalim, who was keener on the idea of a baby sister, would always have the last word. He goaded her into achieving the impossible. Salim, on the other hand, was quiet and never acted out his childish whims.

The boys bolted as quickly as they had appeared. They were never still—always on the run, winging further afield. Boori was reminded of her own childhood. She was always on her feet then. She'd break free from her tether and wander off further and further. No one could beat her at the *ciburi* game. Once off, there was no way she would stop, not even to catch her breath. Sometimes she crashed into a bush or tree, but she'd stop the bleeding by crushing *shialmutha* leaves with her teeth and squeezing the juice on the open cuts. Jalil used to scold her, 'Boori, this really tops it! How can you bear all this? It would have driven me nuts!'

'You shouldn't have been born a boy!' Boori would guffaw. 'Why don't you become Boori and I'll be Jalil! Hey, no sweat! Huh?'

'Hah! What a mad woman!' he teased her. 'What would you do if you were Jalil?'

'I'd run away, never to return.'

'I'd do that anyway,' Jalil replied thoughtlessly.

'Will you?'

'You see, I might one day. But I don't have your fire. You were always so different.'

Now looking back, Boori realized she didn't have that fire in her anymore. She was now drained. She no longer wished to fly away from her cage to infinity. She wished to be a mother. She lost the thread of thoughts as Salim and Kalim went out. She was jolted back to reality. Sakhina was married only last Ôgrôhayôn, and she was already blessed with a son before the year was out. It was as if the finger of fate had marked her out.

Boori folded her embroidery and got up to leave. Feeling the room's silent, scorching heat sear into her, she fled to the courtyard. A dove was cooing nonstop. It made Boori wistful. The sound broke her heart into a thousand pieces.

During moments of greater intimacy, Boori would sound out Gafoor. He'd laugh it off. Back to his grinning old self. He felt sorry for her childlessness and his heart would go out to her. He would never get mad or find fault with her, the way his neighbours would. The neighbours sometimes called her 'barren', which would infuriate Gafoor.

'What is it to you if she is barren?' he'd scream back. 'Do you feed her? Do you take care of her?'

The more the neighbours trashed Boori, the more Gafoor worshipped her, calling her his new fairy. In his eyes, her desire to be a mother was entirely natural. He was not so keen though, as he already had two sons. If she were to have a child, it was fine by him. The only snag was that a baby would want cuddles and undivided attention. The uncertainty didn't bother Gafoor though. He felt that a baby would come along in due time, no matter what quack medicine or shrine she tried. He turned his back to her and went to sleep. Hurt by his indifference, Boori couldn't sleep.

'Why are you buttoned-up?' she erupted, pummelling his back with her fists.

'Don't you think you've tried enough black magic. You've been through everything—tabiz, charms, home-made potions, herb medicine, as well as vows to saints—what more can you do?'

'This is my last chance. Let me try!' Boori urged in a weak voice, clutching at her last hope. 'I won't ever bother you with it again.'

'You don't know how to get to Srinile Dham. It is about six miles away—you have to walk a three-mile slog and go on a buffalo cart for another three miles. It is hard going. You won't be able to make it on your own.'

'Of course I can, please let me go,' she begged him, her voice throbbing with such urgency that Gafoor really felt for her.

'Eh? I'll take you there if it makes you happy. You're my gold mine, Boori! You filled my life with happiness.' Gafoor kissed her fondly. There was nothing in his way.

Burying her face in his chest, Boori felt at peace with the world. That night she surrendered to her husband's wild desire. Her blood raced quickly through her veins and every cell of her body was aroused. She was swept away in an intense wave. She didn't utter a word, she rather enjoyed every second of their lovemaking. The bamboo trees wrestled with the wind. Dry leaves rustled in the courtyard. An owl hooted somewhere. The moon poured a milky light over the horizon. Quietly, Boori and Gafoor walked out to the canal and unmoored the boat.

They didn't go with the intention of fishing but wanted to enjoy each other's intimacy. Her pleasure floated over the water with the tinkle of her laugh, while her husband bided his time to plunge into the river of her blood. The water gently lapped against the canal's mud banks. The tall grasses growing alongside the water cast a pale, silent reflection, even though the water was too dark for Boori to make out her own shadow.

Not that she was bothered, her mind was elsewhere. Sitting on the boat floorboards, she wondered about Gafoor's strong physical desire. What a man Gafoor was! He forgot about fishing when he was aroused. On his boat, he would change into a ball of liquid fire. He preferred the boat for making love. Yet, he was restless once he was on the boat.

Boori saw to it that no one was watching. The boat scudded till they had reached a quiet spot that was secluded enough for their purpose. Maybe he was looking for a place where nature radiated her warmth. Boori tried to read his face, but could not tell the difference between the shadows of his eyes.

Then suddenly she remembered Jalil. Thinking about him flooded her with a burning tide she couldn't stem. Jalil had left for Dacca right after Boori had got married. He was a rickshaw-wallah to start with, but was making a pretty packet and was quite happy with his life, it seemed. He would tell her stories about Dacca whenever he made brief trips to the village. Boori would always hang on his every word.

'I'd take you to Dacca if we were married,' Jalil had whispered one day.

Boori couldn't be angry with him, even though she wanted to. But it was as it should have been. Jalil had left home and done lots of menial jobs working as a tea-wallah, a hotel porter, a motor mechanic and finally a rickshaw-wallah. The small pond fish was thrashing about in the big river! Boori's heart ached after him.

'What harm would have been done if Jalil had married me?' She brooded. She concluded that it would never have been possible. But she also realized that Jalil had left a permanent mark on her whole being. She wanted to feel his presence now.

His memory started flowing through her veins. Her hand suddenly gripped the gunwale and she gritted her teeth.

'What's the matter, Boori? What's on your mind?'

'Jalil.'

'Jalil?' Gafoor frowned and puckered his eyebrows. 'Ya Allah! Why on earth are you thinking about Jalil?'

'He was just on my mind, that's all.' Boori laughed out loud.

The darkness came to life and Gafoor eased up his paddling. They were approaching their nook under the *tetool*.

'What are you scared of?' she asked.

'You joke about so many things,' Gafoor replied. Then he relented, smiling and scratching his head. He jumped into the water to tie the boat. Boori smiled to herself. 'Let it be a joke to Gafoor when I feel the stab of pain,' she thought. She shrank within herself again.

Sundar tomar mukher hasire
Sundor tomar banshi
Surete pagol korlire bandhu
Mon korili udasi.

পৌষ
Poush

Nita arrived just two days before the Poush mela, accompanied by her new flame.

Choron Das had a fair complexion and a cheerful face, but he was a stubby sort of a man. His rough, reedy voice jarred on your ears and was barely audible when he sang.

Whatever plagued her, Boori's pains melted at the sound of the *dotara*. She knew the sound only too well. She took the pot off the stove and ran out of her kitchen. The courtyard was littered with drying paddy stalks. Boori met a different Nita, her face was brightly lit. Choron Das was standing at her side. She went and hugged Nita, then stared at Choron Das with inquisitive eyes, which made Nita giggle.

'What makes your eyes squint? It's my soulmate you're looking at, *soi*!' she said. 'I have found my *moner manush*!'

Boori smiled. She led them across the paddy-strewn yard to the veranda. The farmhands raised their eyes and were thunderstruck. Nita had thrown her bedroll down and lay spreadeagle with her feet and ankles caked with dry mud and her tousled hair in the wind. Her clothes did not cover her body. Everything about her was in utter disarray.

'I love the smell of unripe paddy, *soi*!' she said, taking a deep breath. 'If only I could live a life like this, I'd give anything to be amid green paddy all year long.'

'Nothing can cage you or stop you from going anywhere, *soi*,' Boori replied. 'Your life would dry up if you stayed put.'

Nita smiled, keeping her face averted. 'Can I have some water?' she asked.

Boori went inside to fetch water and Choron Das started to play the *dotara*.

'Your *soi* is not bad-looking, eh?' he said.

'Impressed?' Nita asked him in jest.

'So what if I like her?' the minstrel queried, laughing gently.

Boori returned with a full pitcher. Nita drank half of it and passed it to Choron Das. He drank it in one swig. Boori just gaped at them.

'Why are you two sharing the water? I can get you some more.'

'We always eat and drink that way. We can't have our fill in any other way!'

Nita looked different today, Boori hardly recognized her. She had changed beyond all recognition.

'Will you be going to the Poush mela? That's why I came.'

'Mm-hmm. My husband has gone to hire a buffalo cart.' Boori's eyes blazed with delight. 'Will you go in a buffalo cart yourself?'

'Pff! My feet are my wings. And then Choron Das is coming along with me.' Nita giggled and gave him a meaningful glance.

He winked at her and bent over the *dotara* strings. Boori noticed the exchange and was a bit taken aback. She thought that maybe her own life could have been like this if she was married to Jalil. Different thoughts flashed through her mind as the farmhands herded the buffaloes nearby. The workers were busy with husking, they were raucous. This time of the year was a very busy time for Boori. Her head was wobbling. She was thinking of giving Nita a sack full of rice so that she didn't have to beg for alms. But she was unsure whether she would accept the offer.

'Why do you want to fill my sack?' Nita told her once. 'If it is filled then I wouldn't be able to walk on the roads of the village. Do you want me to stop my wandering? I would be dead then.'

Boori asked, 'Shall I serve food to your *moner manush*? It is almost ready.'

'Let's get going! We should be setting off or we'll be late. You know we have to stop at lots of different places along the way.'

Boori went into the hut and returned with a basket full of puffed rice and molasses.

'Here, have these. Since you are in hurry, and I haven't finished cooking. There isn't much, though.'

'Take it! My friend is giving us this as an offering.' Nita put a handful of *moori* and molasses in her mouth. 'Whatever *soi* gives, we take with pleasure.'

Choron Das kept his head low, his long curly hair hanging down his neck. He plucked the *dotara* absent-mindedly and started to sing.

Na jene mojona pirite
Jene shune koro pirit
Shesh bhalo daray jate
Pirit korar hoi basona
Sadhur kache jange bena
Loha jemon poroshe sona
Hobe sei mote

'What's wrong with you, *moner manush*?' Nita jibed. 'Why aren't you looking at my *soi*?'

Boori stared at him.

'Isn't your *moner manush* a lover boy?'

'See! She is making fun of you!' Nita teased Choron Das, tapping his knees rhythmically.

The player swung his hair back and shot Boori a wide-eyed gaze. Startled and ill at ease, Boori looked away.

'Love and compassion are to be shared or they go to waste,' he answered.

'Tsk-tsk! Your *moner manush*'s way too shy, Nita, but he's

always ready to shoot the arrow of fun and fell his foe,' Boori teased.

She ran off before Choron Das could shout back. Both minstrels had a good laugh. Nita whispered amorously into his ear, 'Are you sure you have hit the arrow in the right place?'

'Mmm, absolutely! Why else would I roam around the world with you?'

Choron Das began to gulp down puffed rice, pretending to be busy. Nita nibbled at a handful of rice while watching the workers as they husked the crops. She felt no connection to such family life. She wasn't cut out for a settled life. She preferred the freedom of a vagrant's life over anything else. She had no idea what a granary full of rice meant. Suddenly, she laughed on her own. She never wanted this kind of bondage. Not everybody was fit to do everything. She smiled back at Choron Das, who was a bit surprised.

'What's so funny?' he asked.

'Nothing!'

'Tell me!'

'I just thought that I'd never be a housewife like Boori.'

'She'd never go for your hurly-burly world.'

Boori looked at Nita and her new flame, and said, 'Well, you have a friend who will make you forget the pain of the road. He will take you on his shoulders when your legs can no longer carry you.'

Choron Das laughed uproariously. He got down from the veranda and stood beside the stack of rice. He played his *dotara* in front of the workers and danced.

'Look,' some of the farmhands said, 'he is dancing like a madman. Let's shake our legs and join him.'

'You're right,' the minstrels said and laughed.

Six of the workers started dancing with Choron Das. Salim and Kalim also joined them. Choron Das handed the boys the *dotara* and asked them to play.

They gave it back to him, crestfallen.

'You play it,' they said. 'We haven't learned how to play it.'

'Okay then I will teach you how to play. I will teach your mother too. Go and ask your mother if she wants you to learn to play the *dotara*.'

The boys ran to their mother.

'Maa! Do you want to learn how to play the *dotara*?'

'No!' Boori shook her head, covering her face with her hands.

The boys ran back to Choron Das and said, 'Baul kaka! Maa doesn't want to learn, but we do.'

Choron Das gazed at Boori.

Nita came close to her and whispered, 'I think my *moner manush* has somehow fallen for you!'

'Stop talking nonsense!'

Nita patted Boori on the back and said goodbye.

'Well, dear, we have to be on our way. We have a long way to go. It's fun to be on the road, but it's hard going, too.'

'When will you be back?' Boori's voice sounded anxious.

'I'll see you at the mela.'

'Will you?'

'Yes, of course. I'll be looking out for you, don't you worry. This time your wishes will come true. You mark my words!'

'Insha'allah,' Boori begged.

The two of them slung their bags over their shoulders and were off. Boori kept watching them until they were mere dots on the horizon. She had lost all track of the labourers, the paddy to be husked, the buffaloes...even the *sojna* tree. Instead, she went to the bank of the *pukur* and just sat there. She rued everything in her rut of a life and felt her heart skip a beat. Tears rolled down her cheeks. She walked back to her hut and wept for a long while, her face buried in the quilt.

Early next morning, Gafoor and Boori set off for the Poush mela. Gafoor felt a divine hand shake off all Boori's cares and stress along the journey. Now she was invincible. She kept silent, her thoughts drifting off with the squeaking of the buffalo cart. Boori stared at the skyline with eyes wide open. It was the first time that she had left Haldi.

She realized there was a village beyond her own, a field beyond their field. New roads emerged from the one they were treading and went Allah knows where! Yet, she was too startled to take in all the countless new sights along the way. Everything looked different. The hues of the villages along the way were very different from her village. Familiar trees wore different colours or had different shaped leaves. The houses by the roadside were built differently too. Boori had never realized that there were so many things outside her village. She breathed in the new atmosphere—the fragrance of Haldi had evaporated and the new air was fresh and tickled her nostrils.

Her thoughts slipped wistfully back to her childhood, as the cart trundled towards Srinile Dham. The buffalo cart ground to a halt. They had to walk along the dirt tracks between the paddies. Boori was oblivious to her weariness. The paddy harvest was over and the bald fields looked parched, but Boori found the walk pleasant nonetheless. She would wander off far and wide. Burning straw, heating date juice or cooking sweet potatoes would be a treat on such jaunts. Those were her golden days which lingered in her memory like a treasure chest and with which she could play at will. As she was daydreaming, Boori stumbled on the paddy stubble, but Gafoor caught her by the arm, guiding her shaky steps.

'You should walk a bit more carefully,' he cautioned her.

'Sorry, I lost my footing,' she said, red with embarrassment.

She walked on, looking at those strangers milling around her on their way to the shrine. As they drew closer to Srinile Dham, the smile on her face said it all—she could barely contain her excitement as she jostled with the crowd—a swarm of dark-bodied insects. The roof of the makeshift mela pavilion was still some distance away. A low rumble reached her ears. Walking along the paddy dyke, Boori came down to a flat area, her bare feet caked with dust.

'Hey! Slow down, Boori,' Gafoor urged.

Boori nodded with a smile. Gafoor whispered to her,

'You look very beautiful, mashallah! You have come to this mela looking like a fairy.'

Boori covered her face with her sari *anchol*. Her face was flushed and she walked more gingerly and shyly. She paused to weave the dream of her life in the shade of a neem tree that sliced the sunlight. Hugging the pouch tightly to her chest, she went to the *dham* and tied up the pouch onto a branch of the neem, making a vow in the name of the saint. She went on to daub her whole body with dust from the *dham*, but unlike other devotees, didn't roll herself on the ground. Something inside her told her that she should complete the ritual. Her faith shouldn't be found wanting. One minute she found it unseemly to be making a scene of herself, the next, she pushed her way through the crowd. As a mark of faith and respect to the saint, she forced herself to bow down and touch the earth with her nose. She couldn't, however, quite bring herself to bow too low. So, she rushed through it all, rubbing holy dust over her skin.

'Will I be blessed, even though I didn't kiss the earth?' Boori wondered out loud.

Gafoor laughed it off; her doubts and hesitation were a source of amusement.

'It doesn't matter one jot. Only faith can get you everything. You've paid your respect to Kesa Baba, and that's that.'

Boori felt relieved at his words. Gafoor had no more to say. He was in two minds about the whole thing. His head ruled his heart when it came to blind faith, and he acted according to logic rather than impulse, although this time he relented for Boori's sake.

Gafoor sat more confused than he cared to admit; would Srinile Dham's neem tree be able to fulfil her dreams? Would it end her six year-long wait? Would Namita's belief make Boori's dream come true?

He looked ahead and saw a huge crowd around them. People were still coming and going. This mela would spill over the next two days. Everyone had one goal—to hang a pouch of five *annas* on the neem tree with a wish. People came from far and away. Some even waited a whole year for this. All their hopes were vested in the mela, so they ran like scared rabbits, just to have their wishes fulfilled.

Jaded, Gafoor kept staring at the palm tree. He was easily exhausted these days. He was missing his hookah right now.

Once her devotional duties were over, Boori fluttered about the mela with Gafoor, feeling like a feather in the wind. She joined the throng snaking its way around fire eaters on stilts and a *khelnapheri-wallah*. The ambulant vendor had a rainbow display of toys and trinkets to fulfil every child's fantasy—there were clay dolls, *kaporer putul*, wooden toys, spinning tops, tom-tom drums, paper cranes and even homemade food on display. Boori hunted for gifts for the boys. She didn't care much for *teer dhonuk* or *gulti*. Instead, she bought wooden horses and elephants for Salim. Kalim had requested a flute. Boori also bought some glass bangles, a nose ring and a set of earrings for herself.

'What would you like to have?' she asked Gafoor, her voice brimming with excitement.

'Me? I don't need anything,' he replied.

'How about a *gamcha* and a fish basket?'

'Why would I need them if you won't go fishing with me?'

'That's why you should buy them. If I come along, you never try to fish. You always come home empty-handed.'

'Easier said than done,' he retorted. Against his better judgment, his dreams of a miraculous catch always came crashing.

'When was the last time you landed *mrigel* or *shorpunti*?' she taunted.

'Remember all those *kachki* and *katla* fish kissing goodbye to the river just to have a peek at you!' he bantered in turn.

Boori caught the twinkle in his eyes and then looked away. Gafoor's voice gave her a sharp tingle of excitement. They bought the *gamcha* and basket. Wandering on, they spotted Nita and Choron Das sitting amid a cluster of people under a large *koroi* tree. Boori watched them. Nita was singing, with her eyes closed, in a soft voice to the tune of Choron Das's *ektara*. Boori hardly recognized her friend. This Nita wasn't exhausted and worn out. She seemed to be an entirely different person. She belonged to a different world. Boori was not part of that world nor did she understand it.

She felt like running up to her friend and begging her, 'Please make me like you, or my wish may not be granted.'

Gafoor pulled her back. Under Nita's spell, Boori chose to follow in Gafoor's footsteps.

'She's in deep meditation, she wouldn't know you,' Gafoor pleaded.

'Uh-uh! She's singing.'

'Pretty much the same to these folks,' he pointed out.

'I suppose so,' Boori admitted, realizing that singing was Nita's only refuge.

Boori melted into the motley crowd. The tone of the *ektara* stilled the young woman's nerves. She couldn't forget Nita's face. She longed to be rejuvenated like her two friends, Nita and Namita.

Sauntering about the mela recharged Boori, as she could seldom have such a free rein. The dusty air, the northerly chill and general chaos of the mela couldn't take the wind out of her sails.

Gafoor was winded like a spent horse. His eyes smarted and

he coughed continuously, blood rushing to his face. The hustle and bustle of the crowd taxed his patience. His discomfort soon wore off, however, as he caught up with Boori. His wife seemed to have sloughed off all cares and worries; she had recovered her youthful grace and enthusiasm. He marvelled at the way she found the energy to keep going, whilst for him everything was an uphill struggle.

'What are you thinking about, Gafoor?'

'Nothing, let's go home, Boori.'

'It's only noon,' Boori's voice sounded cautious.

'Days are still short and we've got to get back before it gets dark.'

'It won't matter one way or the other,' Boori chipped in. She craned her neck and stretched her limbs ready to go. Gafoor beamed.

'All right then! Let's get some food.'

They went to a stall with bamboo walls. After their lunch, Gafoor dozed off leaning against a tree, while Boori had her eyes on the magic show. Her titter and clapping would soon wake him up from his catnap.

On the way home, Boori beamed with excitement. She strode so effortlessly along the dykes running across the paddies that Gafoor lagged far behind. They finally crossed the last paddy field and scrambled into the buffalo cart. Breathless, Gafoor leaned against the back of the cart to catch his breath. He was overwhelmed by the chill of winter and the squeak of the cart wheels. Could Srinile have snatched away something precious?

The fisherman dreaded to think what Boori would do if her wish was not fulfilled. How would he be able to plod on with a woman as cold as a stone? The scene paled and a white dove flew overhead, only to disappear into the darkness. The slow monotonous pace of the buffalo cart presaged an impending rut.

Gafoor was at a loss to read Boori's mind. Magic dreams

would leap off his wife's imagination and melt into thin air. Gafoor didn't figure in this landscape with its brightly-plumed peacock. He would remain anchored in his own world.

'Why do you look so miserable?' Boori asked, all of a sudden.

'Why do you ask?'

'You face looks so pale.'

'It's nothing,' Gafoor said reassuringly.

Boori didn't ask any further questions. She soon fell asleep, lulled by the cart's dull trundling.

Back home, Boori spent her days busily. Gafoor would sometimes eavesdrop or steal a glance to read her mind. Boori acted like a colourful *projapoti* fluttering over the lush green grass; in this case Gafoor's family was the green field over which she flitted. She dispelled Gafoor's worst fears as she no longer sat idle all day, scowling and weeping. She no longer slipped back into her own shell, wringing her hands by the *pukur*. In a show of affection, she would pick on Gafoor or play some pranks. Sometimes she patted the boys' cheeks.

One day, Kalim exclaimed sounding puzzled, 'Maa, why are you so happy?'

'Aha, *dushto chele!*' Boori suddenly blushed. 'What are you talking about?'

'You are so changed. Now you don't curse us as you used to.'

'Have I ever cursed you?' she jested.

'You did on and off. But you've stopped. Tell me, what has come over you?'

Boori tried to ward off further questions.

'You've started asking questions like an ageing father. Go and play *dangguli*. I'll make some coconut sweets for you this afternoon.'

'I won't go until you tell me,' Kalim replied stubbornly.

'Are you serious?' Boori asked.

'Dead serious.'

And Kalim ran off. Gafoor sniggered at his wife.

'You make me mad,' Boori bellowed, blushing. Gafoor roared and hugged her.

The days prior to their visit to the Srinile mela had been agonizing, but Boori was now back to her usual lively self, humouring Kalim's most childish whims. She would play with him in the courtyard. She was on better terms with her neighbours too. During Namita's visit, a sea of emotions flowed through her body and mind. But Boori never lost hope.

'Your saint hasn't granted your wish, yet,' Gafoor teased her one day.

Boori pressed his mouth with her palm.

'*Chi*! You shouldn't disrespect Baba like that! These things don't happen in the blink of an eye. Be patient. Good things come to those who wait.'

'Yes, it's good to have faith.'

Gafoor was won over. He heaved a sigh. Whether or not Boori gave birth to a child mattered little to him. He was just happy to see her in such a good mood. She deserved a good turn. It was long overdue. He was grateful to Kesa Baba from the Srinile ashram for tipping the scales his way. He had already been blessed with the birth of his two sons.

In the meantime, Jalil came back from Dacca. His mother had approached a *ghotok* to arrange his marriage with a beautiful girl. After getting married, he would move to Dacca with his bride. Long ago, Jalil had lost his father. So his mother, who was everything to him, acted as his *wali*. Upon seeing Jalil, Boori's spirit sank. Before he could say anything, she erupted,

'I won't go to your wedding, Jalil!'

Jalil was tongue-tied. He couldn't figure out what she meant.

'What's wrong with you, Boori,' he blurted out.

'Nothing.'

'Then what stops you from coming to my *gaye holud*?'

Both remained silent for a while. Boori was slicing betel nuts gingerly. No one else sliced betel nuts so fine.

'What will you do with all this betel, Boori?'

'Sakhina is hosting a dinner for the naming of her son.'

'A little bird told me that you visited the Srinile ashram.'

'What if I did?' Boori snapped, her eyes ablaze.

Caught off balance, Jalil fumbled for an answer. 'You didn't have to. You should have asked Gafoor bhai to call on a doctor in the city.'

'What's a doctor got to do with it? I am not sick.'

'That's nonsense and I can't believe it. One of my friends called in a doctor for his wife. After the check-up, the doctor said that she could never give birth. Doctors can find anything through medical check-ups.'

Boori didn't buy his 'I know better' line. She glanced at him vacantly. She knew that people went to see a doctor when they were sick.

'What are you up to?' Boori asked, with a certain amount of scepticism.

'I mean it, Boori. Trust me, I'm serious.'

'Well, I don't want to talk about it,' Boori shrugged it off, piqued.

Then she accidentally cut her finger with the betel knife. 'Ya Allah!' she screamed and ran off, wailing and clasping her finger. She looked for a rag to wrap round it.

'How bad is the cut?' Jalil queried.

'It's nothing.' Boori came in sight of the *pukur*.

Jalil thought she'd be better off left alone. He was annoyed at her haughtiness. He had wanted to talk to her about his wedding. But Boori had pricked his happy bubble. He went to the bazaar instead.

Boori sank her ankles into the water. Jalil's sudden appearance would always leave her in a state, and this chat made her feel the worse for wear. Boori no longer liked him.

The pain in her chest was searing and it had no outlet. Under the monkey jack fluttering in the breeze, she stared at the canal to cast adrift the words which ran riot. She watched the swift current. She loved looking at the tides. The bank was full to its gills, which made her heart leap with joy. Floods meant a fresh start. She envied the lotus and *kochuripana* afloat on the water. All her sadness vanished all of a sudden.

Jalil's wedding took place amid a grand fanfare, with choruses and wild singing. A couple of days later, he went back to Dacca with his bride. Once again, Boori was overcome with nostalgia.

All of a sudden, Boori's ageing mother passed away after a protracted illness. Her death marked the end of a painful chapter in the family's life. Taking care of the bedridden old woman had left its toll on Boori too. When her mother breathed her last, she wailed. True, Halima Khatoon had lost her spite as she swam against her tide of woes and troubles. Yet, Jalil's wedding rankled more in Boori's heart.

Before leaving for Dacca, Jalil asked Boori,

'What do you think of my Korimunnessa?'

'She's a pretty, pretty girl just like a full moon. Mind her when you take her to the city, though,' Boori replied, avoiding eye contact.

'What are you getting at?'

'Just a thought,' she said, giggling.

'I don't understand you,' Jalil grunted, a scowl on his face.

Jalil didn't chance running into Boori while getting ready to leave for Dacca, but he left her with bitter memories.

Eight years into her married life Boori finally became pregnant. With the first symptoms of pregnancy she became restless. The moment she felt the baby kicking in her womb, she rushed to Gafoor while he was sound asleep. She poked his ribs and pulled the quilt off his body.

'What's the matter, Boori?' Gafoor asked, half asleep.

'Wait till I tell you the good news.'

Boori wildly rubbed her face against Gafoor's chest. He had never seen his wife in such a state. She had not been this physically close to him since Allah knows when.

'What's the matter?' he asked, lifting up her face. 'What's been bothering you?'

'The saint has blessed me.'

'Really?'

'Yes, I can feel it.'

Boori felt elated and Gafoor whooped it up, drunk with joy. He had no idea he would be so excited to hear about Boori's pregnancy. He couldn't keep his eyes off her. Salim's mother had not been over the moon in her time. Being as fertile as the overflowing Shomeswari, she conceived only days into their marriage. It was almost a routine event. At the time, Gafoor was indifferent to the news.

'Fat lot of good that is!' he had grouched to his first wife.

'Aren't you happy?' she pleaded.

'For all I care!' he had spat.

'I don't like the feel of it either,' Salim's mother had muttered.

Gafoor could clearly recall the whole scene, and then four months after the wedding, their marriage had sailed into stormy waters. But this time Gafoor couldn't pin down what had triggered the change in Boori. His wife had become a devoted soul. Gafoor could see in her the supernatural influence of the saint. Boori would thus heed every word of caution that came her way from the elders, their every admonition about what to do, what not to do; what to eat, what not to eat; when to bathe, when not to bathe; about not going out at night and what not. She would follow every piece of advice to the letter. Although she winced at these restrictions, she didn't dare challenge the unwritten law. She'd just lump it. She would hum a tune as she sewed her *kantha* in the afternoon. She was told to pray some extra *rakas* everyday. She was very careful while moving around, lest she met with an accident.

'If you pray to Allah all the time,' her neighbour had exhorted, 'then he will give you a healthy baby.'

'Oh God! Boori, how changed you are!' Gafoor would often marvel at her, with a smile on his wrinkled face.

'Changed? Not likely. Just trying to be ready for it,' Boori stared wide-eyed.

'You've turned into an angel!' Gafoor said, pulling her leg, 'Only a few days ago, your auntie next door was giving you a piece of her mind.'

'Don't say that. That was ages ago.'

'Was it? Okay, now be a dear and get me my hookah.'

Boori brought him his water-pipe. She rarely humoured him. Gafoor could read her deadpan expression and would stop troubling her or asking her to do things for him.

She missed Nita a lot and also Choron Das. The minstrels hadn't been around for a long time. Boori tried to look as far as her eyes could reach. There was not even a shadow of the couple's presence. Maybe they would drop by one day when she had a baby in her cradle, insha'allah! That would be a ray of sunshine. She hugged her embroidered *kantha*.

অগ্রহায়ণ
Ôgrôhayôn

Right after her eighth month, Boori gave birth to a baby boy. There was a saying that a baby born in Ogrohayon was blessed with a good star. Boori didn't want to tempt fate by reading into the future. Just one glance at the baby was enough to feel a sea-change within her.

Gafoor watched his third baby. Boori would scream at him if he stared for too long.

'Don't gape at him like that! You will make him ill!'

'*Pagol!* Am I not his baba? How can I make him ill? Look at yourself! Aren't you over the moon with joy?'

Boori laughed uproariously.

'Have I gone mad or become a witch? Why not a mermaid while you are at it? Or a fairy perhaps? Red fairy? Blue fairy or White fairy, Ummmm?'

She held her child tight and sang the fairy lullaby.

Sat rajar dhon, laskmo manik,
Ek maniker sonar mohor,
Manik jabe pankhiraje,
Tepantorer math periye.

Her child's little face tugged at her heartstrings. Boori's new role as a mother had made her serene. The boy was named Rais. However, the arrival of the baby boy in the family put a damper on the moods of Salim and Kalim. They welcomed their new brother with little enthusiasm.

'We asked you for a sister, Maa, and all you give is another brother.'

'Okay, boys, next time round you'll get a sister.'

'A brother's no good. It's all cuts and bruises.'

'Please, Maa, can I have him in my lap?' Kalim sat close to Boori. Their curiosity was boundless.

'No, son, he may slip off your lap. Can't you see how delicate he is?'

'Mashallah! He is not made of clay. Can I hold him?' Salim asked.

'No! Not right now, dear!'

'Yea, yea, I can see that you love him more than you love me.'

'No dear, not at all. I love you the most.' Boori planted a kiss on Salim's forehead.

'When you walk out of the room, I'll hit you with my *batul* and snatch the baby. See who'll be sorry then!'

'Who's the cry baby round here?' Boori chided the boy and broke into laughter.

Salim took Kalim by the hand and both left the house. Whatever he might say, it was Kalim who drooled over Rais. When no one happened to be in the room, he would tiptoe to fondle his little brother, which was bound to disturb his catnap and the little tot would start crying.

As the days went by, Boori noticed something strange about Rais. His eyes seemed to be lifeless. He had the dull, vacant stare of a deaf and dumb child. Even a sudden sound failed to startle him. Boori felt a millstone in her chest weighing her down. She tried to brush aside the suspicion—but couldn't—that the boy was going to be deaf and dumb.

Yet, she tried to steel herself. Without revealing her suspicion to anybody, she kept a close watch on the boy. But with every passing day, her worst fear was confirmed. One day, she couldn't help letting out a shriek.

'Look, Rais isn't responding to me!'

Boori's cry just confirmed what Gafoor had been suspecting

for a while. He too watched the boy and tried to elicit a response. He was shocked to find that the boy failed to respond. Rais played all by himself, and he laughed to himself when there was nothing to laugh at. He wouldn't pay any attention to his parents' or brothers' anxious words. This strange behaviour disheartened Gafoor. Admittedly, the boy wasn't as lively as Sohrab Ali's daughter next door. A similar sense of guilt saddled Gafoor, as if he were to blame for this stroke of kismet. He even avoided eye contact with his wife.

In the following months, Boori's hopes evaporated one after the other. She couldn't keep herself busy with her household chores long enough to avoid thinking about her son. All she wanted was to look after Rais—her sole source of light and joy. She held him close to her heart, spinning dreams of all the things she had been denied in her childhood. Her son would grow up to be a fine young man. A dream girl would steal his heart. He would marry his lovebird. Boori hummed a lullaby:

Chader kopale chad ashbe.

The boy responded only to her and did not bond with his own father. He didn't even sit comfortably in his father's lap. One day, Gafoor fondled Rais a bit roughly, but the boy gave him a bloody nose.

'Get him off me!' Gafoor huffed and hurled the baby onto the bed.

She ran from the kitchen hearing Rais's wail. She picked him up and asked, 'Why is he crying? Did you hit him?'

'No, I just threw him on the bed.'

'What did you do that for?' Boori's voice cracked. 'Isn't he your son?'

Gafoor's attitude shocked Boori. It seemed unduly cruel. She could not stomach it.

How could anyone behave like this with his own children?

'Since you've got other children, you can't feel how special he is to me,' she protested. 'I've never treated Salim and Kalim like this. I took them as my own. No one can say that I've ever raised my hand against them.'

Gafoor went out without a word. After that incident, they didn't speak for a week. Things got back on an even keel after Gafoor admitted that he had acted out of character and promised that he would love the boy the same as Boori loved his two sons.

Kalim took great interest in Rais. But the boy's dumbness left him cold. He would leave the house to play with the other children when he got too upset.

'Maa, why can't he speak? It's awful. I wish I could box his ears to make him speak.'

'Don't be silly! God has made him like that. You must look after him when he is older. Will you?'

'Yes, Maa, we will take good care of him. We'll feed him whatever he wants!'

Boori put her hand on Kalim's head. She could feel the world weighing her down, but couldn't share her pain with anybody. Sometimes, she would hug Rais close to her and break down. Boori's world was meaningless without Rais and so was Rais's without Boori.

When Rais turned three, Boori and Gafoor paid a visit to the Srinile ashram. There they made another vow to Kesa Baba and hung up a bundle on a neem branch. This time Gafoor agreed without any resistance. He only chuckled after Boori made the offering.

'Even if you hadn't asked, I would have taken you to the ashram, because I knew that in your heart you were still not satisfied.'

'Oh, don't say that.'

'Well, tell me honestly, are you satisfied with Rais?'

'How can you say that as a father? The boat of love rides the tide.'

Boori knew the conversation would lead nowhere. A disabled son could be nothing but a source of perpetual pain. Gafoor was aware of that too, yet he needed to hear it from Boori.

The journey to the ashram turned out to be harder than expected. Unlike their last visit, Boori's spirit was dampened. A little walk exhausted her. Worst of all, Rais wailed and whined all the way. After a long plod along a muddy road and frequent breaks in the shade of wayside trees, they eventually reached the mela. But no sooner had they arrived than Boori wanted to get back. She didn't like wandering round the mela all day long anymore. A dark shadow veiled her face. Gafoor couldn't read a hint of hope in her eyes. He was afraid that she might vanish from his life. Muting his dislike of ashrams, he had braced himself just to accompany her. What he wanted most was to restore her to her youthful self and regain the bliss and happiness of married life.

But the dream remained a delusion. Rais had become indispensable to Boori's being. When Gafoor left for a day's work and Salim and Kalim were off to school, Rais was the only one left with her. Clutching the hem of her sari, he would shadow her wherever she went—to the *pukur*, the kitchen, the rice-husking room, the *boroj*. Boori developed a habit of talking to herself, as she could not talk to Rais. Boori had changed somehow, and Rais was at the heart of this change. Muttering to herself kept her happy. While gathering red betel nuts from under the trees, she would finally speak her mind.

'Rais, my precious,' she would cry out, 'you're breaking your maa's heart. You'll always be a thorn in my flesh. Still, it's nice to have you with me. You're the brightest star in my dark sky.'

Boori laughed off her own observation. She needed a good laugh to take her mind off things. At such times, she would also revisit her childhood days. She could almost picture herself walking with Jalil along a dusty road. Pointing to the clouds of dust, Jalil would tell her, 'See, Boori! How the sunlight shines through the dust? One day, I'll show you the rainbow!'

She had never seen a rainbow before in her life.

'Will you? Really? When?'

'I don't know when. When it rains, the sun will come out and the seven colours of the rainbow will be yours forever.'

'That'll be the day, Jalil!'

'It will! You will see.'

Jalil ran to the river after that. He didn't look back.

Boori looked at Rais, thinking of Jalil. He never showed her the rainbow.

Her life didn't turn out exactly how she had dreamed it, but she had to be content with it. 'You have to take the rough with the smooth,' she thought half-grudgingly. As she stopped to gaze at Rais, she told herself, 'I want much more than this. Why should my luck run out here? I will pray to my kismet, "Let me pick up my life where I left off." Let's go inside, Rais.'

The child had a mind of his own and sometimes he expressed his likes and dislikes. He had put a betel nut into his mouth, but Boori took it out and put it back into her bag. She placed him on her lap, hugging him and showering him with kisses. The boy tried to struggle free, but Boori wouldn't let him go.

Rais began to wail. She put him down with a thud. 'You don't like your maa's fondling, do you, wretched boy?'

Her eyes moistened with tears, which she dried with the hem of her sari. Rais wriggled free and picked up another betel nut from among the bushes. He stole a glance at his mother and smiled.

'*Dushto chele*! You're making a fool of your Maa, aren't you? Don't pick up those nuts. Look, what a wayward boy you are! Well, son, will you look after your Maa in her old age? When you grow up, will you still love me as you do now? Mind you, don't turn into a wimp of a husband!'

Rais hugged her knees and lifted up his little arms to his mother's face. Boori took him in her lap and walked home with her bag of betel nuts slung across her shoulders.

Sometimes Gafoor marvelled at Boori's unflagging patience. She never beat Rais or showed any signs of displeasure. She'd always keep the boy under her wing. Rais was happy.

She thought to herself that Allah had made her content in a very different way. Unlike mothers who had bright-vowelled children running around like chickens clucking for their attention, a mother whose child couldn't respond to his name had much more. Boori's heart, head and eyes were focused on one thing only and that was Rais. She put the boy on a pedestal and everyone around knew it.

Puffing at his hookah, Gafoor said, 'You're remarkably patient, Boori. I've never seen a mother like you.'

'If I don't care for him,' said Boori, a little offended, 'who will?'

'Can you tell me why the boy was born this way?' He blew out smoke.

Boori didn't reply. She went on husking betel nuts. After a while, she looked up at Gafoor, venturing, 'Perhaps I've done something *kharap*. Giving birth before my term was a bad omen.'

Gafoor stopped smoking. 'Boori, this is crap! You have not sinned.'

Boori forced a smile. 'The old folks say so. They say that I am cursed because I roamed the fields when I was young.'

'Ya Allah! Don't pay them any attention. They have nothing else to do but grouch, complain and cackle all day!'

Gafoor resumed his puffing and Boori busied herself with the betel nuts. Neither spoke. Only a few garbled sounds escaped, but they vanished into the night. Outside, there was a full moon. The boys were fast asleep. Boori cut the wick of the lamp and went out of the room.

Gafoor tried a thousand ways to get Boori back on an even keel. He knew that his indifference would break her heart. Tears began to roll down his cheeks. He trudged to the stairs leading down to the *pukur* and brooded there quietly, on his own.

No, Boori was no sinner. He couldn't believe it. She never lied and never did anything wrong. She loved Gafoor's children like her own. She was as pure as the water running down a stream. How could she be blighted by sin when she had never deceived or cheated anyone? Life got tangled like a fishing net. Time went by and youth faded into memory. Still leaves continued to fall in *Sit, Bôshonto* and *Bôrsha*. Days ebbed quietly.

From time to time, Jalil would visit the village, but he refrained from seeing Boori. He was now the father of two daughters. Boori felt aggrieved, yet she asked some of her neighbours about Jalil. In the event she ran into him, she would give him a real telling-off. 'How could you forget me? How could you forget the time we spent together? I treasure those precious moments! How could you, Jalil?'

She found out that he was quite well off. The former rickshaw-wallah now owned a grocery store in the capital. Jalil's sister came to visit her with Jalil's two daughters; his wife never joined them. Korimunnessa visited many other homesteads when she came to see her in-laws in the village, but never went to Boori's house. Jalil's sister informed her that both girls had taken after their beautiful mother. They were very smart, and they warbled non-stop.

'Your brother is very lucky to be blessed with two lovely children! Allah has given him everything.'

'But he's still hurting, you know, because of you!'

'Is he?' Boori stared at her with amazement.

'He let me in on his secret. No one else knows.'

'What did Jalil tell you?'

'He said he would have been very happy if he could marry

you.' Khodeja giggled and added, 'He said if you hadn't married at such a young age, he would have eloped with you to a town.'

'Did he really say that?'

'Oh yes, he did!'

'He never said anything like that to me.'

'Well, he said that there was no use crying over spilled milk now. "Boori and I should have shared our fate, but our stars got crossed."'

'Is he happy, Khodeja?'

'Not at all, they are always picking fly droppings out of pepper.'

Boori got sad. Khodeja looked at the courtyard and said, 'Look, the girls are having fun with Rais!'

'Here, have some betel leaf, Khodeja.'

'Thank you, I love the way you cut the betel nuts.

Khodeja put the betel leaf cone made by Boori into her mouth and said, 'My brother no longer pulls a rickshaw; he has a grocery shop in town. He said he would take me to Dacca this time. I'm dying to see the capital. Shall I get you some red bangles?'

Gafoor didn't feel like himself these days and suffered from severe bouts of asthma. He couldn't sleep a wink at night and stared at Boori with his pale sunken eyes. Boori felt that old age had struck Gafoor a little too early. It was obvious that his health had deteriorated, but no medicines would help. People said that if you had a fit of coughing, all you had to do was to stop breathing for a while and it would just go away. He might be worse off in winter, but once the season would change he would get better again.

Boori was at a loss on what to do. She was half Gafoor's age and was physically fine. She could manage all the household work on her own. It didn't wear her down. She was happy with her life. True enough, she had her share of hurdles. But she looked forward to Rais's future. This challenge kept her going.

Gafoor had a limp and walking had become quite painful for him. He would sit on a stool in the veranda. He took no interest in anything whatsoever. He thought his days were numbered and harked back to his youth. A sense of helplessness soured his mood. He would flare up at the slightest pretext. He even beat Rais and scolded his wife. She hadn't seen it coming. Boori took care of him and nursed him as gently as possible, but it was never good enough. She'd get sick of her husband's constant nagging on the one hand and of her disabled son, on the other.

One day, Boori had had enough.

'Can you tell me what's wrong with you?'

'My boat's past it, I just want to die.'

'What are you talking about? Don't people get old? Don't people get sick?'

'Course they do! But when men get old, they lose it. You, you are still young. I just wish I were still young and healthy. I envy you.'

'Didn't it cross your mind when you married me?'

'No, it damn well didn't! Why would it?' He spat out phlegm. 'Your brother asked me to marry you and I did...' Gafoor paused. 'I was happy to have a young bride then,' he said, after a dry, hacking cough. 'I am not so happy anymore! My flute has broken.'

'Serves you right! Now you'll have to make do with your broken flute!'

Boori stormed out of the room.

Sometimes she felt like running away, leaving all her cares behind. She wondered whether it was actually worth having a family. But then she realized that if she didn't have a family of her own, she would have to live off someone else. In those melancholy hours, she often thought of Jalil. It had been such a long time since Jalil last came to see her. She longed for him. When he was in the village, she did not long to see him so much, but now that he was far away, she missed his presence.

One day, she found a bright rainbow in the sky. The rain had washed the sky clean of clouds and everything around was silhouetted in golden sunlight. If only Jalil came to the village once! If only he asked her to see the rainbow just this once!

'Jalil, where are you? Please hold my hand!' she screamed inside.

There was no one around. Boori wiped her eyes dry with her *anchol*. She heard Gafoor coughing, his laboured breathing, but she didn't feel like going inside. Gafoor's whingeing was the last straw! True, she was young. 'But why would he be jealous of my youth?' she wondered. Her age didn't matter one jot when he made love to her, did it? Then why was he making a fuss about it now? If that was the case, then let him stew in it. She came out of the room to talk to the labourers. They were busy filling the sacks with paddy, which would be taken to the paddy husker to make rice. Some of the rice would be sold in the bazaar. Salim was in charge of all this, but he was away for his exams.

Boori had no clue why Gafoor had changed for the worse in his old age. The man who had guarded the wall between her and the world was now as unmanageable as an old buffalo. That buffalo was now hell bent on trampling her to the ground. She drew no succour or pleasure from her married life anymore. She poured out her frustration in front Rais, as she gathered vegetables from her kitchen garden.

'Look here, Rais, your father is a slug. Hai Allah! I've never seen such a *jook*! I'd have been better off marrying Jalil. I'd be living in town where I could watch trains whistling by. Oh, that would have made my day. Well, Rais, when you grow into a man, you must get yourself a job in town. Then, you must allow me into your house. Six months a year, yes, that'll be enough for me. Hello, son, can you do that for me? What are you gawping at?'

Rais stared at his mother, cocking his head sideways. He picked up a leaf of red spinach and held it out to her. Boori gave him a hug and went back to the kitchen. Squatting in the veranda, she began to sort out the betel nuts. Gafoor coughed in the bedroom and called out to her several times. Rattled, she didn't respond. Then Gafoor fell silent.

Gafoor had been poorly for a long time. He fluctuated between lethargy and bouts of delirium. Boori couldn't calm his coughing. Then one day, she remembered Nita rambling on about the miraculous cures of a Baul fakir.

By the time the old woman arrived, Boori's husband had spat blood. The haggard-looking healer went into a trance. She took the sick man's left hand and drew circles, while chanting mantras. Oblivious to what was taking place around him, Gafoor stared into a blank space. The fakir leapt to the ground and drew a diagram. There were wild incantations of '*tomar angate byamo mukto*'.

She pronounced that a snake spirit had taken hold of Gafoor's soul. The healer mixed *maankochu* leaves with herbs and roots. She added mustard oil and a yellow liquid from a phial, and then she poured the solution onto his ears and eyes. She gave Boori some *tabiz* to ward off the jinn.

The fever subsided after a week, but it reduced Gafoor to a bag of bones. He fell ill again, his arms and legs twitching. Then one day, after running a fever for forty eight hours, he passed away. Rais was just thirteen.

The *namaaz-e janaza* left Boori stone cold. Sohrab Ali came back with Maulana Hamid to hold a *milad mahfil* on the fourth day to ask for Allah's forgiveness, mercy and blessings for Gafoor and his family.

'Our beloved brother has passed away—*innalillahe wa innailahe rajeun*—we ask Allah that he be given *jannat* as his abode in the eternal life. Please keep the departed soul and his family in your prayer, *Alhamdullilah*!'

Boori had no time to sit back and ponder the situation. Her

husband's death was an unexpected blow. During his illness Gafoor had caused Boori much trouble, but now that he was dead, she had lost her tongue. Never had she missed him so much. She felt a wrench within her. Flashes of memory shot through her head; images of love and moonlight tumbled over one another and blurred with the tumult of time. Boori became an old woman overnight. Her hair had greyed.

Salim took up the responsibilities left behind by Gafoor. By now he had grown into a more patient, more sensible young man and developed a knack for their family business. Within a few weeks, he took charge of everything. His grasp of land rights also served him in good stead. The smell of paddy would make him restless. During the threshing season he'd spend whole nights brooding in the veranda.

And what was Rais up to at this time? He loafed in the veranda all day, wearing a clownish expression on his face. All of a sudden, he would dive at a *doel* and grin, or he would hug their dog, Bagha, which he considered a playmate. Bagha too liked to tail his friend everywhere and be rewarded with a pat. Kalim had stopped fussing over him and he no longer ventured to play *chhoa chhui* or *kanamachhi*. Whenever Boori looked at Rais, she was overwhelmed by a sense of helplessness. Lately, Rais stopped following his mother to the *boroj* and Boori didn't ask him either. She felt distraught.

Kalim sang in a high pitch. His voice was attuned to the Bhatiali songs. Boori listened to one snatch of music with rapt attention.

> *Amay bhashaili rey*
> *Amay dubaili rey*
> *Akul dariyar bujhi kul nairey*
> *Kul nai kinar nai naiko nadir padi*
> *Tumi sabdhanetey chalaiyo majhi*
> *Amar bhang tari rey*

She felt that this would have been her song if she'd had Jalil in her life. The song reminded her of her unfulfilled dreams. It gave her some joy and solace. The son had inherited his father's voice. Kalim rose before dawn to go fishing and he'd call his sleeping mother to fetch his net and fishing reel. He wouldn't leave home without his tackle.

Boori generally kept it ready at hand the evening before, but that was not enough.

He would mutter under his breath, 'Trust my luck, if you don't hand me the net yourself, I may not have a catch!'

Boori was aware of this strange streak in Kalim from his early days. However, she didn't feel bad about being woken up at the crack of dawn.

Salim and Kalim had taken to fishing like ducks to water. They could barely walk when they started to play with bamboo canes and jute strings and would use ant eggs or earthworms to land their priceless fish. Gafoor had also shown his boys the trick of using cow dung on paddy straw to lure *magoor* and *singhi* into bamboo frame nets or earthen pots. As they grew sturdier, they were taught the ropes of 'proper fishing', as Gafoor put it, and he would proudly coax them as they worked their nets to create waves and trap fish in the cold winter water. During the monsoon, Gafoor also showed his boys how to arch a bamboo shaft overhead and spear *katol* in the shallows of the swamps, but the boys were not so keen on spear fishing.

'Maa, I'm off,' Kalim would call out to Boori. He hopped onto his boat and broke into a song.

Ami bhatir belai nao bhashailam;
Mridu mondo batash bohe,
Beguni jole nouka bhashe.
Nodir baake etel matir ghor,

Oparete shobuj ghasher bonee
keba shukhai tar neel sarita petee,
Ami bhatir belai nao bhashailam re.

Shajer aloi jai milaye shob rongin chobi
Mondirer ghonta baje toong toong
Kapiye nodir jol.

Kar tonoya ghate ashe
Jhumur jhumur pai?
Amar pane chai?
Ami bhatir belai nao bhashailam re.

Tar mukher pane cheye amar ridoy neche othe,
Ami preme pagol para,
Kemon kore thakbo ami ekon ghore feere?
Jhokon ami bhatir belai nao bhashai re!

He soon melted into the dark, rowing and singing, but a haunting echo of his song lingered on in Boori's heart, taking her back to those sweet old days. She reminisced. She too had such vocal dawns locked up in her memory, still fresh, still untarnished, with the only exception that Gafoor stopped singing when she joined him. Holding Boori's hands, Gafoor would cross the grove quickly; sometimes he would clasp her and plant stolen kisses on her lips half way down the grove. She would get scared by the birds flapping their wings nearby and would hold him ever so tightly as if to burrow into his skin.

Boori bolted those memories safely away. With the distance that time offers, she was able to move on. She thought there was nothing unseemly or untoward in her stepsons' lives. The river flowed its course—tilling, sowing, harvesting, threshing, rowing, fishing—everything went smoothly. Only, Gafoor was no more.

Yet, despite Gafoor's absence, there was no noticeable hitch in the fabric of their lives. They had not weathered a storm big enough to uproot them; they didn't have to grope in the dark. Only a shadow no longer hovered in the yard. Nor would he walk to the canal holding his young bride's hand, his fishing net hanging from his shoulder. No longer would he play the game of love on the canal or call out to Boori, late at night, after his weekly jaunts to the bazaar.

When all these memories submerged her, Boori would seek refuge in the past. Flashes of her life with Jalil would run randomly through her mind. She recalled the day the two of them had gone fishing on the canal. The wind was picking up. Suddenly, a gust flipped over the ramshackle bamboo raft and Boori pretended she was going under just so Jalil could hug her and pull her safely to the ghat. She had been mesmerized by the beads of water and the tingle of his skin against her wet clothes. Jalil's eyes crawled over her hungrily and she held his gaze. Her own skin was like molten lava and she had felt as if her body melted into his. They had carried on as though nothing had happened. What if the dice had rolled the other way? Things might have been different.

An earlier memory resurfaced and she smiled wistfully. A game of *bouchi* had the children work up a sweat. They flew towards the ghat and jumped into the pond to cool off. The air was still and the cool water felt heavenly. Most of the youngsters waded in the shallower parts. To impress the girls, the bigger boys, who were up to their necks in water, ducked under, spouted jets or splashed like belly-flopping frogs. Boori dived into the deep end with hardly a splash or a ripple. As she emerged, she suddenly lost her balance. Realizing that something was not right, Jalil, who had just bobbed up from underwater, swam to her and dragged her to the water's edge. Boori gasped in pain. She pointed to her ankle and asked whether there was a water snake wrapped around it. Jalil held her in his arms and told her it was a mean old root that got entangled with her as they clambered up the ghat.

Boori felt that the very thought of Jalil swept away all the worldly impurities. To her Jalil was a hero, the ever-flowing spring of *jannat* lifting her from the temporal world into a realm of heavenly ecstasy.

When Salim and Kalim went out, the house would fall quiet. It was Boori who broke the silence now and again.

'Rais, my love, you're a sweet boy! Can't you call me "Maa", just once? You don't know how desperate I am to hear you call me "Maa". I had so many hopes for you. I tried my best to draw out that one word from your lips, but I've failed. Well, son, how can you be so dumb? Allah! Rais, oh my Rais, please just say it once. I'll press my ear against your lips. Please call me. Please! Your call will be like peals of thunder exploding into the night. The villagers will rush round you to get a glimpse of you. If you can manage that, it'll be enough for me. You're helpless—you cannot plough, go fishing, raise a family. You just whip your arms about wildly. This pain is more than I can bear. I want you to become a legend, Rais. Oh my Rais…'

Boori shook him suddenly, tugging at his shoulder. Rais gave his mother a blank stare. Tears rolled down his cheeks; his lips quivered, but no sound came out. Boori felt defeated. She held his head close to her chest and cried silently, just like him.

Boori turned her back on her family duties. She thought that she had come to a stage in her life where she would just eat and sleep. She needed a change. But the truth was that she was caged to this life. She would never be able to get out of Haldi. Salim came and sat beside her.

'What's on your mind, Maa?'

'Nothing,' Boori replied, laughing the question off.

'You don't busy yourself with the housework like the other aunties. You don't pop round the neighbours, poking in their business. You never talk behind anyone's back and you don't get mad. You just sink into silence,' Salim remarked.

'I think I'll marry you off so I can bring in a pretty daughter-in-law into this house. She will look after the family and I will get to put my feet up more often, which I have wanted to do for some time now.'

'I see. That'll give you a good excuse to run around freely. Fat chance I'll let you do that!'

'I'm getting on, son. It's time we looked for a bride for you. You're out all day and I feel so lonely with no one to talk to. You cannot imagine how painful it is for me.' Boori clasped Salim's hands tightly.

Salim shook his head and looked down. 'Well, I want someone who will show you respect, who will take care of you and won't talk back at you. So look for the girl you think is best, but don't blame me for any *tamasha* that the bride may cause. It might be a jump from the frying pan into the fire.'

Salim went out, crestfallen. The idea of marriage had caught him off guard. He wasn't ready for it yet. He felt like diving into the *pukur*, never to emerge.

One day Nita staggered into the courtyard, taking Boori by surprise. She had her *dotara* and her pouch of clothes with her. Her hair was dry and tousled; her feet, dusty. She looked puffed out. She seemed to have walked a thousand miles. Boori was making the workers spread a layer of cow dung and mud over the yard. She came forward as she saw Nita and said, 'Come inside!'

'I need some water.'

'You go and sit there and I will get some water for you.'

Nita went to the other side of the yard and sat down. She put her *dotara* and pouch down. She combed her hair with her hand. As Boori brought the earthen bowl of water, Nita drilled her shrewd eyes into Boori.

'Your face looks as though you've aged, dear.'

Boori smiled. She pulled a stool to sit beside her and said, 'Here, have some water. Why should I get any younger?'

Nita sat down, stretching her legs on the ground. She was alone today.

'Where's your soulmate, dear?' Boori enquired.

'We aren't on speaking terms. He just told me he was fed up with this life and went begging for alms.'

'He seemed rather withdrawn.'

'I told him off and left. I'm sick and tired of all this.'

Boori was taken aback.

'Why are you pulling such a long face?' Nita sulked. 'Get me some food quick! I must go back soon, or he'll give me the cold shoulder.'

Boori went indoors to get her some food. 'Nita has changed,' Boori said to herself.

'Oh, Boori, come on! When you think about it, haven't you changed as well? This happens all the time. Nothing remains the same forever. Hey, I don't have all the time in the world! Get me some food,' Nita shouted.

She hastily cobbled together something to eat. But Boori's efforts to rustle a quick meal still fell short. So when she did appear with the food and water, Nita snarled, 'You've been slacking so badly of late! It took you so long to prepare so little food! How come you've changed this much, dear?'

Pushing a handful of rice on a banana leaf towards Nita, Boori forced herself to smile.

'Don't try to pull one over me. Just one look at a rice grain tells me if all the others were properly cooked,' Nita said, gulping down the rice.

Despite her criticism, Nita seemed content once she had had her fill. After that she got ready to go. She struck her *dotara* just once.

'Tell Choron Das that I sent him some rice,' Boori said. 'Also tell him that he's in my bad books because he didn't come to my house. I don't want to see you alone, *soi*.'

Boori gave her another helping of rice for Choron Das.

'My dear, you've saved me from begging today,' Nita said, smiling with gratitude.

Boori sat wistfully, leaning her back against a pillar in the veranda. Nita seemed like a whirlwind which blew everything in all directions and raised puffs of dust, dying down as quickly as it started. The banana leaf rolled on the ground with the few leftover crumbs. Boori looked at it. Though Nita licked the leaf clean, Boori felt as if she had left something behind. Nita pranced off the yard as proud as a peacock. The tinkling of her ankle bells and bracelets grated on Boori's mind.

Within two months Salim was married off in a grand manner.

Kalim had announced that there would be a feast in the house for three days when his elder brother got married.

'How does that sound to you, Maa?'

'You go ahead, Kalim. Salim is my elder son. There has to be lots of feasting and merriment for his *gaye holud*.'

'Thank you, Maa! You just saved my day. I have already told my friends in the village that we'll have a huge *gaye holud* party. I'll smear him with turmeric. He'll be glowing like fireflies. No one will recognize him.'

Boori laughed a good, hearty laugh.

'Never in my wildest dreams did I ever imagine that something this joyful would happen.'

'You're a very lucky, Maa! You've got the luck of a queen. Should I be calling you Rani Maa?' Kalim added, tongue-in-cheek.

'You're crazy!' Boori beamed.

Salim said little, if anything about the whole matter. He was very happy, though. The whole house was in a festive mood. Young children decked the hut and courtyard with crepe paper garlands. Girls made red and blue paper flowers, which they pasted on the walls. Someone came up to Salim and recited a poem:

Selim bhai er mukh ranga tuktuk.
Shukher naye bheshe, bou ashbe sheje.

'Just go away,' said Salim, pretending to be angry.

Peals of laughter tinkled throughout the house from the girls' corner. Their trills and jokes were music to Boori's ears. Nita and Choron Das came to stay at their place for three weeks. They were Boori's guests. They sat under the *sojna* tree with their musical instruments. They could be heard now and again playing the *dotara* from afar.

'This is what a *gaye holud* should be like,' passers-by would say, as they walked past the house.

Boori was happy. Jalil had arranged everything. It was Khodeja who did the matchmaking. Ramija was related to her in-laws. When they were looking for a bride for Salim, Jalil asked his sister to come up with the proposal. He said to Khodeja, 'Why don't you talk to them about Ramija? I like the girl, she is your husband's cousin's daughter, she is educated, hard-working and sharp.'

Khodeja brought the proposal herself.

'Jalil bhai would very much like you to see Ramija,' she said. 'She is so beautiful and hard-working too.'

Boori scolded her, 'Hold on! Am I bringing a wife to work in my household? I would like her to take it easy, have fun for a few years!'

'Oh, I have the picture! You are out to spoil your daughter-in-law! She won't be running her household!'

'So when are we going to your in-laws, Khodeja?'

'I have come to visit my parents. But, if you like, we can go back tomorrow. Would you like to come with me?'

'Yes I will. I think Salim won't say no if I like her.'

'Of course! Salim is not at all like that! You are so lucky!'

'Just pray that I can die with this luck! I don't want to be unhappy.'

They rode back on a boat the next day. Boori returned after staying overnight. She really liked Ramija. They set a date. The festivity started after that. Boori was in a trance for a while. She just hoped that she could die with this happiness. She couldn't ask for more. Suddenly she felt a knot in her chest. She looked at Jalil from afar and thought that he was playing the role of Salim's father. Ages ago they had a family together, Salim was their first born. Then there was Kalim and Rais. Now they were together once again in another time, another village. One day this village would change in front of them and they would still find the traces of its spirit in the palms of her hands.

The next day, *holud* and *mehendi* were mixed with mortar and pestle to make a paste. Some of the women would apply the paste to Salim's face, neck and body, later in the afternoon. Boori had prepared some *kheer* with thick milk. Women would feed it to the bride and bridegroom while they applied the paste. The festivities began in the afternoon. Some clay lamps were lit around where Salim was sitting. A song rose.

> *Brishti parey tapur tupur*
> *Node elo baan,*
> *Shib Thakurer biye holo*
> *Teen konney daan.*
> *Ek konney radhen baren*
> *Arek konney khaan,*
> *Arek konney na khaaye*
> *Baaper baari zaan.*

'We are the groom's party,' guests clamoured, 'though there's no problem being the bride's party either, since she will eventually come here.'

'That's right!' others said in unison. They all started singing; the house was raucous with cheers and chants:

Holud bato mendi bato,
Hato fuler mou,
Biyer shaje shajbe konna!

'But then we don't have a bride, we only have the groom,' said
Maliha, one of the women singers, correcting them. The brightly-
coloured guests were served *borhani* and *pati lebur* sharbat. Lips
were licked and teeth tucked into gulab jamun, *rôshogolla*, *shondesh*,
kalo jam and *chom chom*.

Kalim mixed dyes with water in a large vat. Sinewy youths
would spray coloured water at each other. They soon looked like
exotic snakes and rainbow birds. The bridegroom's *holud* ceremony
was completed before dusk. The following day they celebrated
with colours once again. Nita and Choron Das smeared colours
on their bodies and swayed their hips to the music. The boys and
girls sang along.

Salim smiled and hugged his mother.

'You've made it all possible. I'm so grateful, Maa'

Five days later, the nikah took place at the bride's house. To
mark the *bidiyy*, Salim brought his bride home two days later.
Boori welcomed her home. She arranged a huge feast on Walima.
They killed a cow from their own farm and the rice served to the
guests was from their own fields. People from all around Haldi
came to attend Salim's wedding feast. Boori was so happy to see
people just coming in and out of her house these past few days.
To hear them sing and have a good time. The wind was spreading
their happiness.

Fortunately, she had set aside some food for the poor. Two
unwanted guests, Mansoor and a *taluqdar* had engaged in an
eating match. They seemed hell-bent on spoiling the party as
they were locked in their battle. The music barely drowned their
slurping and belching after they had gobbled up an umpteenth
ball of rice and beef *bhuna*. Sweat dripped from their brows and

greasy chops. The tension was palpable between the two contestants. Even the guests were holding their breath. Mansoor saw his rival off, as the *taluqdar's* head fell into his plate with a clatter and he just snored away. The crestfallen elder with the ballooning gut was carted home. Mansoor too had bitten off more than he could chew. He knocked over a lantern and broke its chimney. His white pajamas caught fire. Some guests nearby doused the flames with buckets of water. The landowner was drenched from head to toe and was soon on his way home, looking like a soggy *kaak tarua*.

Ramija, Salim's wife, was a shy and pretty wisp of a woman. She cut a fine figure. The day after the marriage, Boori showed her round the garden, the house and the lands.

'This road leads to Dacca. See the railway line. You can go to Dacca by getting on a train from here. There is the river; you can go wherever you want from here on a boat.'

Ramija covered her face with her hands. Boori put her hand on her shoulder and said, 'Let's go home. See how the first ray of light makes the world look beautiful! The sun has yet to rise, but how radiant the sky looks! Don't you like it?'

'Hmm. I have never looked at the sky like this before. No one has ever taught me to see such things.'

'It's okay. You will see a lot more from now on. You will see and learn in your own good time. Have a look! There is another beautiful scene.'

They saw Salim, Kalim and Rais walking towards them. They rushed to meet Boori and Ramija.

'Where did you go?' Salim asked.

They smiled.

The two women talked over a lot of things. When Salim was out of the house, Ramija tailed Boori everywhere as if she were afraid of losing her way. Later on Boori told her about her duties around the household.

'Listen, my dear, from now on all of this will be yours. You must take care of these. Just give me a few scraps of food and it'll do me just fine.'

Ramija said nothing, but she kept her eyes wide open, staring through the *anchol* covering her forehead.

'Do you like it, dear?' Boori asked.

Ramija nodded.

'Will you cope?'

'I can if you tell me what to do.'

'Hai Allah! What a naive child! Why get me dragged into it? I'm past it.' Boori gave a motherly pat on the girl's chin and pulled her *anchol* off.

'How can you look after a family from under that veil?'

Ramija blushed and Boori chuckled.

'Why are you ashamed to look at me, *bouma*? I'm like your mother now. You can trust me with all your troubles. I'll always be there to help you.'

They walked arm in arm across the garden. Everything impressed Ramija, although she had never been here before. Some of the girls her age were unhappy at their in-laws'. They complained of daily beatings at the hands of their mothers-in-law. They had to slave away night and day. Some girls were so battered they had to flee for their lives and get a divorce. But she felt that her new house was like a heaven. There was no quarrel, they were all at peace. She had left behind a pleasant part of her life at her parents' home, but she put a brave face on it, as she found a new affectionate mother. She felt at ease. She dipped her feet in the water. It cooled her whole body. She covered her face with her wet hands. She wanted to keep her sorrows underwater.

While standing by the *pukur*, Boori asked Ramija to cater to Salim's needs.

'He's a funny boy. The slightest disorder ruffles his feathers. He's very sensitive.'

After a few days, Ramija got the hang of the domestic chores. She took over all Boori's duties. She was a charming, smart girl.

Boori breathed a sigh of relief. Now that the weight of family responsibility had been lifted from her shoulders, she felt like sleeping under a large tree, or walking through a deep lush green forest. Golden leaves had fallen around and birds sang sweetly. Her sleep was undisturbed. Only helpless Rais was left as her charge. She would bathe him in the morning, feed him twice or three times a day, and dress him as though she was fooling with a freak doll in her old age. Rais had grown into a healthy youth, a sturdy young man whose appearance won over everyone. He looked much older than his years, though. On seeing his face, people could not imagine that he was dumb. He never appeared fully conscious, never all there. But one mere glance at him grieved Boori.

She recalled her childhood—the sweet landscapes of the gently flowing Shomeswari, the lush bushes beside the *pukur*, the riot colours of the *shimul* swaying in the sky and people streaming to the station. Now Boori was free. Her mother was not around to spit a volley of curses. There was no husband to call her home. Her stepsons were busy with their own work. Ramija was cooking in the kitchen. Sometimes she would think of Rais, but often she didn't. Thinking about him didn't pain her half as much now as it did before. Boori collected betel nuts or picked up vegetables from the garden, tucking them under her arm. Occasionally, she went fishing in the *pukur*. She was allowed to live her life and her heart was filled to the gills with joy.

Ramija loved Boori deeply and she took good care of her. She was lucky. Since childhood she had been fed tales about quarrelsome mothers-in-law. She felt that she must have been very pious in her previous life, whatever that meant. But happily, she got a good mother-in-law in Boori. Her respect was tinged with gratitude. Massaging Boori's ankles with an ointment, she would say, 'Whenever you need something, please ask me, Maa.'

Boori enjoyed the care and respect Ramija was showing her. Content, she closed her eyes. Boori had no daughter of her own. A daughter would always help her mother comb her hair and make her bed. After her arrival, Boori knew what she had been missing. She had no idea what it was like to have a girl around the house. She used to roam around the village at Ramija's age. She knew the village's ins and outs. Haldi was her world. She knew she would never be able to see the whole country; it would remain a dream. She felt that she found a friend after she met Nita. But she knew that she would never be able to cast her net beyond that. In her dreams she knew thousands of people. It was like the song she heard when she was young.

Once lunch was over, in late afternoon, Ramija would recount her childhood to Boori—kiting, fishing, her parents, her playmates, endless games of *putul biye*, *kutkut*, kabadi, *hadudu*, *dariabandha* and other village tales. Boori tapped into her own childhood memories as she listened to her daughter-in-law. Sometimes, Ramija switched the conversation and Boori tossed and turned in bed, trying to get some sleep. The young woman had no clue as to why Boori was bored when the conversation ran off course and threaded into a number of different rivulets.

'Maa, oh Maa! My stories always put Maa to sleep,' Ramija would complain.

Boori could see that Ramija was fond of reminiscing about her childhood memories of her village and parents. In the past few days, her parents had become like a fairyland, a magic place to which she could never go back. Ramija was now bound to this new life. Salim would not allow Ramija a trip to her father's, despite all her requests. Boori could not figure out why Salim was bent on stopping her from making the short trip, but it changed the way she saw her stepson. He had grown into someone that she didn't recognize anymore.

Salim was busy at work all day, so when he got back, like a

spent bullock after dusk, he went straightaway to dinner and then to bed. Any questions would nettle him and Boori could not get through to him.

Ramija bombarded Boori with questions.

'What has been on your mind so deeply all day, Maa?' Ramija enquired.

'Nothing.'

'Come on! I know something's the matter.'

Boori was startled at Ramija's insistence. She wondered whether she actually knew what was niggling her.

'Are you concerned for Rais, Maa?'

'Yes. I do feel for him. I don't know what fate has in store for him.'

'Allah will bless him and take him under his wing, don't you worry, Maa.'

Ramija spoke with an air of worldly wisdom.

'Take Shamsul, our blind cousin, Maa. He may act stupid, but you can't take him for a ride. He has ways of knowing what's going on. And he's got such a sweet voice. All the girls are in love with him, one way or another.'

Boori liked it when Ramija acted like a guardian. She was a very simple girl who never thought ill of anyone. Boori felt sorry for the way Salim hit her and rode roughshod over her feelings. Her stepson complained that she didn't do any work. He had a long list of grudges against her. But Boori knew how hard-working Ramija was. Sometimes, he would lock her in the kitchen. At night, Boori would hear Ramija whimper in the next room. Salim picked on her all the time, which worried Boori sick. But his behaviour towards his mother was completely the opposite. This hypocrisy perplexed Boori. She got bogged down by it all. A lot of things happened which were beyond her. Life was like a pendulum swinging this way and that, from hope to despair, from anguish to ecstasy. In the early days, she had tried to knock some sense into her stepson, the way his elders would, but Salim swatted her concerns about his behaviour towards Ramija as he would a mosquito.

'You wouldn't understand my problems, Maa, so save your breath and stop meddling.'

Boori felt humiliated by his mean, harsh words. She left the room silently. She couldn't overlook his demeanour, let alone suppress the pain from her mind for the next few days. She decided not to interfere, but later almost changed her mind when she heard Ramija weeping again.

He was his own man. She shouldn't poke her nose into his affairs, Boori scolded herself. She would have to bear Ramija's tears. Was there any other way? Salim was her husband and so he could do whatever he liked to her.

Boori was in two minds. At times, she wanted to prise out why Ramija could not please her husband. At other times, she kept away from the danger area. Once, in the middle of the night, Salim threw Ramija out of his hut. And she came to Boori, sobbing. Boori said nothing, but comforted her by wiping her tears. Ramija sniffled until her eyes were dry. Later that night, Boori woke up to the sound of Salim's gruff voice and she found him dragging his wife back to the hut. Boori bit her lips to keep quiet and she left them to their own problems. Since then, she left them alone. She just visited neighbours or went to the *pukur* when she heard them bickering, laughing aloud or shouting at the top of their voices. She turned a deaf ear. She would return home once Salim had left. Stepping inside the room, she'd stretched out her arms to draw Ramija to her heart. Both women wept in silence. Boori was puzzled as to why the young woman bore her suffering stoically, almost wordlessly.

Kalim, by contrast, was polite. Boori liked him. She made plans to marry him off. Although he was reserved and well-behaved now, once married he could turn out to be cruel. Like some shy men who only reveal their mettle and true nature to their wives; when they can't compete with their fellow men outside their homes, they pour out their frustrations on their hapless wives. Maybe Kalim would turn out to be different, he was a good boy. So when she went fishing for a bride, she thought of Osman Mridha's daughter.

Over dinner, Boori brought up the subject of Kalim's wedding. Salim had been out all day, but was not worn out yet. After dinner he would fall asleep straightaway. So Boori wanted to sound him out while she could get his attention for a change. It wasn't that easy as he kept himself busy and was reluctant to talk about household matters. Boori watched as Salim shovelled rice into his mouth.

'Son, Kalim should get married now.'

'What's the rush?' Salim grumbled between his teeth.

'Why not now?'

'I said not now, Maa!'

'Why not? Will you do something about it after I die?' Boori fumed.

'You get your head all muddled up with nothing these days, Maa,' Salim exploded peevishly.

'You would say that, since you're so grown up now!'

'Look, Maa, cool your head. You don't know half of it. All you care for is your own little patch. The country is in a state. It's going to the dogs.'

'What's wrong with the country? Has it caught a fever?'

Boori burst out laughing. Ramija giggled too. This time Salim flared up.

'Don't scoff at what you have no idea about. We are going to have it out.'

Salim drank a glass of water. Kalim kept his head down, chewing quickly in silence and Boori toyed with her plate. She wrung her hands. The hut was shrouded in silence.

Salim emerged as a leader of the village. He had a glib tongue and talked wisely, arguing with the neighbours and discussing their problems. He had gained authority and self-assurance, which Boori was proud of. While witnessing the change, she had no doubt that the decisive chin of his would still be there in ten or fifteen years' time. Someday, Salim would lead the country.

Boori thought from now on she would keep an eye on Kalim. She might not have borne him in her womb, but surely there was a love-bond, an umbilical cord. A tie that could not be severed in this lifetime.

People would stream to her veranda, sometimes talking aloud, sometimes in hushed tones. Boori could make no sense whatsoever of what was happening to the country. She only knew about ploughing, harvesting, winnowing, husking; she had some idea about drought and flood, about poverty or a full belly after a good crop. Nothing worse punctuated her days and nights. Now there was some lurking threat, but where did it come from? She had no inkling. The air was ominous, but she couldn't imagine what the future held in store. Salim stepped out of the hut after dinner. When she looked at him, she realized that he had changed into a man, almost overnight. Whatever trace of youth was left in him would also be shed off in a few months. After he had gone, Boori caught up with Kalim and asked him, 'Son, what is the matter? I've never seen the country in such a state.'

'You may see something you've never seen before,' Kalim replied.

'But you must tell me what the matter is.'

'What's the point? You wouldn't understand.'

Ramija barged in. 'Kalim bhai doesn't have a clue himself. What would he tell you?'

'It's the call to free ourselves,' Kalim shot back, rattled.

'What call?'

Boori looked worried and twitchy. Kalim played on her ignorance.

'That's why I said you wouldn't understand.'

'That's all nonsense, boy. In fact, you brothers won't come to your senses unless you've got your backs to the wall,' Boori teased him with a touch of affection.

Ramija giggled, her musical laugh filling Boori's ears, she went out to the kitchen to wash the plates. Tongue-tied, Kalim walked towards the doorstep to light a bidi. After a while he began to sing.

Mon majhi tor boitha nere, ami ar baite parlam na
Mon majhi tor boitha nere, ami ar baite parlam na
Shara jibon ujan bailam, bhatir nagal pailam na.
Ami ar baite parlam na,
Mon majhi tor boitha nere, ami ar baite parlam na.
Dukkher deshe dukkher nodi kaindya boiya jai,
Shukher ashai mon majhi tui kandos hai re hai.
Mon majhi tui bebhul jemon, ami kopal pora temon
Sukh dukkher kinar pailam na,
Mon majhi tor boitha nere, ami ar baite parlam na.

ফাল্গুন
Falgun

Boori was on the edge. She stretched out in the veranda. She would always remember Gafoor when trouble knocked on her door. She gazed at the sky with its scintillating stars.

Darkness engulfed the area around the bamboo trees. She had never come anywhere close to war. She didn't know what it would be like. Calls for 'Pakistan Zindabad' had reached the village a few days after her marriage to Gafoor. She didn't understand how the new country was born. She just knew that they had been 'liberated', hearing from her elders that the English had 'washed their hands off India' and left the country in a stampede.

'See we've got a bright new country,' Gafoor told her after they were married. 'I'll buy you a flag with the star and the moon. We'll fly the flag when we go fishing.'

Boori had laughed her heart out. How many people were lucky enough to have a new bride and a new country, she had thought.

No one talked about war then. No one was terrified of it either. She recalled boys playing joyfully with green and white flags, like butterflies fluttering in their hands. Some of the villagers had made a fuss about it, whilst others cheered and sang prayers. It was all in good humour.

But now the word 'independence' meant war.

Why did it change Salim and Kalim beyond recognition? What had happened to her country? Something was definitely afoot; otherwise they wouldn't consider postponing Kalim's engagement.

Boori began to fret. This was not just like any drought or flood devastating the whole area. Maybe that's why Salim and Kalim had changed so much. The two of them looked apprehensive, yet they were on the ready. Boori saw a new kind of trouble lying in ambush. Tidal waves threatened to wash away Haldi. Her senses on the alert, she could smell a whiff in the air. Even her dog's barking had an eerie urgency. Boori roamed around the village. There seemed to be a fire smouldering under the ashes. No one could take it in anymore. The people who suffered in silence now raised their voices. Boori's heart skipped a beat. She paced the neighbourhood back and forth for clues. Their heads held high, the starving humbled people stood tall, banding their pride together.

Boori led the cow to graze in a grassy patch. She ran into Sohrab Ali on the way.

'Where are you off to, Sohrab bhai?' she asked, puzzled by the look on his face.

'To the bazaar to hear the news on the radio. Something terrible is going to happen, Salim's mother. This time, we'll not let them get away with murder. They'll see who the "monkeys" and the "chickens" are around here. We'll stand up to the arrogant Biharis.'

'What will happen, Bhai?'

'I'll tell you later.'

Boori couldn't get to the bottom of their agitation. What had seized everybody? Bagha barked and whined at night for no reason, rushing in the dark to the garden to chase the enemy. Boori would tell the panting dog to be a good boy.

'Why are you scared witless? What's the matter with you, Bagha? Can you get a whiff of what is to come? I'm trying to imagine what's going to happen, but I can't. I thought it might be a drought or a flood, but I was wrong. I can't put my finger on it, but it's definitely something more serious.'

'Maa, why are you talking to the dog?'

Boori blushed at Ramija's question; she forgot she was around. She'd get lost in her own thoughts and begin talking to herself. Bagha was a ready listener.

'Maa, what's the matter? Have you become like them?' Ramija asked.

Boori was at pains to respond to her daughter-in-law. Though she didn't look her in the face, she thought Ramija cocky to nose into her affairs. Boori kicked the dog in a huff and walked off to the *pukur* with Rais. For Boori every day was a new beginning. Shedding her misgivings, she felt rejuvenated as a bright morning light welcomed her. A gentle breeze refreshed her whole being. The first thing she did was to open the door of the chicken coop. They all came out at once. Then she went to see the cattle. She stroked Kajoli and Dholarani and patted her calf, which gave a snort.

'That's a good girl, Champa!'

The animals trailed behind her.

She enjoyed everything she did. She didn't notice how the day rushed on. A wedge of swans flew above the bamboo grove, casting a shadow over the yard. They spelled the morning light. There was a spring flowing somewhere. She could hear it, but couldn't locate it. She felt it would signal a flood, blessing the land with fertile silt. Boori walked to the lake. The water flow seemed to be changing; the size of the lake, the water, the waves, everything changed. Even the water weeds were changing; so were the ghats, the texture of the soil. Even its heartbeat was not the same.

Her eyes followed the road leading to the station. In her younger days, she used to walk to the station, just to look at the train, secretly holding hands with Jalil. The mimosa, green dense grass, clusters of bamboos and *maankochu*—all these sights jogged her memory. Now, however, she felt almost as though she was walking on a road unknown to her.

The dust slithered in the sunlight. The road led ahead, inviting Boori, challenging her to go.

'Come and see where I'm taking you! You have been meaning to follow me for a long time, haven't you? The time has come.'

Boori got restless mulling over things. Haldi. The war. Salim and Kalim. Ramija. Rais. They were so many worry beads. And she couldn't just leave her son behind! Who would look after him? She stood near the road and watched people come and go.

Crowds were pouring to distant places. No one spared a glance at Boori, who stood on the edge. They all walked on with long rhythmic strides. They had a deep, mystical, essential bond with the land. Did it speak to them? Had the spirit of Haldi been slumbering at the bottom of the pond? Whose invisible hand had lulled this little village to sleep for so long? Could that road reveal the secret of this sudden burst of energy?

So this was what war was like. She saw people running towards freedom. Sheik Mujib's name was now on everyone's lips. Who was he? Had he called the Bengali people to war? Was he to guide them to independence?

Oh Allah! Only last year they had an election and all the talk was about voting for the Awami Party's sampan. This year, it's all about war, war, war! Boori stood near the road, thinking about Nita. Had the minstrel gone to war too? Why had she stopped coming to Haldi? She really wanted to learn from Nita how to sing. Then she would sing songs sitting on the bank of the *pukur*.

Boori walked up to the big *shimul* tree on the outskirts of the village and sat under its shadow. She watched attentively as the schoolboys played. They seemed to be more subdued than usual, and talking in a different voice. They were getting keener by the day to break away from the village. The grave, patriotic swank of the lungi-clad boys! Boori could not have pictured it before. How could these starving children fight the enemy? Boori wondered if Rais would ever be like them. She worried how her handicapped boy would compare with these militant boys. She sighed. Rais was a misfit, cast adrift in Haldi. Her boy wouldn't be able to do anything with his gormless mouth. He would be useless in the uprising. He was worthless.

The shadow of the *shimul* grew bigger while Boori kept an eye on the boys. If only she knew why they had stopped playing *shatchara* or bat on ball, why her beloved village had changed beyond belief, why they practised shooting, why they got drunk and dreamt of conquering a new empire. What were they after? What did they lack? What really drove them to call for blood?

Boori tried to get up, but sat down again. This place fascinated her. She could see the whole village from her vantage point. It was like peeling the outer shell away to see the life within. Poverty, drought, torture, oppression and exploitation had made Haldi pale and drab. The fever that gripped the village moved Boori deeply. As a soothing breeze blew Falgun's scorching heat, a flock of chattering birds flew over Boori. Some *tuntuni* perched near her head as she lay on her back. People, like *shimul* seeds, she mused, burst in anger and scattered all over the earth. These people moved purposefully towards some white fluff like *shimul* cotton. The *shimul's* red flower reflected the people's blood-shot eyes.

Like a mother hen over her brood, Boori fussed, fretted, flurried. No one bothered to ask her help. Was she unfit to play her part in the war? The young men claimed that this great struggle of theirs against evil wasn't for old folks.

'Do you think I can just sit here and do nothing?' Boori huffed and puffed.

'Look, this is our *muktijuddho* and you stay well out of it,' the reply came.

Boori asked Sohrab Ali, a neighbour, 'What's going on, Sohrab bhai?'

'You wouldn't understand it.' After a while, he added, 'We're repaying them with our burning hatred for our exploitation. "The low lying land of the low lying people" will teach them a lesson that they'll never forget.'

'Can we count on those half-fed boys in lungi to take up this cause?'

Sohrab Ali flared up at her words. 'My word, you're really a hoot, Salim's maa! We were cowed into silence so long because we didn't trust ourselves. But they kept working us to the bone. Now we, Bengalis, must break our chains.'

'I don't understand a word of what you say, Sohrab bhai.' Boori stared at him wide-eyed.

'You wouldn't. Why don't you go home and put your feet up!' Sohrab Ali scurried across the field, while Boori went indoors. She couldn't believe what she'd just heard. She sounded out Salim who dodged her questions. No one filled her in on what was going on, as if she had nothing to do with the national problem. But Boori had an inquisitive mind and she didn't take no for an answer.

So she tried to eavesdrop on conversations in the living hut, pressing her ear to the door. Salim would launch into a high-pitched tirade and all the villagers would discuss some momentous subject. She didn't fully grasp the nature of the problem. Yet, she put two and two together and she braced herself for the storm.

Boori remembered the radio speech delivered by the man with a lion's voice on 22nd Falgun. All the men and women in Haldi gathered and listened with rapt attention to the speech. Boori herself was mesmerized by the great voice that came out of the air:

'My dear brothers...
    I have come before you today with a heavy heart. [I]t is a matter of sadness that the streets of Dacca, Chittagong, Khulna, Rangpur and Rajshahi are today being spattered

with the blood of my brothers, and the cry we hear from the Bengali people is a cry for freedom, a cry for survival, a cry for our rights.

Ours has been a long history of lament, a never-ending flow of blood and tears…'

The voice drowned in a sudden burst of static to everyone's disappointment and died. They said the man with the magnetic voice was Sheikh Mujibur Rahman. The voice crackled to life again.

'Mr Yahya Khan, you are the President of this country. Come to Dacca, come and see with your own eyes how our poor Bengali people have been mowed down by your bullets, how the laps of our mothers and sisters have been robbed and left empty and bereft, how my helpless people have been slaughtered.

On that day, right here at this racecourse, I pledged to you that I would pay for this blood debt with my own blood. Do you remember? Today I am ready to fulfil that promise!

If a single bullet is fired upon us henceforth, if the murder of my people does not cease, I call upon you to turn every home into a fortress against their onslaught. Use whatever you can lay your hands on to confront this enemy. Every last road must be blocked…

And the seven million people of this land will not be cowed down by you or accept tyranny any more. The Bengali people have learned how to die for a cause and you will not be able to bring them under your yoke of oppression!'

The speech struck a deep chord in the village. All she knew was that the man was addressing their problems as though he were targeting Haldi. He talked about their hearts' desires. The village, its trees, fields, crops, cattle, plants and animals expressed their deepest desires in that magic voice. Siraj Miah taped the speech, and ever since they'd listen to it every now and then, with whoops of excitement. Salim memorized the speech for her. Although Boori didn't understand every word, she remembered the odd sentence he had bellowed:

> 'You must prepare yourselves now with what little you have for the struggle ahead.
>
> Since we have given blood, we will give more of it. But, insha'allah, we will free the people of this land!
>
> The struggle this time is for emancipation! The struggle this time is for independence!
>
> *Joi Bangla!*'

Boori couldn't remember more than these last few sentences charged with fire and electrifying energy. She would forget them and ask Salim to repeat them over and over again. She was obsessed with the echo of the man's fiery speech, trying to tease out its meaning and wishing to approach the hero.

One day, she asked Salim, 'My son, can you take me to see the great man?'

'Just like that, eh!' Salim replied, bursting into laughter. 'I've never come across him myself. I can see his face in my mind's eye though. Moreover, Dacca is far away.'

'I can also picture his face,' Boori hastened to reply. 'But as I have never seen him, it looks different all the time.'

'You are right! Last time he came to give his speech I was ill, so I couldn't go. Maybe I'll never get to see him.'

'Oh yes! You will live to see him.'

The villagers would huddle together to listen to Bangabandhu's voice or Tagore songs, broadcast from the Free Bangladesh Radio. *Amar shonar Bangla, Banglar mati Banglar jol* and *Joi Bangla, Banglar joi, hobe hobe hobe hobe nischoy* were among the favourites and the notes would bring tears to people's eyes. The radio spluttered other tunes that never failed to whip up their spirits. *Amar bhaiyer rokte rangano ekushey February* was one such song that primed them for war:

Selina Hossain

Amar bhaiyer rokte rangano ekushey February
Ami ki bhulite pari
Chhele hara shato mayer ashru goriye February
Ami ki bhulite pari
Amar sonar desher rangano ekushey February
Ami ki bhulite pari

Jaago naginira jaago naginira jago kalboshhekhira
Shishu hotyar bikshove aj kapuk busundara,
Desher shonar chhele khun kore rakhe manusher dabi
Din badoler krantilagne tobu tora par pabi?
Na, na, na, na khun ranga itihase shesh ray dewa taroi
Ekushey February ekushey February.

Sedino emoni nil gogoner bashone shiter sheshe
Rat jaaga chand chumo khaiyechhilo heshe;
Pathe pathe fote rojonigandha oloknanda jeno,
Emon somoy jhorh elo ek khepa buno.
Sei andharer poshuder mukh chena,
Tahader tore mayer, boner, bhaiyer charom grina
Ora guli chhore edesher prane desher dabike rokhe
Oder grinya padaghat ei sara Banglar buke
Ora edesher noy,
Desher bhagya ora kare bikroy
Ora manusher onno, shanti niyechhe kari
Ekushey February ekushey February.

Tumi aj jaago tumi aj jaago ekushe February
Ajo jalimer karagare more bir chheley, bir nari
Amar shaohid bhaiyer atta dakey
Jaago manusher supta shalti hate mathe ghate bate
Darun krodher agune abar jalbo February
Ekushey February ekushey February.

Boori didn't lose hope. She roamed around the whole village, then went home. Ramija came up and sat beside her.

Salim was so full of Bangabandhu that he stopped beating his wife overnight. Ramija had become withdrawn these days. She was pregnant and would soon be a mother. Unlike Boori, she had no problem conceiving a baby. She felt cheerful and serene at the thought of receiving a gift. Boori was pleased for her sake. She sat beside her daughter-in-law and could see the concern in her eyes.

'What happened to you, Maa? Your face looks pale.'

'I walked round the village and I can't get my breath back. Something has happened to Haldi,' Boori said.

'Not likely!' Ramija laughed it off. 'You're just imagining things and overreacting like those wild youngsters.'

Ramija's tinkle infuriated Salim. He couldn't stand it and chided her.

'Stop giggling, it's not funny!'

'I don't have much to think about, that's why I always laugh. Has all the family forgotten how to laugh? Maa, I can't feed Rais, he refuses to have food from me. He's mad and he's waiting for you.'

'Rais, Rais, Rais...Where are you?' Boori suddenly tapped her forehead, remembering her son, and called him out. There was a time when she would have given anything to have this boy. But now she didn't feel like running after him. For a good many days, she had not been taking proper care of him. He'd loaf about, sit in the veranda or play with Bagha in the courtyard. As he couldn't speak or complain, it was hard to tell whether he was aware of Boori's neglect or missed her affection, and bore his sadness in silence. He was a loner and no one bothered to bond with a dumb boy of his sort.

Boori was silent, sitting still with the boy's chin resting on her folded knees. Ramija was boiling rice on the stove. She would cook in the courtyard if the sky was clear. She enjoyed it more than in the kitchen. She usually collected bone-dry stalks and sticks for the wood-fire oven. Sometimes Rais would come along. He helped her by snapping deadwood underfoot. A smile hung on his lips as he collected the twigs. He couldn't share his emotion, but Ramija was moved nonetheless. The wild flame lapped the rim of the pot.

'When love comes,' she muttered to herself, 'it bubbles like frying peas. When love leaves, it pounds you like paddy in the husking.'

Boori stared at the stove. It felt as though the mantra *Joi Bangla* had leapt out of the fire into the stove. The people of the village were always full of *Joi Bangla* these days. Boori could hear an echo inside her heart. Her thoughts travelled to many places. She imagined her village ablaze. Who was behind it all, she wondered? It just burned and burned, day after day. It burned people, homes, animals, trees; anything it caught in its path, it just burned. But what had the pot of boiling rice to do with it? Was Haldi the only village alight or was the fire raging all over Bangladesh? Again Boori got restless. She called out her daughter-in-law, 'Ramija! Ramija!'

'Amma! Over here! I am here.'

'Why don't we chant *Joi Bangla* together?'

Both Ramija and Boori screamed *Joi Bangla* at the top of their voices and circled around the yard. Boori held her fists aloft in celebration. Rais ran up to them and clasped Ramija's hand. He made a squeaky gurgling sound as he danced around.

Both women couldn't believe their ears. Rais hugged his mother and cried with that same stifled sound. Boori was fired up and she let out a wild whoop.

'Rais! Baba Rais! Say *Joi Bangla*! Say *Joi Bangla*, please?'

Rais danced holding his mother. Boori howled with delight.

'What are you crying for, Amma?' Ramija asked in disbelief.

'Haven't you heard? Rais is saying *Joi Bangla*?'

'Is he? Did you hear him?'

'You can't hear him, but you can see his words. His face is jubilant. Amma, he speaks with his whole body.'

Boori was aware of a different Ramija standing before her eyes.

'What are you saying, Ramija?'

'That he speaks with his whole being. You have to read his body, Amma. You'll never be able to hear him otherwise.'

'I'm sure you're right.'

Boori sat near the veranda. Rais settled beside her. She couldn't take her eyes off him. It was as if his body was on fire too. He could get burned, get drowned with *Joi Bangla*. He could even join the war. Falgun was in its last weeks. Winter was gone. So was Rais's sickness and the boy was now in fine fettle. Ramija looked different too. She was expecting. She talked like an elder one these days. She was so proud and happy. If only Rais could be like that. If he could just say the words, 'See mother, I can do everything too! There's no need to be sad.'

Boori stared at the sun-drenched yard.

চৈত্র
Chôitrô

Falgun was followed by Chôitrô's scorching sun. The earth dried up and cracked. Boori couldn't venture outside for fear of the heat. Her tongue was parched and her skin peeled off. She'd drink like a fish. The *pukur* water glistened invitingly.

'Look dear,' she said to Ramija, shielding her eyes from the glare, 'I've never seen such a heat wave. It's boiling hot as if someone had opened the gate to hell and forgotten to close it. The furnace is burning up the village. There's no escape.'

'Don't walk about in the sun. You'll get sick. Be a dear, and promise you won't step out of the house from tomorrow.'

'Says who? I could never pin myself to one place. I'd sorely miss the bustle and excitement. Can't you see that?'

'Let them play their wild pranks. They don't want you there,' Ramija scolded Boori as if she was a young girl.

'You shouldn't say that. When I hear them shouting *Joi Bangla*, or *moder gorob, moder aasha, a'mori Bangla bhasha*, I can't sit idle at home and do nothing. You can't understand how my soul bubbles over with that roar. Let's shout a thunderous *Joi Bangla*!'

Ramija stared at Boori with wide eyes. Her wrinkled face glowed with the sunlight. Boori became thoughtful.

'You know, Ramija, I lose track of everything but this call. I can't forget it. I don't know why, but I simply can't. Do you know what I think when I hear it?'

'I couldn't possibly guess, Maa,' she replied.

'I imagine that Haldi is swept away by this call. I've never felt anything like it! I feel like dying. I wouldn't be sad if I died now.' Boori's heart was brimming over with joy.

'What makes you so thoughtful, Maa?' Ramija wondered out loud.

Boori didn't reply. She withdrew into her shell. Ramija was quiet too. She didn't like too much noise. Besides she was pregnant. She was getting bigger by the day. The small being inside her kept her on her toes. Boori looked at the sky.

'Why do you worry so much?' Ramija queried.

The sunny Chôitrô's sky turned turquoise. The huge branches of the trees were alive with the chatter, twitter and cackle of birds. Boori loved listening to birdsongs.

A sparrow trilled, stopped, trilled again in the bamboo grove. A cuckoo sang overhead.

'The *kutum* is calling for guests, Ramija,' she remarked casually.

'Someone from my father's family will definitely come over,' Ramija replied. 'I haven't seen Baba for quite a while. Maybe, he will drop by with my sisters. I'm sure Nilima and Rashida miss me.'

Boori watched Ramija's face awash with tears. Her daughter-in-law was always emotional when she talked about her family. Boori tapped into her own memories from another world. She didn't know what it felt like living far from her family. Her father's and her husband's home were one and the same for her. Gafoor's memory had almost faded into ashes now. She couldn't recall anymore the faces of Salim and Kalim when they were young.

Boori felt sleepy sitting in the veranda. She drifted off by noon when the sun was at its hottest. Salim and Kalim had not returned yet. No one had lunch since the boys were not home. Boori asked Ramija to start eating. She wouldn't hear of it though. She never ate before her husband. Boori waited for them. She leaned on the bamboo pole of the house. Startled, she blinked her eyes open. She thought she heard Kalim calling out for rice. He was starving and could not wait. Boori shook herself awake. She looked round, but found no one there. She was edgy. She heard a faint voice calling 'Maa, Maa,' begging for food. She felt the whole of Haldi came to her door, screaming for rice. She would hear this cry during droughts, famines and floods. Screaming for food was Haldi's kismet. In her wild imagination, she conjured up the starving villagers screaming madly for something to kill their hunger pangs. Boori became restless. Something rattled around her with a dry cough, 'Maa, give me some rice…rice…rice.' Her heart beat faster. She yelled, her eyes flashing wildly.

Boori went into the courtyard. She looked at the distant edges of the open fields. There was not a single ghost of a soul to be seen. The cows were tethered on the grazing ground and a couple of goats were wandering here and there. Boori checked the green olive tree for people; the giant tree spanning 40 feet in width, as well as several generations, was a favourite shaded spot with its twisted branches.

The whole village seemed empty. Where had all the people suddenly gone? Boori untethered her cow and goaded it home. It was due to calve shortly. Ramija woke up. Rais was sitting quietly in the veranda.

'Hasn't anyone come?' Ramija asked.

'Not yet. Why haven't you had your meal? Let's have something to eat.'

They began to eat in the kitchen. The soft, white rice tasted dry and hard to Boori. She had to wash it down with water.

'What's wrong, Maa?'

'It doesn't taste good. Too bland.' Boori rolled the rice together between her fingers. Rais wolfed down his food in no time. Boori watched her son.

In the evening, Salim and Kalim returned home after spending the day on empty stomachs. Their faces looked exhausted.

'Where have you been all day, my sons?' she asked them.

'We were at a meeting,' Salim answered briefly.

Boori served them food, after which they put their feet up in the veranda. Ramija had her meal, and she then put away the kitchen utensils. The full moon's milky light spilled over the landscape. Boori was soothed by the moonlight and the gentle breeze. She felt far away from Haldi—the place that had filled her with bliss and bitterness for so long. On such a fascinating night, she was tempted to take a walk in the village and discard the dullness in her mind.

'I feel like singing from the bottom of my heart, Maa,' Kalim enthused.

'Go ahead, son,' Boori coaxed him.

'But I need some inspiration.' Kalim strolled about the courtyard, lit a bidi and patted Bagha heartily.

Ramija joined them in the veranda. Rais also joined them, leaning against his mother's back.

'It's really a charming night,' Salim said, breaking the silence. Kalim stood under a coconut tree and began to hum. His voice was travelling up and down the scale. A little later Kalim sang more raucously:

Nongor tolo tolo somoy je holo holo
Nongor tolo tolo somoy je holo holo nongor tolo tolo
Nongor tolo tolo somoy je holo holo nongor tolo tolo
Nongor tolo tolo somoy je holo nongor tolo tolo

Hawar buke noukar paal
joware vasie dao

Sokto muthir badone badone
Borjobadhia nao
Borjobadhia nao borjobadhia nao

Somukhe ebar dristi tomar
Pechoner kotha vulo
Pechoner kotha vulo
Pechoner kotha vulo
Pechoner kotha vulo

Nongor tolo tolo somoy je holo nongor tolo tolo

Dur digante surjo dake
Dristi rekecho sthir
Sobuj asar sopnera aaj
Noyone koreche veer
Noyone koreche veer
Noyone koreche veer

Ridoye tomar muktir alo
Alor duar kholo
Alor duar kholo
Alor duar kholo
Alor duar kholo.

The two brothers had had a meeting with people from other villages. Bangabandhu Sheikh Mujibur Rahman had called upon all Bengali people to 'turn every home into a fortress'. Everyone was to join the war with whatever weapons they could lay their hands on. The air resonated with slogans from Dacca:

> 'Brave Bengalis, take up arms!'
> 'Free your country, Bangladesh!'
> 'Your address, my address,
> Padma, Meghna, Jamuna,
> You are ours and ours to claim!'

Salim and Kalim returned home intoxicated with these slogans. They chanted their heads off, punching the air:

> 'We will no longer be slaves!'
> 'Now, it's time to fight, get your weapons ready!'

They walked into the courtyard and marched around to imaginary martial music.

'It seems as though war has broken out in the house,' Ramija trilled.

'It isn't funny!' Salim scolded her. 'You didn't hear Sheikh Mujib's speech; we will have to sacrifice more blood! That's what he said.'

Boori was a little confused.

'Why should we give blood?' she asked, looking them in the eye.

'There can be no war without bloodshed, Maa! There will be a river of blood!'

'"A river of blood?" Whatever do you mean?' Boori queried in a cracked voice.

Everyone rallied around her. Rais also came up and stood beside Salim and Kalim. Bagha yelped excitedly.

'Whose blood will be spilled in this war?' Boori screamed.

'Everybody's, Maa! All the blood of this country's seven and a half crore people.'

'What are you saying, son?'

'Don't you worry, Maa!' Kalim hugged his mother. 'Your sons too will shed their blood for the cause.'

'My sons? Oh, right, yes of course!' she replied automatically. 'My sons will give their blood too. If all the people of Bangladesh give blood, then why not my children too? I too will give blood! So will Ramija and Rais!'

Suddenly Boori started howling. She wailed like a baby. The noise pierced the darkness and rippled across the house, the village and the plain like a fish leaping from the water and gasping for air.

'Let me take you inside,' Kalim said, wiping her tears with her sari *anchol*. 'You get some rest. I'll sing you to sleep. Just the way you did when we were young.'

Picking her up gingerly, Kalim lifted her onto his shoulders. He walked to her bedroom.

'What are you doing?' Boori was livid. 'Put me down! Put me down, I say!'

'No! I will not put you down! Somehow I have to repay my debt.'

'Let go of me!' Boori kicked her legs.

'I will go around the yard with you once.'

When things went back to normal, Boori let herself go and hunched her shoulders against her stepson's strong arms. She saw all the others following him around, clapping. After his lap of honour, Salim asked his brother:

'Why don't you let me give her a piggyback?'

'No way! She is mine alone today!' Kalim horsed around with his mother for a while and then he laid her down on her bed.

'Now, you get some sleep!' he said as he touched her feet.

He sang her a lullaby:

Bulbuli-te dhan kheyeche
Khajna debo kishe…
Dhan phuralo, pan phuralo
Khajnar upay ki!
Aar kota din shobur koro
Roshun bunechi.

Boori closed her eyes and felt as if she had hopscotched back to her childhood. Kalim's singing buoyed her heart. Salim kept silent. Ramija felt wide awake. Rais, for his part, walked to the edge of the courtyard and clapped at the moon with wild and gleeful cheers. The whole family enjoyed this quiet moonlit night. They looked blissfully happy and oblivious of the outside world.

On the tenth of Chôitrô, they heard the news about Dacca on their ramshackle radio. Tikka Khan's 'Operation Searchlight' was under way and the army had besieged and captured Dacca. Sheikh Mujib was arrested and taken to Karachi. They couldn't get more news about him. The government radio had declared a blackout.

Salim fumed. He hugged Boori hard and vowed in a stern voice to do something about it. Boori was lost adrift. Salim shouted in a discordant tone, then shot a salvo of abuses. He spewed some slogan: the words that poured from his lips sounded like readings from the Qu'ran.

Boori had never seen her son so agitated. Salim behaved as though he was taking on the entire enemy. A few moments later, he switched off the radio and rushed off to some hideaway. Kalim followed in his footsteps. Their aggressive stance nettled Ramija. The baby was roiling in her womb. It was only a matter of a few weeks before she was due to go into labour. She felt weak and worn out.

'What a mess! What the hell happened in Dacca to make them explode like baked brinjals?' Ramija cried. She scowled at her mother-in-law. 'What's the matter with you, Maa?'

Boori remained silent. She tried to recall the slogan *Joi Bangla*.

Salim and Kalim rushed away from the house with that slogan on their lips. All Boori's limbs were stiff. She cast a hollow glance at her daughter-in-law.

'Why are you looking at me, Maa?'

'Ramija, come over and let's make a chorus of *Joi Bangla*!' Boori suggested.

'What do you mean?' Ramija wondered.

'Oh, Ramija, you don't understand anything.'

'I can't stand all these slogans anymore, Maa!'

Boori left the hut to loiter under the olive tree. She muttered to herself:

'I would like to do something. This village is my only home. Since childhood, the dust, the trees and shrubs, the animals have been my family. I must do something for this village, even at the cost of my life. I would gladly give my life, if it came to it.'

Suddenly a gaggle of boys in the distant field interrupted her musing. Their voices didn't carry though. Boori's throat was parched as her eyes settled on the horizon, faraway. A gander scuttled off, rustling through the dry leaves and twigs on the ground. The *kutum* was cooing in the olive tree.

Boori couldn't help thinking that a tortuous road of struggle lay ahead for her people; they had a pledge to keep. Did those gangling youths, full of wild energy, make a pledge too? After a few minutes, Boori could hear the slogans:

'Brave Bengalis,
Hold your weapons ready!'
'Free your country!
Padma, Meghna, Yamuna,
You are ours and ours to claim!'

They went onto the road which led to the bazaar. The procession snaked its way round a bend. Boori's face flushed from the scorching heat. Cheering them on, she punched the air:

'Your leader, my leader!'
'Sheikh Mujib, Sheikh Mujib!'

She stopped in her tracks and looked round. Her leader was nowhere to be seen. Would she ever be able to see him? She peered into the sky. Kalim had taught her this slogan. How she adored her boys! Boori was so very proud of them. By telling her about Sheikh Mujib and about the state of her own country, they opened up a whole new horizon before her eyes. She paused to gaze at the paddy fields and beyond. She felt that she needed to make a pledge too. A pledge to do something for the country. She was stranded in the middle of nowhere. She raised her arms to the top of her head, even as the *Chôitrô* wind caressed her, and wrapped her sari *anchol* round her head.

Within a week Jalil had fled from Dacca, leaving behind all his belongings. His wife and daughters had been slaughtered by the Pakistani army. The villagers gathered around him in the outhouse. They were all ears to get the latest news from the city. Boori stood near the fence eavesdropping on the conversation:

'I went to Narayanganj that night. The Pakistani army killed my wife and my daughters. I have lost all my relatives now!'

Jalil broke into tears. Boori felt like crying too but she knew that others may end up gossiping about it, so she controlled herself. Jalil was in her heart, but no one was to know that.

Then at one point he wiped his eyes and resumed his tale.

'I went to the racecourse field to listen to Bangabandhu's speech. Thousands of people had gathered there. It was unbelievable. I had not seen anything like it in Dacca before. I joined the crowd and shouted myself hoarse with slogans…'

'Allah, please have mercy!' Jalil cried as if unhinged. We must wring the vultures' necks. We must avenge their deaths, Salim bhai!'

'Yes, we'll have blood for blood,' Salim responded, primed with rage. 'We'll free our country, just as we promised Bangabandhu, *Joi Bangla!*'

'*Joi Bangla!*' everyone replied in unison. They screamed and thumped the air with their fists. Gradually, the crowd dispersed in ones and twos.

Boori overheard the conversation from the hedge. As everyone was leaving, Jalil headed for her hut. He looked upset, demented and his bloodshot eyes looked down. His hair had greyed. He didn't know what to say, how to start when he saw her.

'Dacca was asleep when the Pakistani army swooped on its people, shot men and women, looted homes and set fire to buildings. "Jaldi, jaldi," one commanding officer barked, "all Hindus and kafirs to stand in line." After the men were herded in one place and the women and children in another, he chose at random saying, "This one. That one." People began screaming as the prisoners were roped together, and then, as sudden as winter rain, they were sprayed with bullets. The few children and teenagers who survived the machine gun fire were bayonetted to death.

'While Babu Bazaar was torched, I was away in Narayanganj. I saw corpses piled up, dead kids on dead mothers' laps. Wives hugging their husbands to ward off the bullets. Fathers shielding their daughters from the bayonets. Blood streamed into the Shitolakhya river, which turned crimson with floating dead bodies.

'Almost all the male members in my family died in the fires in Dacca, my beloved younger brothers, Nazrul and Nayeem, my first cousins Mohammad Abdul, Altaf and Fazle. Taher, our next door neighbour lost his baba and most of his relatives in those massacres. He saw Pakistani soldiers pour petrol over the dead bodies and set them on fire. He told me about the tragedy...'

Jalil broke down in tears. 'How can people do this to other people? Allah must have created them differently from the rest of us. When I shut my eyes, I hear the TATA TATA of guns, I feel the heat of the fire consuming those bodies, the wails of the women gang-raped in the hot silent night and the helpless screams of the dying. I can't shut them out, I just can't...'

The veins on Jalil's neck and temples stabbed; the muscles on his face were braced for an explosive release.

Boori looked perturbed. A few moments later she muttered, 'But, Jalil bhai, those who fired on us, they are our fellow countrymen.'

'Yes, we're all citizens of the same country, Pakistan.'

'Then, why would they kill us?' she blurted out. 'We haven't done any wrong.'

Boori stomped her foot in anger. Jalil kept silent. He tried to think of an answer to her questions.

'They hate our guts, they call us "bingo dogs".'

Boori repeated her question, 'What do they hold against us? Why should we have to put up with what they did just because they do not like us?'

'You're right, Boori, this is beyond words. Everyone is crying aloud for blood.' Jalil was fired up too. 'I didn't believe in revenge, but now I feel I must also fight for our freedom, Boori,' he said as he strode off.

All that Ramija was used to was her kitchen fire. The blaze that charred the country caught her napping. The sound of gunshots were new to her. She had spotted the odd hunter shooting birds, but never seen people actually being shot dead.

'If their shots can kill us,' she muttered under her breath, 'then why not kill them too?'

Everything now became crystal clear to Boori. Her inner eye saw it all.

Borgi elo deshe
Bulbuli-te dhan kheyeche
Kkhajna debo kishe

In late Chôitrô, Ramija gave birth to a son, a beautiful, gawky, yet well-shaped baby with a face like Gafoor's. Boori was busy with the baby all day. She rubbed oil on his body and she applied khol around his eyes for protection. The baby was aglow like sunrise.

On most days, Salim and Kalim just took a cursory look at the baby. They didn't have time to play with it. Freedom was on their mind. The army had taken over. They heard of the devastating turns their country took each day through the news on the radio. They were busy mobilizing, painting *chika mara* slogans, and plotting sabotage operations with Jalil.

Meanwhile, Boori had been toying with names for the baby and she brought the matter up with Salim over lunch.

'We must choose a *bhalo nam* for your son.'

Salim remained silent. His mind was elsewhere. Boori could only guess at what he was going through.

'Why not call him Hafiz?' Boori suggested. 'It's been in the family for generations.'

'You choose what you want to call it. I can't be bothered with your petty concerns,' Salim said, visibly disgruntled. 'We are at war.'

'A name is for a lifetime,' Boori's voice trailed off as her stepson walked away. 'A name belongs to you as your birthright...'

Boori carried her grandson on her waist and sang:

Aai aai chad mama
Aai aai chad mama tip die ja
Chader kopale chad tip die ja
Dhan banle kuro debo
Mach katle muro debo
Kalo gaer dudh debo
Dudh khabar bati debo
Chader kopale chad tip die ja

The baby had unlocked something in Boori, a hidden door to a joy that was rooted in her own childhood. Ramija would often smile, watching her mother-in-law's childlike delight.

'Maa, you're over the moon,' she said, a ring of motherly pride in her voice.

Boori looked at her glowing face.

'What are you looking at, Maa?'

'I'm just looking at you. It fills me with such joy. I wasn't half as happy when Rais was born.'

'Why dig up the past?'

Ramija went to the *pukur*, while Boori played with Bagha.

'Are you pleased, Bagha, at the arrival of a new family member?' She patted the dog and sang a snatch of a song:

Khoka ghumalo, para juralo
Khoka ghumalo, para juralo

Borgi elo deshe
Bulbuli-te dhan kheyeche
Khajna debo kishe

Dhan phuralo, pan phuralo
Khajnar upay ki!
Aar kota din shobur koro
Roshun bunechi.

She stepped out of the house with Rais, as she wanted to go to Hanif's shop and buy some sweets for him. Sometimes she watched her grandson in wonder and nodded. Boori regained her confidence and, as time passed, the pleasure she found in her grandson's company only grew. She would press him close to her chest or swing him around in her arms. She would have fun making up her own rhymes:

'You want to go to war,
Who will join you?
There is Rais, then there is the cat.
All set to go!'

Rais didn't respond. But the baby stretched his arms and legs.

She had not laughed so heartily when Rais was his age. Now when she played with the baby's windmilling arms and thrashing legs, she forgot all her pain and wounds.

'Dadu! You are my wealth of seven kings. You are my pearl. You were born to the chants of *Joi Bangla* on everyone's lips. Do you see the world is topsy-turvy now? You don't even know that your own father is seething with revenge. The whole of Haldi is changing its colour and when you grow up, this village will not be same. We cannot share a boat with those who shoot our brothers, can we?'

She would talk to the baby about Haldi and the freedom movement, as he watched and listened to her, in a way that no one else did.

She would get angry at Salim for making himself scarce all day.

'Look, son!' she complained to Salim one day. 'You're almost never home and you never spend time with your own baby, why is that?'

'I don't want to see that shrimp,' Salim said, drowning his feelings. 'Let it grow a little bit older and then I'll have a proper look at it.'

Boori was hurt.

'Look, Maa! You ask me to take the baby in my lap, but I'm afraid that it will slip out of my hands. I don't have time to rock it or fondle it the way you do,' Salim pleaded.

'You're too busy with your work. When the baby is grown up, he won't call you Baba.'

'So you keep saying. I'll take the chance.'

'Don't talk to me about chance, Salim!'

'Maa, why can't you understand that I made a promise to help free this country? I want my son to grow up in a free land,' Salim spouted in full lecturing mode. 'So that when he is older, he will remember that his father fought for the liberation of his country. He will be a proud son. I'm now sowing the seeds of his pride into his mind. You raise our baby by giving it all your care and affection, but my love is of a different kind,' Salim said, more vulnerable than he cared to admit, and then left the hut.

Boori was moved by what Salim had said, much as it pained her to admit it. His words came straight from his heart. She sat silently for a while, etching them on her memory.

Sometimes Rais had a look of disbelief on his face as he stared at the baby. He had never *seen* such a tiny baby, let alone be in a close proximity to one. The tiny legs kicking in the air, the hands that sought to clutch whatever touched its palms, the unprovoked laughter fascinated him. At other times though, the tiny gasps and coughs got on his nerves and he felt like cuffing him. Boori had to keep her grandson at arm's length from Rais. She couldn't leave him unattended anyway, but especially not with Rais around. She'd spend all her time with the baby. Salim and Kalim were rarely at home, if at all. Sometimes they would come home after midnight. And Ramija's domestic chores left her little time to look after her baby, so it fell on Boori to take the baby under her wing. This child meant a whole kingdom and only she could claim access to it.

'Far away and just as long ago,' Boori whispered a fairy tale in his ears, 'there was a reed of a fisherman. Munir was his name. He lived from hand to mouth in the marshes. His house was a cane roof over a nutshell of a boat. Munir knew the waterways like the back of his hand. He had no match and he would smell out the best fishing spots. One day, though, his luck ran out and his prized *rui* were no longer the talk of the bazaar. The "pure-blood gypsy" was a sorry-looking mess. He would spear only lotus pads and when he pulled his net in, worse luck, it was torn by roots or stumps. Bogged down by this twist of fortune, Munir prayed to Nodi for good fishing. Nothing happened and the sad fisherman would sleep through his days, hoping that this was all a bad dream he would wake up from. His nets would flutter on the top of the *kash* grass.

One monsoon night, Munir tried his luck in a remote spot cluttered with *kochuripana* and lotus leaves. He cast his net overboard. After several long minutes, he hoisted it nervously. There was nothing. Peering closer, he spotted a tiny *mrigel* at the bottom.

"Not much of a fish!" Munir spat and cursed his fate. "Still, you'll go into the curry pot."

"Psst! spare me," the fish begged, "and you'll be in luck." The silver fish slipped through his fingers. "Promise me you'll never sell my brothers and I'll grant you three wishes."

Munir took the fish at his word, for he had never encountered a talking fish before, and named his first wish. His eyes popped out when he drew in his net. He was so over the moon with this bumper catch that he fell overboard. He hung up most of the fish on bamboo sticks to dry. The next day, it was the same story with an even bigger haul. Munir could hardly lift the net which was badly torn by now.

"I wish I had new nets," the fisherman said.

His second wish was instantly granted and Munir caught so much fish he gave away lots to the river people. Some fishermen got jealous and decided to ride the same fishing spots. Yet, they had no such luck and, out of spite, they made fun of Munir's "old sieve of a boat."

Munir's bumper catches got the better of his boat which sank one night.

"I wish I had a big, new boat," was the fisherman's third wish.

Munir whooped it up as a new boat floated up to his side. The fisherman rode his luck and thought he was king of the wetlands.

Yet, he was soon to have second thoughts. He didn't have a minute to himself anymore with his fishing business scaling newer heights each day. He had lost any semblance of peace. His islands stank with garlands of drying fish. He couldn't ply the waters without an escort, all the while being hounded by buzzing flies. His friends cast a knowing grin. Even folks at the bazaar pestered him for fish.

When Munir saw simple folks fish with an otter, he remembered the *rui's* words...

My story's done,' said Boori. 'But this tale will go on, as long as grass grows and rivers run.'

A sweet fragrance wafted from Ramija's son like a blue lotus in a pool. Boori's heart was filled with happiness. The flash of a lighthouse beam had picked out her boat bobbing on the dark waves.

বৈশাখ
Boishakh

In late Boishakh, Nita appeared singing. Choron Das wasn't with her this time. Her sari was raised to her knees and her ankles were coated with dust. Her face showed signs of weariness while her grey mane was billowing in the wind. Nita had aged. Her face was like a dried old prune. Boori was shocked at sight of her friend.

'*Soi*, it's been a long time! Come in and have a seat.'

Boori took her to the veranda and arranged some cushions for her to rest. Nita put down her *dotara* and slinging her bag off her shoulder dropped it.

'Is that your grandson'?

'Mmm'

'My, my! You're such a sweetie,' said Nita, affectionately.

'What have you named him?'

'Er, he is Juddho,' Boori finally managed to say.

'Juddho? Ah! That's a nice name. It rolls so well off the tongue. Did you choose the name?' Nita was spurred on by curiosity.

'Who else?' came Boori's ruffled reply.

An ache gnawed inside Nita, from her belly to her deepest core. Coming to Boori's home left her with mixed feelings as she too craved for a normal life. Her longing for motherhood had grown stronger over the years. What with her bohemian lifestyle, she had lost her youth and good looks.

To take her mind off things, Nita fished into the folds of her sari at her waist for her tobacco.

'What's on your mind?' Boori wondered aloud.

'Not having a family of my own like you.'

'Having a family now? What are you on about?'

'As years pile on, I think I envy you, *soi*.'

'You must be pulling my leg.' Boori burst out laughing and stroked her grandson.

Nita looked sombre, sighing quietly to herself as she met her friend's gaze. She mused over her blissful days at the ashram. She could never have lived Boori's cooped up life.

'Where's your *moner manush*, *soi*?' Boori queried.

'My soulmate? Pah! I've left him for good. Now the whole country is my soulmate.' Nita replied as she picked up her *dotara*. She toyed with another thought, clattering the strings. Sometimes when she re-emerged from her hidden world, she would find the burden of reality overwhelming. She broke into song:

Amar shonar Bangla
Ami tomay bhalobashi
Chirodin tomar akash,
Tomar batash,
Amar prane bajae bāshi.

O ma,
Phagune tor amer bone
Ghrane pagol kôre,
Mori hay, hay re,
O ma,
Ôghrane tor bhôra khete
Ami ki dekhechhi modhur hashi.

Ma, tor mukher bani
Amar kane lage
Sudhar moto
Ma tor bodonkhani molin hole
ami noyon

O may ami noyonjole bhashi
Sonar bangla,
Ami tomay bhalobasi!

Boori was enchanted by the song, even more so by Nita's rendition of it. She could feel the song drift off into the air, over the shrubs, ponds, *shimul* and the railway station, and further and further away…

It had a magnetic pull and mesmerized her. Boori saw her friend in a different light. The minstrel was no longer a wanderer fishing for a *moner manush*, but a member of Boori's household. She was no longer a mere speck, twinkling in the sky. The clatter of the *dotara* filled the house. Boori was boiling rice in an earthen pot in the courtyard and threw in a few dry stalks before the embers turned to ashes.

'I'm not in a hurry today,' Nita said as she kept her eyes on the flame. 'I'll have a nap after lunch. You can wake me up in the evening. I guess your stepsons will be back by then.'

'You can stay as long as you need. They are not coming back any time soon.'

'I feel uncomfortable in their presence,' Nita added.

'Why, *soi*? They're very easy to get along with.'

'What are you cooking for lunch?' Nita asked, evading her question.

'Snake gourd with *tengra* fish and fried red leafy vegetables.'

'Sounds yummy, my dear. But, you know, dal and mashed coconut will do just as well. I haven't had such fine food for a while and my tongue has forgotten the taste.'

'It's nothing fancy, and you never have more than a few bites anyway,' Boori replied.

Nita let her arm be twisted and Boori informed Ramija that Nita would be joining them for lunch.

'I'm so glad you're eating with us today,' Ramija said to Nita.

'It would make my mother-in-law so happy if you stopped by more often. Please pay us a visit whenever you find time.'

'I do drop by quite often,' Nita pleaded.

'No, you don't. You've been away for a long time,' Ramija protested.

'I wander from village to village and spend time at the ashram, so it's not so easy to come over every now and then,' Nita explained.

Boori brought puffed rice for Nita in an earthen pot. Rais was lolling idle in a corner of the veranda, swatting the flies around his face with his left hand. Boori lulled her grandson to sleep. Rais pushed aside the dish of *moori* that Nita had offered him heartily.

'Your son gives me the cold shoulder.'

'Don't talk about him. Once I had high hopes for him, but they were all snuffed out.'

'What's the matter, *soi*? If I have offended you, then I'm sorry. Please go and put your grandson to bed—he's fallen asleep.'

Nita was sorry that she had caused discomfort. Boori did not do as she was told. Instead, she continued to cradle the sleeping baby on her lap.

Nita chomped her way through the puffed rice. The stove was blazing with red flames. Nita watched on as Ramija took the *gamcha* and went to the pond. 'Your daughter-in-law is a bit on the heavy side.'

'She is a very good girl,' Boori replied guardedly.

Nita scratched the ground with her toenails, heedless of Boori. She felt the dry puffed rice stick to her throat. The baby was fast asleep by now but Boori didn't have the energy to put him to bed. Observing Nita gaze indifferently at the far-off tree line, Boori wondered what was going through Nita's mind? Sometimes she felt immensely close to Nita, at other times Nita kept her at a distance.

'Where is your *moner manush*?' Boori repeated her question. 'Where's your old flame?'

'He's at the ashram.'

'Why didn't he come along with you?'

'Now I am nothing to him. He found a new woman. Don't talk to me about him. I've never seen such a worm in my life,' she spat.

'What are you up to these days?'

'Akhile is my new companion. He's a soft-hearted and kind soul. He composes lyrics for me. Just now I sang one of his songs. He wants to devote himself to writing lyrics at home, while I am to sing them, wandering from place to place to keep people's spirits up. His patriotic songs will lift up the Bengali people. Every day, folks flock to the ashram to hear his songs. They are so deeply moving.'

Nita's breath quickened, her voice quivered when she talked about Akhile. A broad grin lit up her face. She took a deep breath.

Boori was amazed at how much Nita had changed. She had never seen her friend this flustered. Without a *moner manush*, the wandering minstrel was a lost soul.

'Where did you learn to sing like that, Nita?'

'It's all down to Akhile. One day, he took me into his hut and spent the whole night listening to my songs. I poured out my heart into my music. I had never sung that way before in my life. I was a whole different being. The day it was over with Choron Das, I felt like I had been left hollow inside. I had no choice but to immerse myself deeper into my music. We spent the rest of the night lying shoulder to shoulder in complete silence. His chest was warm and my life had found an anchor.'

Boori was listening to Nita with rapt attention as in a fairy tale.

'"From now on," Akhile told me in the morning, "I am taking

you under my wing." Pointing to where his heart would be, he said, "This house belongs to us both. This chest is your bed to sleep on. And your songs are for the people. I'll compose and you'll sing."

'For three full months, I kept singing mystic, spiritual, and melancholic songs. But after listening to Sheikh Mujib's electrifying speech on the radio, last Falgun, he suddenly said to me, "Those other songs don't inspire me anymore. From now on, I'll compose new lyrics."

'I asked him what he meant. He just answered, "Songs for my country. My music will serve the nation."

'That day was a watershed in our lives and we sang these patriotic songs across the country. Folks had the words of our songs on their lips and they would gather and ask us to sing for them. They'd join in the chorus and cheer us on. What a wonderful feeling that was—you cannot imagine the atmosphere. Our songs drove people crazy.'

'Why didn't you bring that man along?' Boori enquired.

'He cannot walk far. He has a sore ankle.'

'Please ask him to come next time.'

'I promise. I will make sure he does.' Nita wound her hair into a bun.

Boori finally laid her grandson in the cradle. Ramija returned from bathing, her wet clothes slapping her legs. Nita looked at Ramija enviously and she suddenly itched to have a dip herself.

'Let's go to the *pukur* for a bath! What do you say, Boori?'

'Sure, it's hot as it is.'

They both headed towards the *pukur* and Nita eyed the bushes on the bank. Her shadow on the green murky water caught her attention. They stepped into the cold pond water to cool off. A *kutum pakhi* was cooing in a nearby tree.

'The *kutum* often sings these days!' Boori said. 'Maybe some relatives will be dropping by.'

'There are no relatives to pay us a visit though,' Boori mused while Nita swam down to the deeper part of the *pukur*. Nita dipped her head under water, then floated halfway across the pond. Boori waded chest-deep close to the bank. The *kutum* was cooing non-stop, giving Boori a sense of foreboding. No one had dropped by for quite a while and she became morbidly obsessed with the thought of unexpected visits.

Although the sun was high up, the *pukur* was cool under the shade of the trees, with a ring of greenish water and a heady smell oozing from the mud near the bank. Dry, pale, yellow leaves twirled and drifted over the water. Boori felt restless. She waded out of the water, but her friend swam on. Nita's thoughts were full of Akhile, her *moner manush*. Boori, whose life was a blanker page, envied her free-wheeling, independent friend. She didn't have to carry around her baggage of sorrows and memories.

Boori, on the other hand, had struggled to provide her family with a warm and loving home. Could she leave everything behind for good and go wherever the wind blew, fall asleep whenever she felt like it? Was there anyone out there, ready to welcome her weary head on his wide chest? Sadly, she had to muddle on. Her mind was bogged in a tangle of thoughts as she watched Nita swimming silently up and down the *pukur*.

As Boori climbed out of the water, she oozed mud onto the bank. She sat on the stump of a palm tree. Nita was swimming so gently that she looked almost still. Boori changed her dress, water dripped down her skin.

'Are you done already, *soi*?' Nita asked from the middle of the pond.

'Get out! I'm feeling hungry.'

'It's cool and comfortable down here. I'd like to swim a little longer, please,' Nita pleaded.

Boori waited reluctantly. She couldn't help humouring her friend's whims. Nita would have it her way regardless of the time, place and other people's priorities. Boori had no such liberty. She had to wait and was miffed. Peering at the sun to guess the time, she leaned against a coconut tree. Sad thoughts kept nagging her. But after a while, she lost track of the *kutum* and its ill omens.

'It's been a long time since I was last able to cool my heart in a *pukur*,' Nita confessed as she stepped onto the bank. 'Whenever I come here, I always feel part of your family.'

Nita wrung water off her hair with a towel. Boori sank into silence.

'Did you mind that I stayed a little longer in the water? Are you really so hungry? Sorry, I often forget to eat when I'm so blissful,' Nita giggled.

'Okay, okay, now let's go,' Boori replied in mock annoyance.

Boori and Nita walked back to the hut. Ramija laid out the lunch. Salim and Kalim were not back yet.

'My! Ramija, what a spread!' Nita was impressed. 'I never get the chance to sit down and have a proper meal.'

'Why don't you get yourself a good husband, Nita?'

'I couldn't stand married life.' Nita drank some water and she started to nibble at her food.

She rushed through her meal and washed her hands. After the meal, Boori sliced some betel nuts. In the afternoon, Nita took her leave, chewing betel, and carrying her bag on her back. She strummed the *dotara* and broke into a song while walking off:

> *Amar shonar Bangla*
> *Ami tomay bhalobashi*
> *Chirodin tomar akash,*
> *Tomar batash,*
> *Amar prane bajae bāshi*

Nita must have found her answers. There was a strange calmness about her. She had found an anchor within herself. Besides, she had a new *moner manush*. She could stand on her own two feet now.

Ramija would curl up with her son on a mat in the corner. She slept so peacefully as if she had no other worries in the world. Boori wished she were like that. But her sails always fluttered. Sometimes she felt so tied down by fate she could cry herself to sleep, but she would quickly remind herself of how much worse things could've been. Ramija slept like a baby. She worked herself to death day in and day out, only letting her mother-in-law give her a hand now and then. Boori's heart went out to her. She couldn't doze off in the afternoon. All Boori had to do was keep an eye on Salim and Kalim's lunch. This much was left under her care. It was the same story at night. No matter how late they came home, she would wait with the food laid out for them. She'd be sitting out in the veranda, her hand against her cheek. This endless waiting made Boori anxious. The house was eerily quiet. Boori never felt so alone. Time and again, her heart beat fast in her chest like the twang of Nita's *dotara*.

Sometimes Jalil would visit Boori in the evening or on a moonlit night and she would offer him some betel nut to chew. He had become a ghost of a man. He was on his own now. His mother had died a long time ago and all his other relatives had been slaughtered by the Pakistani army. Sometimes Jalil would cook his own food. Often he went to bed on an empty stomach. Many a time he asked Ramija if she had any scraps left. Most of the time, she did. Over his food bowl, Jalil would talk to Boori, his most avid listener. Words spewed out of his mouth mechanically.

'Even though the Bangla people are starving and plod on half naked in lungi, they've got the guts to fight the enemy.' He would then replay memories of the bloody events. 'You didn't see Dacca burning that day. Taher, my next door neighbour told me all about the bloodbath at Jahannath Hall and Rokeya Hall.

"You know, Firoza, my eldest, the librarian," the old man said. "She and her husband have a nice little residential flat close to Iqbal Hall. Well, they were hiding under their bed. They thought their final hour had come. They were like headless chickens, bless them! What with the shelling and shooting, the smoke and fire, the smell of the guns and burning bodies. Every now and again their building shook as the bullets rained. The killings continued all night until six in the morning."

People said after Mujib's "*Ebarer shongram muktir shongram, Ebarer shongram shadhinotar shongram*", the Pakistani army went trigger happy.

Firoza told her father that the soldiers had a list of student leaders and professors to liquidate.'

Jalil was then given a lengthy account of how the army had set fire to Nilkhet slum and machine-gunned the inhabitants; how the soldiers attacked Madhu's place and killed everyone in sight, indiscriminately in the halls—bearers, ayahs, students and professors, Muslims and Hindus; how students and staff were forced to dig their own graves, after which they were all shot and buried in the fresh graves; how for weeks corpses were left on roofs to feed the crows and vultures.

'There were mass protests and *hôrtal* at the colleges, universities, courts and business districts,' Jalil went on, 'flashes of my family's massacre keep coming back night after night. They just won't leave. I see rivers of blood with floating bodies. I hear the gunshots crashing like thunder.'

'Stop working yourself into a state and eat your food while it's still warm, Jalil bhai,' Boori said wearily.

'We had only our bare hands, we were helpless,' Jalil grieved.

'Look, forget it all for now,' Boori goaded him, 'and keep your fire burning for the struggle.'

'I have nothing left to do,' Jalil replied. 'We'll wring the necks of the bloody vultures and the damned *Razakars*.'

'What are the *Razakars*?' Boori queried.

'They are the eyes and ears of the Pakistanis and the enemies of the country,' Jalil explained, clenching his jaws tight.

Jalil polished off his meal and Boori passed him some betel. He chewed it nervously, slurping the juice. Boori sliced a nut with a thwack. Jalil's words kept ringing in her head. She didn't know what 'massacres' meant. She had never been exposed to catastrophes other than floods, droughts or famines. She closed her eyes to shut his voice out, but saw flashes of a giant *shokun* flying overhead during Jalil's terrifying account, carrying away the whole country in its claws. Her betel knife fell to the ground.

জৈষ্ঠ

Joishtho

Joishtho was halfway through. The mangoes hung heavy on the trees, ripe for picking. Ramija's son was growing up, strong and healthy, and Boori was her chirpy self once again. She went round to see the neighbours, holding the baby in her arms. However, she was aware of a sea-change, both within herself and in the country. No one shouted *Joi Bangla* anymore. Salim and Kalim were actively part of the freedom struggle and frequently kept away during regular meal hours. They couldn't be bothered by domestic concerns, for they had bigger plans for Haldi and the nation. Fear was etched on the villagers' faces. Boori could sense an impending disaster in her bones, as much as she tried to put on a brave face.

One morning Salim had gone to consult the elders on an urgent matter. They were at loggerheads over the resistance, as some of the older folks wanted to steer clear of ruffling Pakistani feathers. In the midst of their argument, Rokon, the village boatman ran up to them near the entrance of the mosque. His lips were twitching, his body quivering with fear; he had the wild, bloodshot eyes of someone who had seen Kana Bhoot.

Rokon had gone for ferry duty shortly after *namaaz*. He picked up a sprinkling of passengers, at the lip of the canal. He was about to turn back when he froze and almost dropped his pole. There was an ear-splitting thump thump thump. Then a loud bang ripped through the air. Kana Bhoot had sprung from nowhere. Its huge snout plopped into the marsh, then bounced back up, breathing a big ball of fire. Its long tail snapped and sank out of view. Fearing for his life, Rokon punted away as fast as he could.

It was decided that Salim, Jalil, Kalim and a few folks would follow Rokon to see what was up. They had barely left the bank with the ferryman when a flotilla of small boats festooned the canal. Boys from neighbouring villages had got wind of the chase. Rokon's boat crept up stealthily to the spot. The monster was still there, half-submerged, silent, ominous. Someone speared its ribcage with a bamboo stick. It didn't flinch. Edging his way to the front of the group, Jalil jumped onto the beast's carcass. He poked it. There was a hollow clink, clink. Everything inside was broken, buckled or charred. A broad grin split his face. They had nothing to fear. It was only a military chopper. Jalil had never actually seen one, only pictures. There was no trace of the pilot. As soon as he had told the others the news, the boys jostled for a closer look. There followed a chorus of *shabash*. Then a rain of bamboo spears landed on the 'dead animal'. Salim and Jalil could not make out what a Pakistani chopper was doing here. It bode no good. Gafoor's warning that birds of a feather clawed together rang in Salim's head. Bigger buzzards were bound to swoop in and feast on Haldi. Using their bamboo sticks, the men and the sturdier boys sank the monster deeper in the water.

One day Salim spilled the beans about their plans.

'Maa, we are training in the neighbouring village. Jalil chacha has joined us too.'

'So, you are going to war?'

'Yes we are, Maa,' Kalim said, hugging her. 'Salim bhai will be off first, then I will follow.'

'I will join you too.'

'Will you fight the enemy, Maa?'

'I will cook for you, son. I will wash your clothes. Is there anything else I can do?'

'Yes, you could clean our guns for us. You could sharpen our blades, hide our bullets and grenades, couldn't you?'

'Of course, once you teach me how to do it.'

Kalim touched her feet out of respect. Boori didn't sleep a wink that night. She sat up in the veranda the whole night. She saw the sun rise. Her heart was filled with sadness though. The thought that Rais would sit out the war on the sidelines...

One day, she eavesdropped on a conversation between the two brothers.

'Bloody cheek, those *talukdars*!' Kalim spat. 'I hate their guts. All sticking together. When the dog farts, they look at their own ass. Only a fool can buy what they said about the Pakistani army: "Don't follow every wind that blows...these are malicious rumours...we've got nothing to fear...the jawans will see that we are good Muslims...they mean us no harm...we shouldn't ruffle their feathers..."'

'We can't sit idle,' Salim seethed with anger 'and wait for the Pakistanis to run through us like skewers through kebab and flush out one village after another.'

'If we blow up the bridge across the road leading up to the village, they won't be able to come anywhere near Haldi.'

'No, that wouldn't be a very smart move,' Salim objected. 'It's a narrow canal. They would be able to cross over it with a small barge. We can't stop them from reaching the village.'

'You're right,' Kalim concurred. 'It would put the villagers' lives at risk.'

Both Salim and Kalim fell silent. Evil loomed ahead and there was no escape. Boori went back to the *pukur* to watch people pouring into the station. They talked to one another in hushed tones. There was terror in their eyes. She returned to the hut to have a word with Ramija.

'Ramija, do you know what has taken hold of them?' Boori wondered.

Ramija was taken aback by the question. She put down the saucepan she was holding.

'Who are "they?"'

'The villagers of Haldi.'

'Why is your head filled up with such weird thoughts? Has the sun got to you too? This morning has muddled your brain.'

Ramija took *tangra*, *puti*, *chingri*, *shing*, *magoor* and *batashi* from the basket that Boori had filled and gutted them for cooking. Salim had caught these fish from the tiny pool by the house just now. He liked to fish simply, by just walking to the water and throwing his net. Ramija chopped the fish with a thwack; blood trickled down the crooked cleaver and a red blob fell onto the floor. They were alike in some sense, Ramija and Salim. He didn't let anyone else catch fish in his little pool and she wouldn't let anyone else chop the fish.

'You must have been a fisherwoman in your previous life,' Boori would sometimes tease Ramija. It made her daughter-in-law laugh in her usual off-hand way.

As Ramija hacked at the fish, Boori's attention was drawn towards the blood. This was the first time Boori was scared at the sight of it. She felt as if the blood from Ramija's hands and knife would flow out to the river, which would eventually run red into the sea.

'Uff…' muttered Boori, pressing her forehead.

Once the fish was boned and trimmed, Ramija bounced back.

'What thoughts fill your head all day, Maa?'

Boori laughed off the question.

'The *kutum* is calling,' she remarked instead.

'Let it call. There are no guests left to pay us a visit. My baba came last month, so he won't be dropping by any time now.'

Ramija headed for the *pukur* to rinse the fish she had prepared for cooking.

Sometimes Ramija got annoyed with Boori for her weird ramblings. But as she was her mother-in law, she kept things fairly close to her chest. Boori followed Ramija to the *pukur*. The bank was shaded by numerous trees all around. Water weeds cluttered the surface of the pond. A huge *boroi* tree had fallen into the pond; it was partly decayed and smelt of mould and rotting leaves. Ramija washed the fish, then she stirred the water, making it muddy. Through coconut leaves, shafts of sunlight cut across the water. Boori had a flashback of the flow of blood under the fish knife. Although Boori was used to it, she still found the smell foul. She sensed that the *kutum* was calling in the Pakistani army.

Sleepless nights followed for Boori. Salim and Kalim had been plotting and planning late into the nights. Sometimes, Salim would sneak off over the border in the dead of night, leaving Kalim to take care of the family. One day he hoped to follow his elder brother, but knew things happen in their own good time.

Boori couldn't make out what they were talking about, but eventually pieced together two things from what Jalil had said that evening: it was not safe for them to remain in the village, and Jalil would accompany Salim across the border. Ramija broke down upon finding out. Boori wanted to discuss the details of their plan, but she knew they didn't have much time left.

In her lifetime, Boori had never seen such palpable terror in everybody's eyes. No natural disaster had ever forced the villagers in Haldi to leave their homes. She couldn't yet put her finger on what was scaring them out of their wits. What silent monster was lying in ambush? In her childhood, some doctors from Dacca would come into Haldi to give cholera jabs and the terrorized children would go into hiding. But that was nowhere near as scary as this.

Boori shifted restlessly on her bed. She went out and paced up and down the veranda. Salim called out to her, sensing her agony.

'What's bothering you, Maa?'

'Nothing, son.'

'What are you doing outside then?'

'I feel a wrench in my heart.'

Salim got up, with Kalim and Ramija in tow. None of them could get a wink of sleep. They had all been lying in bed, silently gazing into the dark. They were anxious at the thought of the future. Suddenly Boori began to cry aloud. She couldn't shore up her emotions. The anguish that had built up over the past few days burst its bank.

'Maa, please hush! Or you'll wake all the neighbours up,' Salim chided her.

'Why are you leaving, son,' Boori wailed.

'We've been told that the army is about to raid the village.'

'The army?' Boori's eyes blazed with fear.

'I tell you, they will skin me alive if they ever get their hands on me. I'd rather join the *muktijuddho* than die a coward. Maa, listen, don't tell anyone that I left. It might be dangerous for you. If anyone asks about my whereabouts, just tell them that you have no idea.'

Boori shook her head and Kalim fell silent. They breathed in the darkness. Salim lit a bidi. Ramija clambered back to bed when the baby started to whimper. Salim was going to join the liberation war. They had no clear plan or political perception. They were driven only by their love for the nation. The struggle had taken a violent turn, fanned as it was by their sense of patriotic spirit.

Drawing a last puff, Salim tossed the bidi stub into the courtyard. Kalim's sigh broke the silence.

'Maa, try and get some sleep, it will be hard to get up in the middle of the night.'

Boori rubbed her eyes with the hem of her sari. Salim drew closer to her and leaned against her back.

'Maa, if you whimper like a child, who will give me courage?

If you feel downhearted, who will cheer me on? Folks here will get suspicious and some might even blab it all over Haldi. That's why we have to set off before dawn. Please, Maa, go back to bed and try to sleep.'

Salim took her hands in his and lifted her from her seat in the veranda. Boori shuddered suddenly.

'Son, you too try to get some sleep. I'll go to bed in a little while.'

Salim and Kalim went back to their cots. Boori could hear slight rustling sounds from the bushes at the back of the hut. Her mind was flooded with thoughts of Salim's leave. A bird hooted in the dark. The distant sky over the forest turned to ash. The night was no different from the nights in her youth. Out there lights flickered along the paddy ridges and on the horizon. Were they fireflies in the ecstasy of love? Or tears of falling stars? The whole country seemed to be on the move, spilling its life-blood.

After a long while, Boori went back to bed. Rais was fast asleep, blissfully ignorant. She lay down beside him, but as much as she tried to she just couldn't go to sleep. She pictured a pool, deep within herself. Memories floated up like dead fish from the water. She reached down to capture one, but she could never reach far enough and she only skimmed the surface of the water. A wave of nostalgia overwhelmed her; a strange nostalgia that ran deep within her veins. She longed for the monsoon. The endless days of rain. As soon as the skies cracked open, the rain pounded like bullets and her whole world was turned upside down. Dykes leaked, banks burst and flash-flooded. Jute fields and paddies were waterlogged as far as the eye could see. The sky met the earth like an infinite mirror. A new waterworld emerged to be punted and paddled.

That's another thing she liked about the monsoon. It was a world without boundaries. Pools, *pukur*, canals and rivers merged into a vast waterbody. Water spilling onto more water. Despite the risk, gypsies and hawkers plied these waterways, pushing all kinds of wares from pots and pans to bangles and hair-pins. It was no less than a reflection of how resilient a people can be. The monsoon also blurred the differences between people. Whether they were Muslims or Hindus, maulana or miscreant, high caste or no caste, landowners or landless, all the villagers were in the same boat.

Suddenly, a vivid memory of Gafoor floated up her mind. During a lull in the rainfalls, the two of them had gone fishing in the shallows. The sky was a slatey blue that evening. Most landmarks had vanished as bamboo groves and familiar bushes lay submerged. A few tree tops popped up here and there. Gafoor started to lay traps among the tangle of roots of an old banyan tree. Further on, they tried their luck round the islets of tall *kash* grass. Heron-like, Gafoor prodded and punted through clumps of *kochuripana* that clogged the waterways. He broke into a sweat as the pole squelched into the mud bed. Once they found a gap in the murky water, Boori cast the fishing net overboard. She didn't even glimpse the shadow of a minnow. She almost lost her balance, but managed to catch a *rui* between the patches of canes and reeds.

Their jubilation was cut short by a storm. Gafoor paddled his way to a *kash* grass island. Torrential rains lashed at them. They were drenched and couldn't see a thing. The contours of the wetlands had now completely dissolved. With slippery hands, Gafoor and Boori heaved the boat out of the water and dragged it over the mud for mooring. Their ankles were caked with mud. A makeshift roof was made with canes and reeds. The *rui* rolled over as if trying to flop back into water. The rain eased up much later. The air was pungent with the smell of mud and decaying vegetation. Deep down the bowels of the earth a new world was awash. They made love under the half-moon that night.

Ramija kept weeping in the next room. Ever since her

marriage, she had always wanted to stay close to her husband. Out of frustration Salim would take her to her father's house at times, but he would always bring her back on the same day. He was too proud to tell her he loved her, but his actions conveyed much more than words ever could. Now Ramija was going to be all alone and as much Salim didn't want to admit it, he was worried for her. Boori could hear him talking to her softly. She was pleased with the change in his attitude. He seemed much gentler now. Drawing her to his chest, Salim caressed Ramija, promising her he would return to her as soon as possible. Ramija cried her heart out. Rais grumbled in his slumber due to the commotion. Boori tossed and turned in her bed. She kept herself awake, for she couldn't bear the thought of not saying goodbye to her son.

Salim got up in the early hours of the morning and gulped down a plateful of watery rice. He took the baby in his lap and planted a long kiss on his cheeks. Jalil tiptoed in. He came to say goodbye to Boori and asked her to keep an eye on his empty house, to pick the vegetables from his little plot and, whenever she felt like it, to tidy up the place. But when it came to leaving, Jalil's emotions got the better of him and he broke down in tears. Boori's eyes also welled up.

'Kaka, don't be such a child!' Salim chided them both. 'You can't go to war with tears in your eyes! Let's get going.'

Jalil said nothing and trudged off without looking back. This wasn't the first time he had walked away from Boori, never to look back. Boori followed them as far as the *pukur*. This was a new leaf in her life. Never before had she felt so hurt when someone was leaving. Even words wouldn't come to her. Her heart grew heavier by the second, until she could hardly breathe.

The military swooped on Haldi just two days after Salim had left. They came through the main road leading to the station. The Jaistho sun charred the soil. There was no wind blowing.

The leaves of the trees were still. The mangoes on Boori's trees had ripened red. The soldiers fired blank shots as they entered the village. Boori stood at the back of the road to the station. She was tongue-tied. The *kutum*'s call bode no good. She walked off and plopped down on the doorstep with a thud.

'The *kutums* are in our nest, Ramija,' she said, staring at her daughter-in-law's gloomy face.

Ramija couldn't speak. She held her son tight to her chest. The crooked fish knife was lying in the yard. There was no fire on the stove. The two burners were filled with ashes.

'What is to happen to us, Amma?' Ramija asked in a broken voice.

'Insha'allah!'

Boori stared at the *sojna* with a stern face.

'I am scared!' the young woman quavered.

'There's nothing to be scared of, Ramija. Give me my grandson!'

Boori went to the *boroj* with Juddho on her waist. The camp could be seen clearly from that vantage point. Boori wanted to see what they were up to. She had never seen such *kutums*.

Her heart broke when she looked at Kalim that night.

'Why aren't you off to the war too, Kalim?'

'Why are you saying that, Maa?'

'Since Salim is not here, you shouldn't be here either.'

'Mansoor has been blabbering on about Bhai going to war.'

'Who told you?'

'Mansoor himself. He has become quite friendly with them. The *Razakar* is feeding them all our news!'

'Look Maa, Mansoor was threatening me. "Your lot has been up to no good. Now it's time to pay. You infidels will know your place! We'll make you bite the dust." I was obviously not scared of him. I shot back an answer to his face point blank. I felt like kicking his backside. *Langta kukurer baccha!* The bastard giggled like a jackass.'

Boori froze with sudden fear at what Kalim had just said. She entreated him to go into hiding then and there, but Kalim just looked at her with blood-shot eyes.

'I'm not leaving my own house and that's that.' He snapped defiantly, 'I am not scared of any of them. Let's see what they can do.'

Kalim walked into the courtyard. Boori was so upset that she couldn't swallow her rice. She gulped down a few glasses of water. Still, she felt a lump in her throat.

Kalim twirled a flower stem and softly hummed a *bhatiali* melody:

Fande poriya boga kande re
Fand bosaiche fandi re bhai puti machh diya,
Ore macher lobhe boka boga pore ural diya re.

Fande poriya re boga kore tanatuna
Ore aha–re konkurar shuta holu noa–ar guna re.

Fande poriya re boga kore hai re hai,
Ore darun bidhi, sathi chhaira jay re.

Aar boga ahar kore ashe aro pashe
Aar amar boga ahar kore dholla nodir pare re.

Ooriya jai re chokoya ponkhi bogik bole thare,
Ore tomar boga bondi hoiche dholla nodir pare re.

Ei kotha shuniya re bogi dui pakha melilo
Ore dholla nodir pare jaiya doroshon dilo re.

Boga ke dekhiya bogi kandere,
Bogi ke dekhiya boga kandere.

Boori listened to the song raptly. Her heart was filled with pride, tinged with nostalgia. She stood quietly for a while, enchanted by the lyrics.

'Where did you learn this song, son?' she asked Kalim, mesmerized by the wistful melody.

'I heard it from someone. Everyone is singing these days. People are inspired by our songs.'

'*Bhishon shundor!*' Boori exclaimed, kissing him on the forehead. 'May you live to be a thousand years old!'

Kalim bent down to touch her feet.

Then, much against Boori's wish, he went out of the house. Some villagers warned him not to go anywhere near the military camp. They were hunting down Salim. The *Razakars* had tipped them off about Salim's family.

'Don't they know Salim is not here?' Boori asked.

'What is it to them? They won't be satisfied.'

Walking along the dusty road, Kalim thought of attacking the camp. He needed to talk to Bablu, Azad, Mintu and Shujan, so they could come up with a plan. But when he went to look for them, he found that they had all joined the *Mukti Bahini*. No one had told him. Kalim felt sad and trudged home with a heavy heart.

The Pakistani army was hot on Salim's heels. They ransacked the whole village like a pack of trained dogs. Houses were doused in petrol and set alight to cries of '*bangali kutta bhag gia*'. They didn't credit Mansoor's tip-off that Salim had fled across the border to India. Failing to have Salim in their clutches, they fell back on Kalim. As the morning azaan wafted from the mosque's minaret, Kalim lay crumpled in his bed, still asleep. There was an ominous bang on the door.

'*Tora ke?*' Boori asked, her heart in her mouth.

The moment she opened the door, seven sepoys in army fatigue sprung up from behind the *sojna* tree. They stormed into the hut before Boori could realize what was going on. Ramija ran from the bank of the *pukur* to hide in the *boroj* nearby. Boori remained silent, standing by the pillar in the veranda, too stunned to react. Eventually, Kalim appeared, hands in shackles. The khaki men stomped across the courtyard with their bleary-eyed prey. Boori rushed to the olive tree so that she could catch sight of Kalim, even though he couldn't see her. She helplessly watched them take her son away.

The seven sepoys swaggered along the road back to their base. No one dared to cross their path or utter anything in their presence. Even the *choruis* were frightened into silence.

Kalim's arrest had left Boori in the clutches of fear. She couldn't think straight. She had no idea whether her daughter-in-law was keeping low in the bushes or hiding amid the clumps of lotus and *kochuripana* floating in the pond. Afraid for her *izzat*, Ramija had fled while Kalim was being taken away, leaving her son in the lap of a neighbour. Boori was so shell-shocked from the entire incident that she couldn't even recall what Ramija's baby looked like.

Rais was sitting idle in the hut. His presence made little difference as he rarely responded to what was happening around him. Sitting in the veranda, Boori gazed indifferently at the woods. A cloudless sky filtered through the tree top leaves. A white-hot sun was sizzling the field. Ramija wouldn't cook rice today. Her stove remained cold. Boori felt like lighting up a fire with some dry leaves and straw, just to show the *Razakars* that the villagers hadn't left their homes. Someone had to keep the fire burning. But she was so worn out that she couldn't get to her feet.

Boori felt helpless now, although her face didn't register her emotions. She willed her painful memories to drift away like wisps of cotton in the air. Bagha came and sat at her feet, barking and wagging his tail, but she ignored him. The huge *amra* tree in the eastern courtyard stood forlorn and silent, its leaves barely rustling. There was now a dead silence rolling off the ducks' feathers. However, it was the image of Kalim's arrest that overshadowed everything else. With him gone and no news of Salim or Jalil, Boori and Ramija were mere ghosts, haunting an empty house.

A couple of days later, Boori received news from Sohrab Ali that Kalim had not been brutally tortured. As Salim's 'terrorist activities' put him on the most wanted list, the Pakistanis 'just roughed Kalim up a bit' to ferret out information about his brother's hideouts and bases. He denied that he knew anything.

Boori was filled with rage but she took it out on herself—she stopped eating and idled about in the veranda, or by the *pukur*, staring at the sky expectantly.

'Maa, what will they do to Kalim bhai?'

Boori looked at Ramija. She knew the answer, but couldn't blurt it out. She knew that since they had picked him up, Kalim's days were numbered, as were the days of the other boys from the village, whose bodies were found with gouged eyes and chopped genitals, floating on the canal or buried in shallow graves. She couldn't bear the thought of her Kalim meeting such a fate.

'Maa, say something.'

Boori's lips quivered, but she said nothing. Sensing the unsaid, Ramija broke down. One of Sohrab Ali's daughters rushed in.

'The army patrol is on its way. Run!' Phuli screamed.

Ramija took to her heels and ran for cover. No one else remained in the house except Boori and Bagha. Rais stood on the veranda and knotted a rope.

A few minutes later, the seven armed sepoys in khaki uniforms barked in the courtyard.

'You mother of an infidel, open the door!'

They muscled their way in, rifles at the ready. Kalim was dragged along, hands cuffed behind his back. Boori looked at him for a moment and turned her eyes away. Torture had twisted her son's features. Boori couldn't endure the sight. All of Kalim's patience, worries and sorrow had been snuffed out. What remained was a man haunted by the ghost of a distant dream. The pitiful sight of him would ignite a new red flame of revenge, flickering among ruins, egging people on to fight.

'Why do you keep your head down, Kalim?' Boori thought to herself. 'You must look up, son. Let the flames blaze from your tiger eyes. Let Haldi be born again.'

Struggling to dam her menacing fears, Boori wobbled as she stood up. Glancing at the soldiers' feral eyes, she turned away. One of the sepoys was ordered to guard Kalim in the courtyard, while the patrol stomped into the hut. They ransacked its contents from corner to corner, floor to ceiling, knocking over and spilling everything down. They even stamped their boots on Rais. The defenceless boy couldn't respond to their taunts, and they flung him down the veranda. Terrorized, Rais couldn't even cry out his pain. He crawled towards Boori, rubbing his face against her back. Pointing to the injury on his face, he hugged his mother. Boori took his hands into hers and clasped them tightly. Pain and anger bubbled over in her head.

The soldiers went on a rampage thereafter, taking every object in sight—sacks, cushions, pillows, blankets—and bayoneting them to pieces. Boori could hear them taking her life's possessions apart, but she couldn't care less about the loss of such trifles.

Kalim's whole body was a purple mess covered in sores and bruises. He could barely see because his eyelids were swollen. Yet he stood there—a broken man—watching the photo of his stepmother. His lips quivered. He was trying to articulate something, but she couldn't read the words on his lips. What was his voice struggling to tell her?

Although Boori had not carried him in her womb, she had given him a mother's love and affection. There was nothing she could do now, other than pour her heart out to him. She walked towards Kalim, but was stopped by the soldiers' rifle butts and threatening looks. They pointed their guns at her, motioning her to sit silently. Haldi began to spin before her wild eyes. The entire area blacked out.

A gentle breeze was blowing over the dishevelled forest. Boori wished her pain and fury would drift off on the breeze like airborne seeds. To her, these seven soldiers were an apparition of *Yama*. The soldiers were aware of the brewing tension and were prepared to strike anyone who resisted them. The havoc in the house had fired up their blood. One of them started to yell, asking about guns or any other weapons that Kalim might have stashed away. It was impossible to believe that a village leader like Salim carried no arms. Boori couldn't make out what they were saying in Urdu, except when they mentioned Kalim's name. One soldier gestured with his gun for her to stand. Boori didn't respond. Only a wordless sound escaped from her lips. Who were they? Were they raised in this air, light, water and earth that she was familiar with? Boori remembered the half-naked, starving, disease-ridden sons of the soil from her own village and the image blotted out the spectacle before her eyes. At least, the language of the starving people was intelligible. But these soldiers were aliens. She shouted at the top of her voice.

'Kalim, what are these kafirs talking about?'

The soldiers dumped Kalim on the ground at her feet. One of them kicked him in his back, then slammed him face first into the dust. Another pressed his boot on his throat, choking him. Kalim was like a bamboo cane swaying to and fro. If he were released, his body would just snap. He could no longer move of his own accord. The physical torture he had been subjected to had shattered his very will. His skin was a flag of red and blue, scarred all over with fresh wounds and old sores. Were words the way to win wars, he would have given the soldiers a tongue lashing by now. But his words could only win Boori's heart. The soldiers booted him time and again, shouting that if he didn't squeal, they would kill him. He just lay there, taking one hit after another, numbed by pain.

'What would your Maa do, Kalim? I don't know,' Boori mumbled. 'I'm so helpless. Undone. Why should a human being have to sacrifice his life like this? Don't call me "Maa" anymore. I don't deserve the name.'

Boori wiped her face with her sari. An image of Salim's face superimposed on his brother's flashed through her mind. She had promised Salim not to tell anybody about his hideout. But Kalim was being tortured to death before her eyes. What should she do? Would they free their prisoner in return for her life? It was beyond her ability to endure and she began to cry her heart out.

'Kill me, kill me instead. Just let him go!'

She rushed to the nearest soldier and clung to his boot. The sepoys were taken aback and stared at her. Kalim spurted to life and called out to her. 'Oh, Maa! Maa please don't beg them for my life!' he screamed. 'Please don't fall at their feet. Thousands of Bengalis are dying. If you fall at their feet, you will dishonour those who gave their lives for our country.'

The soldiers lashed heavily into his back. Blaming herself for having made things even worse for her son, Boori fell silent and stepped back to the doorstep. Never before had she been able to visualize what Yama, the soul-snatcher, looked like. But these khaki-clad demons fitted the description.

The soldiers grabbed Boori by her limbs. They barked harsh words, slamming the cold barrel of a gun to her chest. Their beastly eyes drilled terror into her. Kalim screamed. Boori felt like running over to embrace him, but she couldn't lift herself.

'Hai Allah!' she muttered in a frail voice. 'I can do nothing for you, son.'

Boori sobbed quietly, sounds choking in her throat. She struggled to remember a sura from the Qu'ran to gather some strength. She tried to recall Gafoor's face, but she couldn't do that either. Haldi unfolded, leaf by leaf, before her eyes and she imagined Ramija's son crying somewhere on the horizon.

The Pakistani soldiers foamed at Boori's inertia.

'Chutiya ka bheja ghas khane gaya hai.'

They spat another torrent of abuse and discussed something among themselves. Then they shoved Kalim and shot him dead. The young man's body slumped to the ground, face down. The soldiers kicked his body, rolling him up and down like a football. They walked off, cheering and laughing.

No sound passed Boori's lips. Only Bagha barked and clawed at the ground. Staring at the departing soldiers, the dog panted and turned its fiery eyes to Boori. Apart from the wailing Bagha, the house was eerily silent. Rais tugged at his mother to tear her from the scene.

Boori stroked Kalim's head with blood-soaked fingers. The blood streaming from Kalim's body conjured up crimson cascades of *shimul* flowers. Soon, the earth would be soaked through, suffused with the rich flow fraught with the seeds of future blooms. Soon, the land would bear the fruit of Kalim's blood. Suddenly, Boori recalled Salim's vision—Haldi being turned into cotton fluff, with the wind wafting away the white chaff. She also remembered the *muktijuddho* slogan. However long and thorny the path, the struggle for freedom would be like a piece of bright cotton fluttering over the fluffy clouds.

Boori didn't notice when Rais drew close to Kalim's body and began to rub his head and neck slowly. It didn't make sense to him. He sniffed at the blood on Kalim's clothes, dabbed his hands and face, and then rushed to his mother. He rocked her back and forth, spouting weird garbled sounds. Everything around Boori began to shake and dissolve. She screamed her head off and clutched Rais to her chest. Her whole being was shot to pieces.

After a while the wailing and crying ceased. Boori shoved Rais roughly away.

'Why are you silent? Why let them do as they please without putting up a fight?' she erupted. 'Why not explode into a volcano of revenge? I'll come with you. We can do something for the village together. Have you ever planted a bomb? Rais, kill me.'

Boori burst into a scream and wailed again. The neighbours gathered to mourn Kalim's body. Ramija had gone into hiding to a distant place. She was due to return shortly.

Sohrab Ali and a few others lifted Kalim's body and put it in the veranda. All of them kept silent, a nervous twist on their faces. Boori felt numbed. The earth was covered in blood prints. Haldi, she thought, was sucking Kalim's blood in.

'This village is crawling all over with blood suckers,' she muttered.

'What did you say, mother of Rais,' Sohrab Ali asked.

Boori cast him a vacant stare.

'Shall we bury Kalim's body in the *boroj*, Sohrab bhai?' one neighbour queried.

'Look, I'll take care of that, don't you worry,' Sohrab Ali replied, wiping his tears.

Haldi's children rallied round the dead body. Some of them dipped their hands into the blood puddle on the ground. Boori tried to remember Kalim's short lifespan and the way he grew up. She toyed with fond memories of his fishing and hiding with Salim. She thought of Kalim's spilled blood as Haldi's newest surge. Her head began to feel dizzy. She leaned against a door post until she heard the sound of Ramija's footsteps drawing close. Her daughter-in-law gave her a tearful hug.

Days passed. Boori shrank further and further into isolation. Just a few ghostlike creatures still dwelt in their dens; at night they all remained frightened out of their wits. A sudden wail from Ramija's baby would remind them that they were still alive.

When the baby whimpered, Ramija rushed to his side to hush him. Unlike her, Boori wanted the baby to cry aloud, to make a racket that would draw the attention of the foreign butchers and show their *Razakar* henchmen that some villagers still had the guts to stand up to their evil presence. But Ramija would have none of it. Admittedly, she was bound to obey her mother-in-law. Boori seemed to enjoy letting the baby wail. Naturally, Ramija felt jittery about entrusting Boori with the child's care, while she went about her daily chores.

'Let him cry his eyes out, Ramija!' Boori pleaded in a lost voice. 'You'll choke him, gagging his crying that way.'

'What are you on about, Maa? His screams could be heard by the killers,' Ramija replied.

'It's not that easy to slaughter everyone!' Boori objected.

She stood still, recalling Kalim's execution. He was buried by the *pukur* in the shadow of the betel nut trees.

'Peace be with you, Kalim,' Boori sighed. '*Allah yerhamo!*'

Kalim had not fought in the *muktijuddho*, but he had given his life for Haldi. Boori no longer looked for betel nuts in the *boroj*. Instead, she would visit Kalim's freshly dug grave. The place was eerily silent. Once, a gust of wind stripped bare the boughs of Kalim's favourite tree. Out of nowhere, a garland of red and green had appeared on the grave. Boori squatted on her heels, a fistful of dry earth trickled through her fingers. Battling over eggs, columns of ants scuttled into cracks in the soil. Boori would walk back with swollen eyes, staring at the spot in the courtyard where her son had been killed. She thought of digging up the pool of dried blood.

'It's not that simple to slaughter everybody,' she muttered to herself again.

'Everything is child's play for the Pakistanis,' Ramija replied. 'They killed Kalim bhai and they had a hand in the fate of Samoor's mother.' To take her mind off things, Ramija busied herself with winnowing paddy. She couldn't cope anymore. The memory of all these deaths had left its toll on the poor girl.

The day following Kalim's murder, Samoor's family had all hidden chest deep in the waters of a jute field. A group of Pakistani soldiers were on foot patrol along the road nearby. The baby in the lap of Samoor's mother started to whimper and, as she panicked over their own safety, she pushed his head under water. When the soldiers had vanished, all the family filed out of the field. The baby had choked to death. Samoor's mother found out that the baby had died only when she was half way home; she was devastated as she shifted the baby's weight from one hip to the other and it felt stiff. She was too petrified for tears or shrieks. Then, over the next few days, she wailed as though she was her own baby's killer. In tears, Boori could not stand the woman's display of despair.

'What have our lives come to?' Boori and her daughter-in-law moaned. 'Is there to be no limit to our kismet?'

Every passing day brought another tragedy no one would have imagined. Ramija finished winnowing the paddy and began to cook. She went to the *pukur* with the rice pot.

'Maa, please keep an eye on the baby. Don't let him cry. It makes me sore.'

Ramija felt scared for her son's sake. She kept him on her lap all the time, which reminded her of Salim. She even brought up the subject of Salim's departure into the conversation as though she were responsible for it. Every now and then, while she was cooking, sitting by the *pukur*, or simply lying in bed, Ramija would burst into tears as though her heart had shattered into myriad shards. She felt guilty over Kalim's death too.

'Kalim wouldn't have been killed if Salim hadn't gone, would he?' she insisted.

'Who knows, *insha'allah*? Everything is as He wills it,' Boori replied listlessly.

She couldn't tell whether Salim's capture could have saved Kalim or if both boys would have been shot.

What would happen to Ramija if Salim died? Kalim left no debts, but Salim's death would leave Ramija a widow. Boori would not be able to support her daughter-in-law's grief for the rest of her life. Her conscience nagged her, the way Bagha picked at a bone. She prayed for Salim's safe return. Praying soothed her.

Boori couldn't get any information on Salim's whereabouts after he had left home. If only he could send them a message, saying he was alive. Just a few words would rid them of this uncertainty that clouded their days and sleepless nights. Words about his health. His moods and dreams. His plans to clean up these Pakistani dogs. Ramija's son was the only lively thing in the house. His crying and playfulness kept Boori on her toes, while a scared Ramija frowned or tried to hide her anguish behind a smile.

'Just look at him and try to put on a brave face!' Boori encouraged her.

'I too would laugh if I were his age,' Ramija argued.

'Courage comes from within. Age has got nothing to do with it,' Boori said.

Ramija didn't respond. Since childhood she had known that she was a coward. All day she would remain quiet in the house like a dormouse.

The situation in Haldi deteriorated by the day. The Pakistani devils were overexcited at the prospect of a killing spree. They would open fire on the villagers on the flimsiest of pretexts, set houses and crops ablaze, drag dead bodies to dump into the canal or pile up in makeshift mass graves. The bodies would be denied any religious rites. The corpses would be scavenged by foxes and vultures. The villagers were terrorized and never ventured anywhere near these graveyards sprouting haphazardly. Skulls, jaws and bones would be found scattered across the killing fields. Sometimes in the dead of the night, the villagers would wake up at the clatter of a machine gun and sit frozen in their beds, wondering whether it was their turn. At other times, soldiers were on the prowl, hunting for women. They would pick up young women in twos and threes. The women never returned to their families. Some were thrown in prison. Most were raped and then found dead.

During the day, the Pakistani soldiers would rustle cattle and chickens. Later, they could be heard celebrating their loot over lunch and dinner at the camp. They would cheer raucously and the sound of their lewd laughter rippled far away into the night. Boori's bullocks were rustled and when she went to look out for them, she found one slain and the other tethered under a big tree. It looked pale and forlorn. Its bulging glazed eyes stared at her. Its muzzle was red and wet. Returning home, Boori dissolved into tears.

'Don't cry, Maa,' Ramija tried to comfort her. 'We don't need any cattle. We run far greater dangers, you know.'

They could set fire to the house. They could kill Boori, or any other close family members or neighbours. What would quench their thirst for blood? They could even bayonet Boori's grandson.

'Look, Maa! They haven't come near our house, after killing chota Bhai.'

Boori became thoughtful and stopped sobbing.

'Forget about the two bullocks,' Ramija added.

'I can't help it! They were dear to me.'

Ramija began to cool her mother-in-law with a hand-held fan. Boori remained silent in the soothing gust of wind, but she felt a wrench in her heart, nonetheless. She couldn't forget the traumatic scene. Although she didn't want to admit it, she was scared out of her wits for Ramija's sake. However, Ramija sensed what Boori had on her mind—her body left her vulnerable. The soldiers might pounce in at any time and take her away. The more she thought about it, the more her blood boiled. She grew paler and weaker every passing day and didn't feel like doing any domestic chores anymore.

The courtyard became overgrown with weeds and filthy for want of regular care. Ramija cooked food only once a day, instead of two or three times. She couldn't be bothered either to sweep the house as she used to. The whole place was in a state of complete disarray. The earth was no longer burning hot like a furnace and flames no longer leapt at the touch of a match. Everything looked dead. All the villagers were terror-stricken. Boori grazed the only bullock in the field and the forest, or by the *pukur*, but no further. She couldn't afford to lose the remaining animals.

In the evening she cut grass to feed it and she herded the hens and chickens back to their hutches before it got dark. The family would have dinner early and rarely lit up the lamp, as they could no longer afford paraffin for their daily use. They were getting poorer and poorer, and Boori felt the pinch looming over their heads. They could only feed their belly because they had a store of rice for a whole year. Apart from this, they had just enough food to go round. Only the other day, Boori had bartered some paddy to Sohrab Ali for some spices and soap.

She started humming *Amar Shonar Bangla*, to brace herself up. She had learned the first few lines from Kalim. Even though the boy was no more, the song still survived. She would ask the children of the village to learn it. This way she would keep Kalim's memory alive and continue the work he had started for the country.

Meanwhile, Ramija's father, Borhan, dropped by to pick up his daughter. They had only heard the news of Salim's departure a few days ago. Boori heaved a sigh of relief after the care and worry for Ramija was lifted off her shoulder. If she couldn't protect Salim's wife's izzat or if the young woman was abducted by the army, how could she forgive herself? It also dawned on her that the two women might fall prey to thieves. So Ramija had better leave Haldi with her father. On the other hand, how could she cope with the loneliness of living in a haunted house? She talked with Ramija's father from behind the door.

'What do you think?' the old man asked.

'It's a wise decision. I'm also very anxious for her safety.'

'Well, I don't know how you women stayed on your own so long. This haunted house would squeeze the life out of me! Insha'allah, nothing untoward has happened, but I would like to take Ramija home with me.'

Boori was annoyed at the lecture she got from Ramija's father. However, she knew in her heart of hearts that what he had said rang true. She had no right to hold her back. Ramija could have arranged to leave for her father's house long ago, but she had not. Boori didn't respond to the old man's words but Ramija would have none of it.

'How will she cope if I leave her on her own?'

'Don't you mind me. I'm an old woman. I can carry on. I only fear for your sake, though.'

'You don't have to stay on, Ramija. If Kalim were alive, it would be a whole different matter, but you shouldn't be so foolish and take chances,' the old man rebuked her.

'Baba, there are neighbours too.'

'Neighbours have nothing to do with it. You need your own blood,' her father contradicted her.

'But Baba, you can't change my kismet. Wherever I go, I must meet my kismet. You cannot change it.'

'Look, I can't let you die either, now that I know everything!' Ramija's father exclaimed in a harsh tone.

His daughter's outspoken, stubborn stance irked him.

'Hold your tongue, girl, and show me some respect! I grasp

the situation much better. I need not be told off by my own daughter,' the old man chided Ramija.

His temper always got the better of him.

'Don't pay attention to the way she talks, *Shoshur*. She will go. Now you have a rest. I am not so keen on her staying here either,' Boori's voice was so sharp that Ramija had better stop arguing.

The young woman went to the kitchen to rustle up a meal for her father, while Boori sat beside her sleeping grandson.

Neither of them could wink an eye. They both kept their eyes open in the dark. Ramija had made up her mind to stay on with her mother-in-law. Boori could say nothing against it. The very thought of Ramija's absence left her mind blank. The empty house would seem a graveyard without her. But she couldn't help it. She had to stifle her pain and weariness as she did when Kalim was killed. She shouldn't think about her own comfort. Besides, knowing how Ramija's father would worry himself sick over her, a part of Boori felt relieved to see them go.

'If I go, Maa, you will feel so lonely. I can't bear the thought. On top of that, you and the baby can't be parted. I won't go,' Ramija stamped defiantly, despite an inner twinge of anxiety.

'Well, you go to bed now. We'll see in the morning.'

'You tell Baba that I won't be going. He only wants to have it his own way. He has always been like that—a selfish old tyrant. You know, even in my younger days, I found him picking quarrels with others, trying to rule the roost.'

'Well, you go to sleep now or the baby will cry in the middle of the night.'

Ramija went silent and Boori rolled over to go to sleep. But she kept awake all night and saw flashes of Kalim's execution. She hadn't slept a wink for a whole week since his death. Now Ramija had to go. Regardless of what she had promised her, or what she had said to her father, he would take her away. Boori meant nothing to the old man. She felt a racking, unbearable loneliness. Reaching out to take Rais into her lap, she realized that even his untainted, illegible love couldn't fill this gap. No one could. There was nowhere for her to escape to. She pulled Rais passionately to her chest.

As the night deepened, a terrified howl rent the air from next door. The two women listened attentively. They made out a rustling sound. After a while the moaning stopped as though someone had gagged a woman's mouth with a strong hand. Then, they could hear a whimper and grunts. A body was dragged. The sound gradually died down. Nevertheless, it kept hammering on Ramija's frightened thoughts.

'Maa, can you hear anything?' she called out to Boori in a quavering voice.

'Yes, I can.'

'It must be Phuli.'

'I guess so,' Boori answered.

'What will happen to her, Maa?'

'*Insha'allah*! Keep quiet and pray to Him.'

A few long minutes later, the noise died down and all was eerily silent. No one dared step out of the house. Boori got out of bed and was about to unbolt the door to find out what the commotion had been about.

'Maa, why are you getting up?'

'I'm going out,' Boori replied.

'No, don't do that, Maa! Who knows, they may be lying in ambush outside.'

Boori feared that someone might stagger to the door.

'Maa, try and get some sleep. Baba may wake up,' Ramija whispered.

Boori remained still. Her body shook all over with fear. No one dared raise their voices against such brutality. No one raised a protest or cried foul play. No individual or group of villagers.

Phuli was dragged away without resistance. She was left to fend off for herself. No one had rushed to her rescue. There was no young man who loved Phuli, who could have laid down his life to stop her gang rape. Boori's head got dizzy.

The night was quiet, but to Boori, this quiet was deceptive and, by no means, restful. She rubbed her head against a shredded pillow and muttered harsh words:

'Allah, save us! Give us strong, fierce young men who will stand up and have the guts to fight and kick the enemies out of Haldi! May you rouse thousands of people!'

Boori felt a bit braver, having prayed to Allah from the bottom of her heart. Never before had she plunged so fervently into such profound meditation. She stepped out of her hut. The stars still twinkled in the night. She went to the *pukur* and splashed her face with cold water. Her tears merged with the water. Getting out of bed, Ramija's father reminded his daughter that they had to be off.

'Pack up quick. We'll set off before dawn. If we reach Boori Bazaar by noon, then we may be home before dusk. You know the boatmen are chary about paddling at night.'

'But, Baba, what will happen if I go away?'

'Don't be silly, Bitiya. I heard everything last night. I'm not deaf. I can't guarantee that they won't be lurking tonight. It's different at home. Our area is defended by freedom fighters. The Pakistani goons cannot venture there. Get yourself ready, there's no time to lose.'

Ramija prepared herself. The conversation had reached Boori's ears. She cooked a breakfast of watery rice and omelette for Ramija's father. Boori willed her hands to stop trembling as she held out the plate. Ramija stood before her.

'Maa, what is it?'

'Don't waste precious time, you'd better start early. It will be difficult for the baby to travel in the sun.'

'Maa!'

'Get going, Ramija, your baba's right. Who can guarantee our safety after last night?'

'How will you cope on your own? Let's go together,' Ramija pleaded.

'Don't you mind me. Allah's with me. The house shouldn't be left empty. When Salim comes, who will be there to welcome him home and take care of him?'

Tears started to stream down Ramija's cheeks. But she couldn't allow herself to weep as her father stood by. She wiped her eyes and left Boori sitting there. Last night's nightmare had pierced her resolve. She bowed to her father's iron will. Boori accompanied them as far as the canal, with Rais tagging along behind her. Her grandson clung to her and she pressed him against her shoulders. She fought hard to hold back her tears.

Ramija wiped her eyes with her *anchol*. Salim had not sent a message for quite a while and she was leaving Amma to fend for herself. She felt disgusted at this act of sheer selfishness and it took her a while to get over it. Taking off her sandals, she waded through the muddy bank to get on board. The baby on her lap looked at Boori with squeaking noises, his tiny arms flailing about in furious frenzy, as though he wanted to crawl back into her lap. Boori stood still on the shore. The boat glided away on the water as she waved goodbye.

The morning sun had yet to rise and a soft predawn pink glow lit up the horizon. Boori stared at the flowing stream which showed signs of a high tide. A cluster of *kochuripana* with violet flowers floated by. The vast field beyond the waterway caught her eyes. The boat bobbed away to a bend in the stream and was quickly out of sight. Boori's mind felt blank. She lumbered on with the care of Rais, like a *kochuripana* trailing along with the current. It was the course of her kismet to float adrift. Her one and only truth. A mild breeze soothed her and a grey dagger fly buzzed past. Rais tugged at the hem of her sari, hinting that it was time they went home. He disliked staying out in the open for long spells, and when he did so he was restless. His mother watched him, remembering the anguish she had gone through before and after his birth, a pain that was forever imprinted on her mind.

The sun had almost risen by now and the forest was flooded in crimson by the early morning light. Boori walked home with Rais. The neighbours had gathered outside Phuli's door. Her mother was prostrate, weeping softly and her father sat crouched in a corner, digging his chewed-up fingernails into the skin of his forehead. The faces of those present looked drained. They were utterly devastated, helpless. Boori joined them.

'The dogs! What they did to Phuli, there's no name for that...'

'You sent your daughter-in-law away, I suppose?' enquired Sohrab Ali to break the deadly silence.

'It couldn't be helped,' Boori sighed.

'Better not to tempt the devil,' another elder chipped in.

'Oh, what will happen to us, Rais's maa?' Phuli's father moaned and broke down.

Boori was disgusted at the villagers' cowardice. They lacked the balls to fight back. Fear petrified them. She felt an urge to scream right into their faces:

'Don't you have any guts? Hugging and crying together. Why don't you challenge those dogs?'

Everyone was broken. She swallowed a lump in her throat. Who would she be waiting for? She could open her heart to no one.

Mansoor was the only one who was bubbling over with enthusiasm. He walked with a fearless bounce in his step, not scared of anything. He was slimy towards the army officers, which made him brave. People called him a 'sly dog' behind his back. Sometimes his ears must have been burning from the insults, but he would smirk and shrug them away. The coward supplied women to the soldiers at night.

'I will wring his fat neck one of these days,' Boori gritted her teeth. 'I'll flay him alive for all his crimes.'

Before leaving, Ramija had urged her neighbours to keep an eye on her mother-in-law. The villagers who used to ignore her or give her the cold shoulder would often drop by her hut. Kader and Hakim, Sohrab Ali's sons, volunteered to sleep in her veranda at night. Sohrab Ali kept a close watch over his sons, for fear that the two boys may try to escape across the border. They were just in their teens and held no profound convictions, but they were fond of Boori. One day, after Phuli's abduction, the two brothers ran to her house, yelling, 'Look, Khala, we can't go on hiding like this, shifting from place to place. We've set our heart on running away to join the *Mukti Bahini*. Baba is always on our heels, or fingering his worry beads over our safety. The Pakis may snatch us any day and kill us. If we die, we should have a hero's death fighting our enemies. And our baba would be proud. What do you say, Khala?'

Boori was stirred by their patriotic zeal and their concern for their father's feelings. Her eyes brimmed with tears.

'You're right, sons,' she smiled. 'Where did you learn to think so much?'

Kader and Hakim exchanged a meaningful look and had a good laugh.

'You still see the boys in us, because we're already finished with school.'

'No, no, no, nothing like it. It's only the likes of you who can take up the cause. Not these old lizards.'

It had been a long time since Boori was last able to sleep so quietly. Kader and Hakim also slept soundly.

Sometimes Boori would stray into the garden with tufts of

soft, downy white flowers. She peered into the distance for Salim's return from the war. What if the dot on the horizon got bigger and bigger and turned out to be Salim?

Days went by without her dreams ever coming true. She would go and sit by the *pukur*. The shadow of the coconut tree seemed dwarfed. Swans waddled out of the water, shaking and stretching their wings. The *pukur*'s greenish water conjured up an image of Nita, who had not paid her a visit for quite a while. Boori longed to rekindle the intimacy she and Nita shared. The sting of loneliness and melancholy now seemed unbearable. Perhaps Nita was wandering from village to village, singing in her sweet voice. Akhile Baul had gifted her with a new lease of life. In marked contrast, Boori's life was dull and dreary, as grey as the swans' frayed feathers. Nights grew longer and longer, filled with unendurable pain and tediousness. Her existence was now a reflection of the infinite sky.

About a month or so later, Kader and Hakim knocked on Boori's door. Dawn had yet to peek through the night's pitch black curtain, when the sudden sharp noise roused her from sleep and she jumped, startled like a mouse. Thoughts of loot, blood, fire, shooting and killing flashed before her eyes. She froze with fear. The picture of Kalim's death rushed back and numbed her. She remembered how everything had unfurled that day. Outside Kader and Hakim were fired up and in a hurry.

'Khala, Khala, quick!' they called out.

Kader's urgent voice had Boori's blood racing fast.

'Whatever's the matter? Why have you come in the dead of night?'

'We're off.'

'Where to?'

'To join the freedom fighters. We'll take part in *muktijuddho*. We didn't want to tell anyone. Please tell Baba by and by, and try to make him understand.'

To Boori's ears, Kader's voice sounded just like Salim's. Salim had left her just like this, one day, which seemed long, long ago. Her lips trembled. Words failed her.

'Please bless us, Khala, so that we can return victorious.'

They bent down and touched her feet. Boori was overwhelmed. She put her hands on their heads and prayed for their safety and success. They appeared to her like angels and they exuded a heavenly scent. She smelled their palms and kissed them. She felt changed.

'What's wrong, Khala?' the boys queried.

'Nothing, I'm praying, just praying for your sake,' Boori slurred her words. She could no longer speak.

'We're going, Khala. Don't you worry, we'll be back before you know it. If you need anything, ask Baba, he will take care of you.'

The boys soon melted into the dark. Boori felt as though the night around her had receded. They had left with a halo of divine light in their wake. It gave her strength and courage to keep going. All her fears had evaporated.

Boori slept like a log, but was woken deep in the night by the sound of guns booming in the distance.

'Bless Haldi with brave, strong-willed boys, insha'allah!'

Then loneliness enshrouded her again. She could while away her time if Kader and Hakim were around to talk to. But now there was no one to chat with. Just nothing to tear off this *anchol* of loneliness and silence.

She remembered Ramija's fish knife. It was so sharp it could cut a droplet of water in half. Could anyone split silence like that? It was not a live thing, was it? The *kutum* no longer sang these days. Or maybe Boori didn't hear it. Sometimes one or two *shaliks* chirped on her kitchen roof. They sounded strangely prophetic. Boori couldn't figure out what it heralded, but she had been waiting to listen to this for ages. Her days oscillated between menacing silence, shooting, bomb blast or culvert burst, that made her heart stop and her pulse race. Those noises rang truer than ever, more precious than her own heartbeat.

A few days later, a boy from another neighbouring family came to her hut and touched her feet.

'Pray for me, Khala, I am off to the liberation war.'

Boori prayed for him too and waved him on as he left, a smile on his lips. The trickle of boys joining the war soon became a steady stream, eventually turning into a flowing, turbulent river. Where had these warriors sprouted from? Boori had no clue. She gazed silently at the silent boys. They did not turn round. They did not look back, but walked on, proud and confident into the sunlight. The future of Haldi was in their hands. Unlike them, she was but a speck in the wind.

Boori was feeling her age and she didn't have much energy left to fight. Yet, she wanted to do her part for the village that was dearer to her than her own life. Perhaps Nita was involved in the war more directly. At least she must be inspiring people with her songs. Songs that could rouse thousands. But what about herself? How could she contribute?

She glanced at Rais. He was now seventeen, sinewy and strong-built. Saliva drooled from his mouth, though. Sitting in the veranda, he would swat a fly from his face and kick his legs. Sometimes he broke into a wild guffaw and clapped his hands for no reason. Boori had rather not look. What could she have to do with this boy who was left cold by all the events unfolding around him? He didn't even know that his brother had died. Couldn't even know what floated his boat. He was in his bubble and hardly registered any emotion. Had he gone to join the liberation war, he could have avenged his brother's murder.

As Boori brooded over her son, she felt broken. Suddenly she stepped forward, sobbing, to embrace Rais. He pushed her away peevishly when she didn't let go of his head. Resenting her concern, he shrank back into his shell. He started trudging off to a corner of the courtyard and scared the ducks away. Boori was much too wounded to be angry at him. Kalim's death had left a thorn in her heart. She suffered from nightmares; the ghosts of his killers froze her limbs until she woke up each night, struggling to free herself.

A few days later, Sohrab Ali was arrested, chained and taken away by the army. The news was kept secret for a few days, but later spread like wildfire. The soldiers had cordoned off his house and whipped the people inside till their skin was flayed. They beat them black and blue and denied them their basic rights. Boori was lucky enough to be been spared. After Kalim's death, the army had not been back to her hut. The howls of the villagers, the screams of the women, the wails of the children reached her ears. She could only offer her prayers, 'Bismillah, give us more guerrillas, more guerrillas!'

After the soldiers left, the village was as silent as death. Boori felt it her duty to look out for the rat who had tipped off the Pakistanis. Whoever he was, he couldn't have realized how he had betrayed his own village, his own soil, his own motherland. Boori craved to strangle the traitor. In a flash, she saw Mansoor's face—the *Razakar* who had informed the army about Salim's whereabouts. Only a couple of days ago, Boori had been stopped by Mansoor, who was smoking under the olive tree.

'Why aren't Sohrab Ali's sons around?'

'They went to see their ailing maternal grandfather,' she proffered.

'Is that so? Didn't their mother go along with them?' he pressed on with his questions.

'Their mother is not so well herself. Why are you asking about them, Son?' Boori wheedled.

'Never you mind. There's nothing the matter.'

Mansoor's voice trailed off as he strode away over the emerald paddy. His black umbrella faded in the distance. Boori wondered whether he actually believed what she had told him.

'*Tumio ekta manush, telapokao ekta pakhi*! Mansoor, you bastard,' she muttered, her head in a muddle. '*Kuttir baccha*! Pah! You've betrayed your motherland and you're in cahoots with the enemy. I'll hang you upside down on a tree.'

Boori had no other way to express her rage. She had spat at his shadow and now ranted bitterly against the traitor.

'You filth! You gap-toothed blabbermouth!'

She walked to the *boroj* and stopped at Kalim's grave. The place was calm and cool and soothed her frayed nerves. She took a deep breath. Her late son gave her a new lease of life. Her head was spinning, the blood rushing in her veins like a rough river.

The following day, Sohrab Ali returned home with severe injuries and a high fever. Boori went to see the old man. He didn't move a muscle at first, but suddenly broke down and sobbed like a child. His wife rubbed some oil on his sore back. Leaning closer, Boori asked him, 'Where's your pain, Sohrab bhai? In your body or in your mind?'

'In my body,' Sohrab replied in a huff.

'They've joined a just cause, Sohrab bhai.'

'I know,' he spat. Blue flames twirled from his hookah.

'Please pray for them.'

'Didn't Kalim's death break your heart, Rais's mother?' Sohrab Ali smiled back at her.

Boori kept silent. Sohrab Ali had been tortured because Kader and Hakim had run away. She was proud to see that he put on a brave face despite the torture.

Boori took the cow from the shed, tethered her in the garden. After a while she undid the rope, goading the animal loudly, 'Feel free to have as much grass as you like today. I'll let you graze to your heart's content.'

Leaning against the *latakan* tree, she was filled with respect for Sohrab Ali who did not wince under torture nor did he blab about his sons' hideouts. Only the two of them, Boori and Rais, could do nothing for Haldi. She kept hearing horrifying news about other villages where the war raged on—the army ambush, the crash of grenades, the clatter of machine guns and the deaths of young martyrs. Boori wanted to *be* a weapon—a gun, grenade, rocket, mortar bomb or dynamite—primed to mow down countless invisible foes. She missed her fiery youth, a youth that could snatch away all her life's attachments. Sometimes she would feel a tingle in her veins as though people were crawling over her dead body.

Boori felt an urge to stroke the cow. As she sprang from her seat, she tripped over a root and crashed into a tree. She bruised her big toe whose nail got caught by a splinter and blood spurted from the wound. Grinding *shialmutha* leaves with her teeth, she made a paste which she quickly pressed on the gash. Then, she herded the cow back to the shed and tethered her to a pole. She went to lie down on a mat in the veranda. Her head began to swim. She enjoyed the pain, which was a strange, but not altogether unpleasant feeling. She was intrigued by the story of a young martyr's recovered corpse that had a smile on its face. How could young boys die with smiles on their lips, while bullets cracked their skulls?

Pondering over the stories of the brave, Boori stole a glance at her son. Rais smiled his usual smile. Unlike the other boys, he didn't have the slightest clue about what war or freedom meant. Unlike the other villagers, he didn't rush to answer the call to arms. She was flooded with guilt whenever she looked at him. The two of them were surplus to the village, as they could not do their share for the *muktijuddho*. They only ate up Haldi's precious food reserves and had virtually no work to do. Salim had been fighting on the battle-front and Kalim had been killed. However, these sacrifices were not enough and Boori thought it her duty to pay her personal tribute.

News of all kinds poured in from the battlefield as the war blazed on. In the evening, sitting in Sohrab Ali's hut, the villagers would huddle round the radio set to listen to programmes aired by the *Swadhin Bangla Betar Kendra*. They felt proud and perky to hear these broadcasts. Sohrab Ali was highly fond of *Chorompotra*. Although Boori couldn't make head or tail of it, she still liked to listen to the radio programmes. Their ears abuzz with the sound of gunshots, the village boys thought they were wasting their time waiting out there to be ratted out by the likes of Mansoor. Their attitude bothered Mansoor a great deal. Boori thought that the members of the Peace Committee and the *Razakars* were a small vicious lot, but the members of the *Mukti Bahini* were as countless as the grains of sand in the river.

Boori received news from Salim saying that he was well. He had arranged for a courier to leave a gourd with a message hidden inside at the bazaar. No need to worry on his account. She read his letter in the kitchen. She had fed her sons in this little kitchen of hers and felt that this was the perfect place to read the letter. She pressed it to her breasts and then started reading.

> Ammajan, take my *salaam*. I had no pen or paper all this time. I didn't have anyone who could take the letter to you either. That's why I couldn't let you know of my whereabouts.
>
> Maa, you can be proud. I now have twenty brave boys under my command. They lead those Pakistanis a merry dance! You should see their faces when lorries and bridges go up in the air like *patka* fish. The *Razakar* lickspittle gave us a hard time, cutting off our retreat. We fought them off and regrouped under the cover of night. We lived off roots and wild berries for days until we were deep into India.
>
> Now, we move from one *Mukti Bahini* camp to another. We have more men and more weapons and we are breaking their lines all the time. By Allah's grace, we'll give the devils a good licking. We won't let up until they get their bloody paws off our country.

Amma, if I don't return, consider me as a *shahid*. I am not scared of sacrificing my life.

Please send Kalim bhai when I ask you to. Maa, it is for the best that Ramija and the baby stay at *shoshurbaari*. I was a bit of a *ghughu* not to name our baby. I know Ramija wanted to call him 'Montu', but you had a different idea. Amma, I like 'Juddho' better too. It gives me greater strength every day. I'd like to name him Swadhin, once we are free. I promise, there will be a proper *akika* with goats and pulao rice, once the war is over.

Give my love to Kalim, Ramija and Juddho. Please pray for me, Amma.

Joi Bangla!

Much was left untold between his words. Boori cried like a baby as she folded Kalim and Ramija's letters in her sari's *anchol*.

Sometimes, the boom of a gun would blast Boori's silence. At those times, she went to the canal. The autumn sky turned a bright turquoise. She would watch the flowers and crops in the field. Sometimes, she saw soldiers patrolling the paddies, with guns on their shoulders. While she was afraid, she figured that they ignored her, never suspecting her to be a potential enemy. Boori chuckled about this while picking vegetables. They could never measure the blaze in her mind, which could ignite and torch them at any time. Didn't these foreign vultures know that dry hay could turn so easily into tinder?

Often Boori felt like chopping everything with Ramija's fish cutter. The river of blood reappeared. The blood trickled from Kalim's body, from Sohrab Ali's wounds, from the injured pigeon hopping up and down her courtyard, from her injured toe. All these events, tragic or trivial, seemingly disconnected, were related and perpetrated by one and the same hand.

The days and the seasons appeared to have changed Haldi. Hens and roosters called with different cries. Boori listened to those calls, while lying idle on her bed every morning. She pulled the blanket over Rais's body, and her heart was filled with a warm wave for her son. His breathing sounded like the flare that blasted bridges. It resonated in Boori's mind. She failed to grasp why she found such solace in him these days. She liked combing his long hair after bathing him. She liked feeding him and looking at his sleepy moon-like face. In the early days after Rais was born, she had fussed over his every need with a mother's sense of fulfilment. Pictures of those blissful days lingered in her mind.

Almost every evening Boori walked along with her son. She no longer felt lonely. Somebody needed her. She was no longer gripped by a sense of helplessness, nor did cold sweat trickle down her spine, or prickle her skin at the thought of the soldiers. Oddly enough, Haldi seemed more intimate and caring.

Sometimes Boori tried to talk to Rais.

'Son, do you feel pain? You must have so much to talk about. But it must be so hopelessly bottled up somewhere in your mind.'

Rais gave his mother a vacant stare.

'What are you gazing at, son? It must be so hurtful. You'd like to speak out, wouldn't you? I can't express myself all that well these days. And I am no good for the village.'

Rais emitted a kind of gurgle as his mother coaxed him. He didn't like her to stop on the road and pulled her hand, urging her to keep going. He plodded on, leaving her behind. He drew near the house while Boori lingered along the way, looking at the violet *kochuripana*. Before Rais's birth, she used to play with Kalim, when she wandered off in the emerald field to glean vegetables. He was also fond of fishing. Boori remembered how she liked to get his nets and baskets shipshape, and how he went wild if for some odd reason his tackle wasn't ready. These memories made her feel dizzy and she hurried home. She had to rustle up some food, as Rais hadn't eaten anything yet. She squatted down in the veranda. Everything around her seemed blurred as her eyes filled with tears. The village looked as white as goose feathers.

Ramija sent a message that they were all doing well. The baby was growing into a healthy boy. He no longer wailed nor was fractious, but he played in the dust all day long. Sometimes, he seemed to want to babble.

Boori received a lavish supply of cakes, fish and eggs from Ramija. But who was there to eat those? Salim had a sweet tooth, but he was away. Boori would bake cakes for him every day, and if they weren't ready, he'd be cursing Ramija. When he left to join the *muktijuddho*, he forgot to take cakes along with him. He usually forgot the little things for the greater ones.

Ramija, too, had been waiting for news of Salim's return. Boori thanked merciful Allah that her daughter-in-law was safe from the clutches of the wild beasts. The army camp was less than a quarter of a mile from Boori's hut. The soldiers were known to torture and gang rape women whenever their lust was aroused. They would swoop down on young girls as on chained cattle. Rumours circulated that the victims were dumped in mass graves or served as sex-slaves.

অগ্রহায়ণ
Ôgrôhayôn

The cool weather of Kartik was over and there were two days to go before the start of Ôgrôhayôn. A chilly wind needled into the bones of those who remained in Haldi. The vegetables were in full bloom. *Machranga* darted over the canal and warblers flew back and forth in the trees. Bagha wailed into the small hours of the night. Winter was better suited to Rais's health. Yet, he looked worse for wear. His round *pukur*-like face had shrunk and the little gleam of light in his eyes died away. The blue gauze Boori draped her dreams upon was now frayed. Pictures from the past haunted her.

She had begged Rais to be livelier, but the more the village was sucked into the war, the deeper her son crawled back into his own shell. He would lunge at the dog or smash bamboos and shoo birds away for no reason. He would be gone for hours. Once Boori told him off for tearing the wings of a dragonfly.

The floodgates opened and the rain fell in torrents. It had been pouring heavily since morning, like the rainy days of Asharh. The sky was overcast. Everything was dark. Boori unlocked the chicken coop, cleaned the cowshed and gave fodder to the cow in the blustering rain. Despite all this, she didn't feel tired. She remembered a song she used to sing:

Nadir kul nai kinara nai re
O ami kon kul hote kon kule jabo
Kahare sudhai re
Opare megher ghata kanak bijuli chhata
Majhe nadhi bahe sai sai re
Ami ai horilam sonar chhabi
Abar theki nai re.

She tucked the hem of her sari around her waist and busied herself with her work. She didn't feel cold, even after staying in the rain for so long. When she got back, she ran into Nita who was just stepping into the house.

'My dear, what a surprise! How are you doing?'

Nita didn't reply. Weary and bedraggled, she dragged herself to the veranda.

'What are you doing in this downpour?' Boori queried.

Nita remained silent, covering her face with her hands.

'Hey, what happened? Why are you crying, Nita? Please, change into a dry sari, or you'll catch cold,' Boori urged her friend.

Nita didn't carry anything with her. So, Boori brought a fresh sari from inside her hut.

'Put that on and I will hear your news. Today I'm feeling happy. My mood lifts the minute I am in your presence. We'll spend the whole rainy day chatting like old women. I haven't been able to bend someone's ear for a long, long time.'

Boori began to sing, but her heart was not really in it.

Kandiya aakul hoilam bhabo-nodir pare
Mon tore ke ba par kore!
Su-samay-e din guwaiya
Asamay-e, mon, asamay-e
Ailam nodir pare;
Majhi tor nam janina,
Ami dak demu kare?
Mon tore ke ba par kore!
Nao ase, kheoani nai re
Manush nai re pare;
Majhi tor nam janina,
Ami dak demu kare?
Mon tore ke ba par kore!

Nita shivered all over while putting on the fresh sari. She had travelled a long way in the rain and she could feel the cold in her bones. Boori brought her some burning coals in an earthen pot and said, 'This will warm you up.'

'Get me something to eat first! I haven't had any food for two days, apart from some *moori* and water.'

'There's some water rice and I'll roast some peppers.'

They both ate in silence. Boori guessed that something was wrong, but she dared not ask her friend, lest it upset her for the whole day.

'I'll stay here for a couple of days, Boori,' Nita ventured.

'I am blessed! I couldn't keep you here, even though I always invited you to stay.'

Tears rolled down Nita's cheeks.

'I'd feel much better if you stayed on with me,' Boori assured her, 'I've been feeling bored and lonely.'

After the meal, Boori began to slice betel nuts. Nita warmed her hands with the pot of burning coals.

'I was soaked to the skin,' Nita said.

'Where's Akhile, your soulmate?' Boori asked her casually.

'He has been killed.'

'What?' Boori inquired, incredulous.

'He was shot.'

'Oh no, Nita, my dear!' Boori screamed.

'The ashram was burned down to ashes. There is nothing to go back to. Everywhere, death, desolation, despair.'

Boori found nothing to say. Nita went on with a broken voice, 'I can't understand why the ashram was set on fire, why the men were killed and why the women were taken away. I could stand the pain if the Pakistani dogs had done it. But it's our own folks who did all this...our own neighbours! Akhile is dead. The worst of it is that he was shot dead by Ali Ahmad. I have never been so ashamed! Heartless *Razakars*! They spat at our faces and called us "traitors" and "terrorists."

"'It's a damn lie," Akhile protested as loudly as he could, "we've never betrayed our motherland. I wrote lyrics for my countrymen."

"'You call 'em songs?" They railed and roared, slapping their thighs.

"'*Rundi ki tatti pe baithne waali makkhi*," Muhammad Asif blared, "we don't need any buzz flies."

'For heaven's sake, Boori, I have known them since my childhood. Before the war broke out, they used to come to our ashram. They'd listen to the songs rapturously.

"'Pakistan is for pure Muslims," Ayub Khan barked, "not for the likes of you sinners and *haramkhor*."

"'Kafir, that's your reward for writing those songs," Ali Ahmad snarled.

'He fired a shot. Akhile and his followers fell to the ground against a chorus of "Pakistan Zindabad". No one could say anything. I screamed and they kicked me in the back. Then they hit me with the butt of a gun. Susama, Mala and Chandana were picked up. They were crying aloud. I couldn't save them from gang rape. How could I, being an old woman? I only felt like telling them, "You people enjoyed our songs so many times, you liked our art. You called our place "holy". Now, tell me how we could have become enemies of our country! You never said anything like this before.

'I fainted after they left. Eventually I mustered all the strength I could and dragged the dead bodies to the river to let them drift away. The ashram was still smouldering. I spent two days under the tree and remembered you. Then it occurred to me to come over here. All of a sudden the skies opened up. But the downpour didn't matter.'

'I'm feeling cold, too, Nita. Let's go inside,' Boori suggested. 'You lie down and wrap the quilt round you.'

Boori led Nita to the bed where she spent the next fifteen

long days delirious and with a high fever. Boori didn't know what to do. She called in the village doctor who made a concoction to pour over the patient's head. Suddenly, her temperature dropped dramatically. She was ice cold to the touch and her lips turned blue.

'What happened to me, Boori?' she asked in a weak voice.

'You had a bad fever,' Boori smiled.

'Why are you smiling? How long have I been lying here?'

'About fifteen days.' Boori smiled.

'Fifteen days, eh!' Nita exclaimed.

She tried to recall what happened, but couldn't. She rested her head on the pillow again. Boori brought her some hot barley. She helped the minstrel to sit up on the couch in the veranda. Nita peered at the sky with pale eyes sunk deep in their sockets and surrounded by dark rings. She slurred her words, struggling to articulate. Boori sat by her bedside and nursed her back to health. She would catch fish from her *pukur* and cook them with vegetables for her friend.

'From today, you'll have rice, dear.'

'I don't feel like it,' Nita objected.

'But how can you survive if you don't regain your strength?'

'My strength? It has ebbed way and there's none left,' Nita smiled wanly.

'What nonsense!' Boori chided her friend. 'You're safe now. Hai Allah! You went through such a bad time!'

Nita remained silent for a while. Then she added, 'They burned my *dotara* as well. Akhile clasped it close to his chest. The damn *Razakars* smashed it to pieces.'

'Why are you still going on about them?' Boori argued. 'We've got an army of guerrillas fighting for *muktijuddho*.'

'War, war, war! This war is getting to my head, my dear. When will it all end?' Nita replied wearily.

'Look dear,' Boori ventured, 'this country will be free one day.'

'Your son may come back to a free country,' Nita shivered with a surge of emotion and she took Boori's hands in hers, 'but where shall I go then? I don't have a *moner manush* and I've lost the shelter of my ashram. There's nothing to go back to. I don't want to leave Haldi. Ever!'

'Now, Nita, you have a rest. You don't have to worry yourself sick. We'll talk about it later.'

'You tell your Salim to build a small hut for me on the edge of the village, once he comes back. I'll spend the rest of my days holding out my begging bowl,' Nita broke into tears.

'Nita, you can stay with me. It's so lonely here. I won't let you go anywhere this time.'

'Can't even walk straight the state I am in. Where the hell should I go?' Nita said, looking away.

'I'm going to get you some rice.'

Boori didn't want to see her friend weep. When she had been delirious, Nita had rambled endlessly, 'I'm a poor lonesome woman, always wandering about the world with no family, no nothing. My head is killing me. In the name of the Peace Committee, they have shot us, raped us, set fire to our homes, stolen our things. They say they're the patriots and we're the enemies of the nation. They branded us "traitors."'

Boori laid out Nita's food. She thought long and hard about this woman with a bad kismet. Nita had lost everything, but she didn't miss them. Boori was shocked by Ali Ahmad's roughshod treatment of Nita. She was brooding over all this when Rais stepped into the kitchen, showing he was hungry. Nita was still frail. She couldn't leave the hut. Memories of the fire, killings and rapes were still raw.

'Why are you so heartbroken, Nita?'

'I've never seen so many innocent people killed,' she replied in a strained voice.

'I've never seen so many deaths either,' Boori echoed.

She and Nita spent long hours staring at nothing or wading through the mire of atrocities.

The war outside took its toll within as Boori tossed and turned in her sleep. Bad dreams woke her up almost every night—dreams of blood rivers, snakes stalking the swamps, the moon pouring molten lava over mangled bodies. Kalim's eyes would taunt her no end. Once she dreamt she saw a *devdaru* sprout from his grave. The tree had huge roots sticking out. It shot up branches laden with bombs and rapidly overgrew the village. The skylight was blotted out. She no longer fretted over Salim because she felt like he was in charge of things. Her elder son would root out the *Razakars* and peck at the Pakistanis till they fled Haldi for good. She was certain that her Salim would be the village headman one day and would help rebuild homes and the school. He would take the children of Haldi under his wings and their dreams would stretch over the paddies to the horizon.

She fussed over Rais though and didn't get a wink of sleep. The boy would spend most mornings in a dazed state. He would throw tantrums, biting himself or kicking Bagha viciously. Then he would vanish all afternoon. Once, Boori found him on the spot overlooking the Pakistani camp. He was marching up and down with a stick on his shoulder and a fierce, but vacant scowl on his face.

One day in the forest, Boori ran into Mansoor face to face.

'Talk of the devil!' she said to herself.

'*Salaam alaykum*, Rais's mother, I hear you have given shelter to that woman!'

'*Wa'alaykum assalaam*! She's no refugee! I urged her to stay with me, as I am on my own in the house, so she keeps me company. She's my friend and honoured guest.'

'Tell that old hag to leave at once, or you'll be in serious trouble,' Mansoor bullied.

'What are you talking about? I've already lost a son. Perhaps Salim has also been killed in the war, so nothing else could scare me anymore.'

'Who told you about Salim's death?' Mansoor took the bait, fishing for news.

'There are rumours about it,' Boori rubbed her eyes with the hem of her sari.

'Please, don't cry. Hush now, Rais's mother,' Mansoor wheedled, pretending to give Boori a pat and a few words of comfort to ferret out more information. 'You're a wretched soul. Your one and only son is deaf and dumb. Please, let us know if you need any help. But do tell that woman to leave today! There's no place for infidels like her in Haldi!'

'Yes, yes, like you…' Boori strode towards her hut.

Mansoor shared his umbrella with her for a few minutes. He grabbed her arm and then asked her point blank, 'Is it true that Salim died in the war?'

'People say so, but I didn't see it with my own eyes.'

'True enough. But you fussed over the two boys like a hen over her chicks. I consider it a blessing that both your stepsons died. Now all the lands will go to Rais. Are you not pleased about it, eh?'

Boori's heart was about to burst out of her chest. Hatred was written all over her face. She took a deep breath as she endured Mansoor's prattle.

'I'm so pleased for you, you know. I'm off to the army camp to tell them all about it.'

Mansoor hurried on, a grin on his face. Boori fumed with rage and spat on his shadow.

'*Chil*, bloody carrion sucker!' She kicked at the bushes angrily, muttering to herself, 'Your flesh and bones will be dog's food after Salim returns. I'll throw your rotten body to the dogs and foxes. The blabbermouth was licking his chops at the news of

Salim's death! Oh, my head is killing me! The sly dog made me sick with his weasel words. Believe me, Salim, you'll live to be eighty, Allah bless you! I lied to that *kukur* and said that you were dead just to stop him from making trouble for Nita and me. For Allah's sake and for your own sake, believe me, Salim, I am no sinner. What would I do with your lands? I don't want any of it.'

Boori returned home in a confused state. Her mind was obsessed with a feeling of guilt, which needled her throughout the day. She couldn't even make a clean breast of it to her friend.

'What happened to you, dear?' Nita asked.

'I've circulated a rumour that Salim died in the war,' Boori replied in a harsh voice.

'Why would you do that?'

'Salim's death will please those *Razakars* no end. It will silence their wagging tongues. They won't be bothering us about your stay. Mansoor scares me a lot more than the Pakistani army, because he's a neighbour and he knows all about my private life.'

As dusk fell, Boori broke down and cried her eyes out. Nita stared at her vacantly. She could not fathom what Boori was talking about, nor could she read her face for a clue. Her friend seemed like a stranger to her.

The news of Salim's death spread like wildfire through the village. Mansoor circulated the rumour to every passing villager that he ran into on his way. Those who awaited Salim's victorious return to Haldi dropped by Boori's house.

'Is it true about Salim, Rais's mother?' Sohrab Ali enquired.

'Alas!' Boori replied in a sad tone.

'Who brought the news?'

'A messenger,' Boori answered.

'It's a lie, a damn lie,' Sohrab Ali bellowed when he heard the news. 'Salim can't die. It's all the doing of that *Razakar* dog!'

Boori said nothing to Sohrab Ali. His shouting provided some reassurance and hope.

Days went by without anything significant happening. Boori's thoughts flew beyond the boundaries of Haldi. She kept her ears trained for the booming of guns. At times Sohrab Ali pressed her, 'Why don't you tell me the source of the news about Salim? You say you got it from a messenger, but we have to take your word for it. We didn't see him, did we, Rais's mother? Can we possibly have missed him?'

Boori wore an innocent and foolish expression on her face and abruptly averted her gaze.

'What ghost gave you the news, only Allah knows?' Sohrab Ali raged.

Boori watched her neighbour striding away. 'We need the sting of your anger,' she rambled. 'We want furious and arrogant men like you.'

Her thoughts danced like motes in a shaft of sunlight. Her feelings swelled up like balloons to a victorious horizon. Hope had chased away her ache and despair. It was only when Mansoor paused by the pond and snarled, baring his yellow fangs, to ask her how she coped, that she felt like lashing out at him. Boori turned her face away and tried to swallow a lump in her throat. Mansoor was his usual self, wearing his sympathy on his sleeve.

'Oh, you must be fretting now. Though Salim was your stepson, still you raised him as your own.'

Boori started to walk off before he had mouthed his tirade.

'Rais's mother! Rais's mother!' Mansoor heckled, but Boori didn't respond.

Boori untethered the cow, picked up a bamboo stick and began to collect some wild grass to feed the cow. But her anger wouldn't let up. She longed for her greener days, when everything was lush and fresh and full of life. Memories of Gafoor bubbled up inside her. She stifled a cackle and rubbed her hands together. There was a rumour that the boys had that Mansoor rat cooped up in a hut till he shrivelled like a prune.

পৌষ
Poush

The relentless drip drip of fear frayed the fabric of the villagers' lives. It seeped into their flesh and every pore of their skin. Tore into their guts. Stopped their hearts. Shattered their spirits. They heard the whoosh-bang of bullets in their dreams. They watched the imminent line of grass. Dreaded the serpent of a canal. The slightest storm pummeling the roofs or the thwack of cranes would now send shivers up and down their spines. They would drown back to sleep, drunk with fear. They were too scared to go beyond their courtyard, let alone venture out as far as the bazaar. Few folks chanced getting caught listening to *Chorompotra* war stories on the radio. When Boori was restless, she had flashes of Kana Bhoot, the one-eyed river monster that had held her childhood in its talon grip. The moon's cauldron mothered new tales of terror.

On the first day of Poush, they were all startled up by the constant sound of gunshots. It was too close for comfort. Boori threw the quilt off her body and sat on the bed.

'What's going on, dear?' Nita asked, drawing quietly closer to her.

'Perhaps the *Mukti Bahini* have raided the army camp in our village.'

'Allah! What will happen next?' Nita sobbed.

'Nothing will happen. Just our brave boys warming up the chilly winter night,' Boori blurted under her breath. 'We'll lead you, *Razakars*, a merry dance. Just you see!'

Rais was snoring under the quilt. No one woke him up. Boori walked to the bamboo door, her pulse beating faster with every step she took. At first she couldn't hear the crossfire nearby. Soon, however, the guns were firing louder and closer than before. Boori heard the neighbours whispering. Everyone panicked. Terrorized women fled with their babies slung across their waists. It was easier to get away under the cover of darkness. In the pitch-black night, a glimmer of hope flashed across Boori's mind. Sohrab Ali stepped into the courtyard, calling out, 'Oh, Rais's mother!'

'What's the matter, Sohrab bhai?'

'We should leave now!'

'Whatever for?' Boori wondered.

'We don't want to be caught flat-footed.'

'What are you talking about, Sohrab bhai?'

'The firing has started and the minute they fire back, we'll get killed.'

'I've never heard such rubbish! Our boys will win the day.'

'I'd be the first to cheer them if they do,' Sohrab Ali admitted, 'but what if they lose? Let's go right away!'

'I am not going to run off, come what may. I'm a harmless old woman. I haven't done anything wrong,' Boori pleaded.

'Are you out of your mind?'

'No, Sohrab Ali. My son's asleep. Where will I go in the bitter cold night if I leave my hut? You go and count me out.'

'Do you wish to die? Please follow me right now! You don't have much of a choice,' the elder insisted.

'No, I won't.'

'You mean you won't be going?' he chided her.

'No, Sohrab Ali. I won't budge. Please, you go safely.'

Sohrab Ali left, frustrated and fuming. Crouched against the wind, a huddle of dark shapes trudged away into the night. A buffalo dragging a rickety cart. Boori remembered Kalim's death. The spot where he was shot was clearly visible from the hut. She shivered. Bullets meant death. Nita was aware of it too. Still Boori remained sitting quietly in her corner.

'Dear?'

Boori was startled when she heard Nita's voice. Nita squeezed her friend's hands tightly in hers and pleaded, 'My dear, please go with them. What if things took a sinister turn?'

'How can you imagine that I'd leave you behind?' Boori argued.

'Then we'll keep our heads down,' Nita said, reining in her emotions. 'Let's see it through to the end.'

TATA TATA TA TATATA, TATA TATA TATATATA.

TATA TATA TA TATATA, TATA TATA TATATATA.

Boori heard continuous firing. Never before in her life, had there been such a rousing winter night. A group of *Mukti Bahini* led by Kader and Hakim had besieged the army camp. They had the upper hand to start with. Their surprise attack killed a few Pakistani soldiers. However, since they were a small band, the guerrillas couldn't sustain the combat for long. They were also running short of ammunition. When they realized that they were about to be outgunned, they beat a hasty retreat.

Kader and Hakim knew the topography of the village like the back of their hands. It was no trouble for them to find their way in the dark. The only difficulty was that the meandering paths slowed down their retreat. They were chased by four sepoys that kept firing their guns at them. Bullets whizzed past their ears. Kader and Hakim ran like the wind. They climbed down a paddy field, leaving the open road to the soldiers. The sound of a stampede in the courtyard startled Boori. She had her heart in her mouth, wondering whether the shooting had ceased. There was no crossfire. Boori clasped Nita's hands.

'My dear, have they lost?'

'No, they can't have lost. I can't believe it!'

Tears rolled down Boori's cheeks. Nita shuddered. Both women crept to the veranda and peeped through the keyhole.

'Khala?'

Boori was all pins and needles. Who were they? The voices sounded familiar, though.

'Khala, open the door, quick!' a voice called desperately.

Boori was ready for it. Her brave fighters had returned. They needed shelter and succour. Once they made their getaway, they would gather strength to carry on the fight. Feeling strong and inspired, Boori unlatched the door. Kader and Hakim scrambled inside.

'Khala, they're after our skins. We couldn't go to our parents' house. Please let us in,' they begged her.

In a split second, Boori made up her mind and rushed them to a dark corner of her hut, where she stowed them in a large empty earthen jar. She slid the lid over the jar. Then she threw a bag of old jute on top. Nita watched Boori intently.

'Dear, what are you up to?' she asked her with some trepidation.

'Who will fight for us if they are caught?'

Boori sat by the bamboo door. After his arrest and torture, Sohrab Ali didn't have the will to stay behind. If Boori had run off too, who would help these boys? No one had the spine to conceal them. Her heart leapt with pride and joy at the thought. But what was she to do next? What would happen if the soldiers realized the men they were after were inside? The soldiers were bound to search every house.

Boori felt wistful as though she were lost in a thick jungle. A pride of leopards was on the prowl, ready to pounce on their prey. She was at a loss what to do. Should she try to stop them? Should she ask them to kill her first before they could walk into her hut? What good would that do? Could it save the lives of these two boys? She could not save them at the cost of her own life. She felt like pulling out her hair. Their very lives were in her hands now. And theirs were precious lives, ones that must live on.

'What should I do, Nita?' Boori nudged Nita's shoulder. 'How can I save them?'

Nita had nothing to say and wiped her tears. Boori was incensed, 'You're always crying, Nita! You must have run out of tears by now!'

Boori paced up and down the room. A few minutes later four sepoys stormed in like hungry felines. They swept a luminous searchlight across the village and picked out everything. The villagers had never seen the glare of the white light. They were petrified. The sepoys barked orders at the top of their voices. They couldn't figure out whether the two guerrillas had hidden in someone's hut or had melted away in the bushes. The Pakistani soldiers talked among themselves. Posting two guards in a courtyard, they herded out all Haldi's remaining male folks and lined them up.

Boori shuddered with fear as an owl hooted from a nearby tree. The sound was maddening. Rais had thrown the quilt off his face. He was snoring, unperturbed. Boori peered down at his face and inhaled his breath. It smelled like the sweet faces of Kader and Hakim, the day they left their home for *muktijuddho*. She felt she was at the centre of her people, huddled together with lights cupped in their hands. An oracle whispered in her ears, 'There's no time to loiter and stare. Life is full of fear.'

Time was tearing Boori's life apart.

'Today, dear, all of us are fated to die,' Nita said hurriedly.

Boori didn't reply. All she could think of was that the boy who couldn't avenge his brother's killing had no right to survive in this world. Thousands of innocent people were being slaughtered and Rais would be one of them. Horrible thoughts flashed across her mind. Without Rais, Boori's world would cease to be. Images of Haldi flickered before her eyes—scenes of her childhood and youth with the lungi-clad dirt poor Bangla folks.

Boori shook off her terror. She heard the sepoys muttering under their breath and closing in on the hut. There was not a minute to lose. She woke Rais. He was taken aback and dazzled by glare of the light. Boori pressed the light machine gun into his hands. Rais was puzzled and for a few agonizing minutes, tears of joy glistened on his bewildered face. There was muted laughter and his head was shaking uncontrollably. Cock-a-hoop, he pressed the gun to his chest. Boori quaked, looking at his face.

'What on earth are you doing, Boori?' Nita asked in a strained incredulous voice.

She rushed over to Rais to snatch away the gun from him.

'No, Nita, you shouldn't take it away,' Boori stopped her in her tracks. 'It belongs here. I gave it to him.' Her eyes were defiant.

Two sepoys burst into the veranda as Boori shoved Rais out of the room, the gun in his hands. The sepoys shouted. Boori stood at the door, barring the entrance. They had to kill her first before smashing their way in and wrecking the hut. But the soldiers had no second thoughts about collaring Rais. They had their man and that was all that mattered. Boori wanted to cry her heart out. She felt like going into the courtyard, but was petrified. She had to keep an eye on two more lives that were equally precious. Kader and Hakim would fight on and avenge the deaths of thousands of Kalim. They were fighting for the freedom of *Sonar Bangla*, at the cost of their own lives. Boori was no more Rais's maa, she was the mother of all Bangladeshis.

The sepoys thanked Boori in Urdu and promised to reward her service to the country. She couldn't figure out what they meant and stood still at the door. Rais had eyes only for the gun in his hands. The villagers in the courtyard had no idea what was going on. No one said anything about the gun in the hands of gawky, foolish Rais. Silence prevailed.

Boori's eyes smarted as the sepoys stormed out with their

prisoner, hands tied behind his back. They left no doubt about his fate. They had their prey in their power. Boori felt as though the sepoys were tearing her heart apart. She walked onto the veranda. Night was in its last throes and the light of dawn pulsed on the horizon. The owl stopped hooting.

The villagers gathered round Boori. She couldn't make out what they were saying. Freeing herself from the ring of people, she approached the corner of the courtyard when she heard a gunshot. She ran to the spot. Under the *jamrool* tree planted by Kalim, Rais lay in a pool of blood. Boori reeled, feeling as if a bomb had blasted her chest away. Rais's body was a crimson mess. The four sepoys swaggered back to their camp. When all the neighbours rushed to the dead Rais, Boori ran back to the hut. She slid the lid off the earthen jar and called out the two boys. Kader and Hakim clambered out with a throb in their veins. They looked puzzled.

'Quick! They have gone!' Boori urged them.

'Have they?' They couldn't believe they had escaped by a tiger's whisker. Nita was wailing. 'Who's crying, Khala?'

'Get going! It's your fight now!' Boori spoke in a harsh voice.

'We were saved by your kindness, Khala,' one of the boys said.

Boori saw them out with a heavy heart. She came an inch away from giving the devils what they wanted. An inch, a whisper, a blade of grass was the distance between life and death.

There was a river of pain swelling up in her, but she couldn't cry before the boys. Kader and Hakim touched her feet and were gone. They were aghast at the sight of Rais's body. When they heard the full story from a villager, they went back to Boori.

'Why did you do it?' Tears rolled down their cheeks. 'Your only son?'

'Don't stand like sore thumbs, boys!' Boori chided them. '*Mukti Bahini* don't want cry-babies.' Her tone barely changed, but her words spooled out with terrifying urgency. 'If you don't run off right now, Rais will have died for nothing. Go! Go!'

They looked her in the eye.

'Bless you, Maa!'

They melted into the dawn with the shard of her pain.

Boori struggled to keep her balance and she had to lean against the fence. She could hear crying from under the *jamrool* tree. Everyone was in tears. Boori felt an intolerable wrench in her heart.

'You never called me "maa", Rais, the soil of Haldi will take you to her breast. You'll never call me "maa". The tendril that haunted me since my childhood and youth is nipped in my old age.' Waves of sobbing shook Boori's body.

Memories welled up. Flashes of the two of them locked in embrace. Rais chasing the dog's shadow. Rais brooding and cooing in the bamboo grove. Rais strutting his stuff or squelching like a bullfrog in the mud.

Life and death were not two different threads. Boori tried to articulate her son's name, but couldn't. She remembered the pain over his birth. She had stuck with Rais through thick and thin. That's what mothers did. Give and give and give. For whose sake did she purloin Allah's gift? Only a mother knew how it felt to lose a child. 'Rais, you cannot guess how I ached for you, son. How your maa could change. This soil is awash with the blood from my flesh. Rais, please, please forgive me, son!'

Boori struck her head against the fence. Nita lurched forward.

'Stop crying, dear. Did you see how your Rais changed into a blood lotus?'

Boori mustered all her strength. She gave her friend a hard stare.

'I don't understand you' Nita said helplessly. 'Once you were mad for a son from your own loins. Today, you killed him with your own hands.'

Boori gasped like a fish out of water. The floodgates were open and her broken heart was fertile soil silted by countless rivers.

'Let's go, dear,' Nita whispered, clasping Boori's hands.

Boori knelt down before Rais. She gingerly stroked his head and tilted it up, scrubbing the clotted blood. His eyes were wide open, bloodshot. Closing his eyelids, she kissed him for the very last time.

Her heart was ash where his body lay. In the background there were a few people bowing their heads or clawing at the dust.

The grudge of love stained Boori's knuckles. She had a fleeting glimpse of Salim returning home as a war hero. He would lead them onwards to Bangla's new dawn. She staggered. Cranes flew off, setting the floodplain alight with crimson buds.

Phuli—Akhile—Kalim—Rais—Haldi—her hut—her pond—her land—her river—her hands caught between the crosshairs of history. Everything turned red.

Translation of the Songs

Catok bance kemone
Suddh megher borison bine
Tumi hey hobo jolodhor
Catokini mole ebar
Tomar songe sokol somoy
Rekho vubane

O Mind! I have discovered the truth,
How can the swallow survive?
Unless the cloud sheds a sacred shower to revive.
You are the preserver,
But the swallow dies here from thirst.
Keep me, my Lord, forever with you.

*

Karo robe na e dhon jibonjoubon
Tobe keno mon eto basha
Ekbar soburer deshe
Boi dekhi dom kose
Uthis na re vese peye jontrona.

O Mind! I have discovered the truth,
None can forever preserve the days of his youth.
Then why are you filled with countless desires?
At last you try once the essence of waiting,
And do not give it up, when engrossed with pains.

*

Aami tor piriter mora
Tui chaiya dekhna ek nazor,
Bondhu re!
Oporadhi hoileo aami tor

Aami jodi jai moria
Ke korbe tore aador?
Oporadhi hoileo aami tor.

Age ke jane gou emon hobe
Gaur prem kore amar kulman iabe
Chilam kuler kulbala
Prem fandhe badhlo gola
Tanle to aar na jai khola
Bolle ke bojhe

I have lost my Self in your love
Will you not bless me with your glance?
O intimate friend of mine!
No matter how much I oppressed my soul
Forever I am all yours…

When I depart for the land of death,
Who else will remain here to caress you?
No matter how much I oppressed my soul
Forever I am all yours.

Who could know that such things would happen?
I would lose all my caste and creed for the love of Gaur
I was a married woman
But suddenly I fell in love
I cannot leave it if I am forced to do so
None, however, understands my trouble.

*

Milon hobe kotodine
Amar moner manuser sone
Chatok prai ohornishi
Cheye ache kaloshashi
Hobo bole charandasi
O ta hoina kopal gune

When shall I meet
My soulmate?
I am like the *chatak* bird that longs
For the new moon day and light,
I want to offer myself a service woman to him
But luck does not favour me

*

Sundar tomar mukher hasire
Sundor tomar banshi
Surete pagol korlire bandhu
Mon korili udasi
Na jene mojona pirite
Jene shune koro pirit
Shesh bhalo daray jate
Pirit korar hoi basona
Sadhur kache jange bena
Loha jemon poroshe sona
Hobe sei mote

Lovely is your smile
Lovelier still is the melody of your flute
I am mesmerized, friend
My mind is not within me
Do not fall
In love unwisely
Be cautious
while testing this nectar
That you do not repent
Profusely at the end

*

Amay bhashaili rey
Amay dubaili rey
Akul dariyar bujhi kul nairey
Kul nai kinar nai naiko nadir padi

Tumi sabdhanetey chalaiyo majhi
Amar bhanga tari rey

You've set me adrift
You've sunk me
The endless waters have no shore
Limitless, with no shores, the waters have no banks
O row with care boatman, my riven boat.

*

Ami bhatir belai nao bhashailam;
Mridu mondo batash bohe,
Beguni jole nouka bhashe.
Nodir baake etel matir ghor,

Oparete shobuj ghasher bonee
keba shukhai tar neel sarita petee,
Ami bhatir belai nao bhashailam re.

Shajer aloi jai milaye shob rongin chobi
Mondirer ghonta baje toong toong
Kapiye nodir jol.

Kar tonoya ghate ashe
Jhumur jhumur pai?
Amar pane chai?
Ami bhatir belai nao bhashailam re.

Tar mukher pane cheye amar ridoy neche othe,
Ami preme pagol para,
Kemon kore thakbo ami ekhon ghore feere?
Jhokon ami bhatir belai nao bhashai re!

At sunset I go rowing my boat,
The breeze is sweet, the waves look purple.
Where the river takes a winding course, I see a house of red clay.

Across the river on the green grass,
Whose blue sari is spread to dry?
At sunset I go rowing my boat.

The evening shadows seem to be stooping,
From the temple across the stream
The sound of the bell comes ringing.

With anklets on her feet ringing *jhumur jhumur*,
Whose young daughter comes to the ghat and stoops
While at sunset I go rowing my boat?

In the flashing light of her charming face I have gone mad.
This time when I go home, longing for her, how shall I live,
While at sunset I go rowing my boat?

*

Brishti parey tapur tupur
Node elo baan,
Shib Thakurer biye holo
Teen konney daan.
Ek konney radhen baren
Arek konney khaan,
Arek konney na khaaye
Baaper baari zaan.

Falling raindrops go pitter patter
The river is at high tide,
Shiva got married
To three daughters
One of them does the cooking
While the other one just eats.
The third gets cross and goes back to her father's house.

*

Mon majhi tor boitha nere, ami ar baite parlam na
Mon majhi tor boitha nere, ami ar baite parlam na
Shara jibon ujan bailam, bhatir nagal pailam na.

Ami ar baite parlam na,
Mon majhi tor boitha nere, ami ar baite parlam na.
Dukkher deshe dukkher nodi kaindya boiya jai,
Shukher ashai mon majhi tui kandos hai re hai.
Mon majhi tui bebhul jemon, ami kopal pora temon
Sukh dukkher kinar pailam na.
Mon majhi tor boitha nere, ami ar baite parlam na

O boatman of my heart! Take your oar from me, I cannot row it anymore.

O boatman of my heart! Take your oar from me I cannot row it anymore.

All my life I rowed up the stream, could never find the downstream flow.

I cannot row it anymore.

O boatman of my heart! Take your oar from me, I cannot row it anymore.

The river of sorrow flows in the country of sorrow

Why do you cry for happiness and say hai! Hai!

I am as ill-fated and forgetful as you are.

I could never find the head or tail of happiness or sadness.

O boatman of my heart! Take your oar from me, I cannot row it anymore.

*

Amar bhaiyer rokte rangano ekushey February
Ami ki bhulite pari
Chhele hara shato mayer ashru goriye February
Ami ki bhulite pari
Amar sonar desher rangano ekushey February
Ami ki bhulite pari

Jaago naginira jaago naginira jago kalboshhekhira
Shishu hotyar bikshove aj kapuk busundara,
Desher shonar chhele khun kore rokhe manusher dabi
Din badoler krantilagne tobu tora par pabi?

Na, na, na, na khun ranga itihase shesh ray dewa taroi
Ekushey February ekushey February.

Sedino emoni nil gogoner bashone shiter sheshe
Rat jaaga chand chumo khaiyechhilo heshe;
Pathe pathe fote rojonigandha oloknanda jeno,
Emon somoy jhorh elo ek khepa buno.
Sei andharer poshuder mukh chena,
Tahader tore mayer, boner, bhaiyer charom grina
Ora guli chhore edesher prane desher dabike rokhe
Oder grinya padaghat ei sara Banglar buke
Ora edesher noy,
Desher bhagya ora kare bikroy
Ora manusher onno, shanti niyechhe kari
Ekushey February ekushey February.

Tumi aj jaago tumi aj jaago ekushe February
Ajo jalimer karagare more bir chheley, bir nari
Amar shaohid bhaiyer atta dakey
Jaago manusher supta shalti hate mathe ghate bate
Darun krodher agune abar jalbo February
Ekushey February ekushey February.

Can I forget the twenty-first of February
Incarnadined by the love of my brother?
The twenty-first of February, built by the tears
of a hundred mothers robbed of their sons,
Can I ever forget it?

Wake up all serpents,
wake up all summer thunder-storms,
Let the whole world rise up
In anger and protest against the massacre of innocent children.
They tried to crush the demands of the people
by murdering the golden sons of the land.
Can they get away with it
at this hour when the times are poised
for a radical change?

No, no, no, no,
In the history reddened by blood
the final verdict has been given already
by the twenty-first of February.

It was a smooth and pleasant night,
with the winter nearly gone
and the moon smiling in the blue sky
and lovely fragrant flowers blossoming on the roadside,
and all of a sudden rose a storm,
fierce like a wild horde of savage beasts.
Even in the darkness we know who those beasts were.
On them we shower the bitterest hatred
of all mothers brothers and sisters.
They fired at the soul of this land,
They tried to silence the demand of the people,
They kicked at the bosom of Bengal.
They did not belong to this country.
They wanted to sell away her good fortune.
They robbed the people of food, clothing and peace.
On them we shower our bitterest hatred.

Wake up today, the twenty-first of February.
do wake up, please.
Our heroic boys and girls still languish in the prisons of the tyrant.
The souls of my martyred brothers still cry.
But today everywhere the somnolent strength
of the people has begun to stir
and we shall set February ablaze
by the flame of our fierce anger.
How can I ever forget the twenty-first of February?

*

Nongor tolo tolo somoy je holo holo
Nongor tolo tolo somoy je holo holo nongor tolo tolo
Nongor tolo tolo somoy je holo holo nongor tolo tolo
Nongor tolo tolo somoy je holo nongor tolo tolo

Hawar buke noukar paal
joware vasie dao

Sokto muthir badone badone
Borjobadhia nao
Borjobadhia nao borjobadhia nao

Somukhe ebar dristi tomar
Pechoner kotha vulo
Pechoner kotha vulo
Pechoner kotha vulo
Pechoner kotha vulo

Nongor tolo tolo somoy je holo nongor tolo tolo

Dur digante surjo dake
Dristi rekesho sthir
Sobuj asar sopnera aaj
Noyone koreche veer
Noyone koreche veer
Noyone koreche veer

Ridoye tomar muktir alo
Alor duar kholo
Alor duar kholo
Alor duar khulo
Alor duar kholo.

Take up the anchor, it's time
Take up the anchor, it's time
Take up the anchor, it's time
Take up the anchor, it's time

Sail the boat through the wind
at high tide.

Make the knot tight with strong grips.
Make the knot tight.
Make the knot tight

Now look ahead of you,
Don't look back, forget about the past.
Forget about the past
Forget about the past
Forget about the past
Forget about the past

Take up the anchor, it's time.

You keep your gaze on the sun of the sky
Your eyes are filled with dreams
Filled with dreams.
Filled with dreams.
Filled with dreams.

Your heart is filled with dreams of freedom
Open the door to freedom
Open the door to freedom
Open the door to freedom.
Open the door to freedom.

*

Borgi elo deshe
Bulbuli-te dhan kheyeche
Kkhajna debo kishe
Bulbuls have eaten the grains.
Aai aai chad mama
Aai aai chad mama tip die ja
Chader kopale chad tip die ja
Dhan banle kuro debo
Mach katle muro debo
Kalo gaer dudh debo
Dudh khabar bati debo
Chader kopale chad tip die ja

Come, come, Uncle Moon, put a bindi on his brow.
My own moon-child wants a bindi on his brow.
when I winnow paddy, the rice grains will be yours;

when I slice a fish, its head will be yours;
when the cow gives birth, the calf will be yours;
when the black cow gives milk, it will be yours;
and a dish to drink the milk will be yours.
My own moon-child wants a bindi on his brow.

*

Khoka ghumalo, para juralo
Khoka ghumalo, para juralo

Borgi elo deshe
Bulbuli-te dhan kheyeche
Khajna debo kishe
Dhan phuralo, pan phuralo
Khajnar upay ki!
Aar kota din shobur koro
Roshun bunechi.

When the children fall asleep, silence sets in
When the children fall asleep, silence sets in

The *bargis* come to our lands
Bulbuls have eaten the grains
How shall I pay the tax!

*

Amar shonar Bangla
Ami tomay bhalobashi
Chirodin tomar akash,
Tomar batash,
Amar prane bajae bāshi.

O ma,
Phagune tor amer bone
Ghrane pagol kôre,
Mori hay, hay re,
O ma,
Ôghrane tor bhôra khete
Ami ki dekhechhi modhur hashi.

Ma, tor mukher bani
Amar kane lage
Sudhar moto
Ma tor bodonkhani molin hole
ami noyon
O may ami noyonjole bhashi
Sonar bangla,
Ami tomay bhalobasi!

My beloved Bengal
My Bengal of gold,
I love you.
Forever your skies,
Your air set my heart in tune
As if it were a flute.

In spring, O mother mine,
The fragrance from your mango groves
Makes me wild with joy,
Ah, what a thrill!
In autumn, O mother mine,
In the full blossomed paddy fields
I have seen spread all over sweet smiles.

Oh mother mine, words from your lips
Are like nectar to my ears.
Ah, what a thrill!
If sadness, O mother mine,
Casts a gloom on your face,
My eyes are filled with tears!
My Bengal of gold
I love you!

*

Fande poriya boga kande re
Fand bosaiche fandi re bhai puti machh diya,
Ore macher lobhe boka boga pore ural diya re.

Fande poriya re boga kore tanatuna
Ore aha-re konkurar shuta holu noa-ar guna re.

Fande poriya re boga kore hai re hai,
Ore darun bidhi, sathi chhaira jay re.

Aar boga ahar kore ashe aro pashe
Aar amar boga ahar kore dholla nodir pare re.

Ooriya jai re chokoya ponkhi bogik bole thare,
Ore tomar boga bondi hoiche dholla nodir pare re.
Ei kotha shuniya re bogi dui pakha melilo
Ore dholla nodir pare jaiya doroshon dilo re.

Baga ke dekhiya bogi kandere,
Bogi ke dekhiya boga kandere.

The heron cried as it got trapped,
The trap was baited with a tiny fish.
The greedy heron flew to the trap seeing the fish.

The heron struggled to get free from the trap
The trap had countless iron hoops.

The heron regrets sitting on the trap
What a fate! His companion left him too.

The other birds came and fed around him
But alas! My heron came to feed on the bank of the Dholla.

A chokha flew off with the bad news
Your mate is trapped by the Dholla river.

Hearing this, his hen spread her two wings.
She flew to the bank of the Dholla to see the heron.

The hen cried and cried seeing the heron.
The heron also cried seeing the hen.

*

Nadir kul nai kinara nai re
O ami kon kul hote kon kule jabo
Kahare sudhai re

Opare megher ghata kanak bijuli chhata
Majhe nadi bahe sai sai re
Ami ai horilam sonar chhabi
Abar dekhi nai re.

The river has no bank, no shore
Which bank shall I leave, to which shall I go?
From whom this shall I know?
The cloud on the other bank, is painted fiery gold,
The rain-swollen river speeds on.
I see a golden picture, I see it no more.

*

Kandiya aakul hoilam bhabo-nodir pare
Mon tore ke ba par kore!
Su-samay-e din guwaiya
Asamay-e, mon, asamay-e
Ailam nodir pare;
Majhi tor nam janina,
Ami dak demu kare?
Mon tore ke ba par kore!
Nao ase, kheoani nai re
Manush nai re pare;
Majhi tor nam janina,
Ami dak demu kare?
Mon tore ke ba par kore!

Wasting my time all these days,
I've now come to the river bank at the wrong time
I don't know your name, O boatman,
Who shall I call for?
Who'll row me across?
The boat is here,
but there's no boatman,
There's nobody on the bank
I don't know your name, O boatman,
Who shall I call for?

Glossary

Akika or naamkoron: naming ceremony

Alhamdullilah: Praise be to Allah

Allah Yerhamo: 'May God have mercy of his/her soul,' Arabic expression used when someone dies

Amra: hog plum (*Spondias dulcis*)

Anchol: the sari's end piece

Anna: currency unit formerly used in India, equal to 1/16 rupee

Asharh: the third month of the Bengali calendar, corresponding to June-July

Ashvind: the sixth month of the Bengali calendar, corresponding to September-October

Ayah: maid or nanny

Baba: father

Babui: baya weaver bird

Bangali Kutta Bhag Gia: the Bengali dogs have flown (abuse in Urdu)

Barui: farmer

Batashi: small fish (*Neotropius acutirostris*)

Batul: tiny toy made of wood and rubber band used to hit birds

Bauls: mystic mendicant, associated with devotional songs known as Baul songs

Beel: marshland or swampland

Begun or brinjal: eggplant or aubergine

Bengali calendar: Boishakh, Joishtho, Asharh, Srabon, Bhadro, Ashvind (Ashwind), Kartik, Ogrohayon, Poush, Magh, Falgun, Choitro (Bôshonto: spring, Grishsho: summer, Bôrsha: the rainy monsoon, shôrot: autumn, Hemonto: the dry season, Sit: winter)

Betel nut: areca nut or seed of the areca palm. It is chewed wrapped in betel leaves with lime for paan

Betel quid or paan: mild stimulant from the Areca palm leaf (*Areca catechu*)

Bhadro: the fifth month of the Bengali calendar, corresponding to August-September

Bhagoban: Hindu term for God

Bhai / Bhaiyya: common address to a younger brother or friend (Dada is used for an older brother)

Bhalo nam: legal name, literally good name, as opposed to dak nam, the pet name

Bhaluk: bear

Bhasha Andolon: Bangla Language movement

Bhati(y)ali: traditional boatmen folksongs (from bhati, meaning low lying areas, flooded during the monsoon)

Bhuna: curry

Bidi or beedi: thin cigarette filled with tobacco wisps and wrapped in a tendu leaf tied with a string at one end

Bidiyy: departure from the bride's home

Bie: Muslim wedding

Bismillah: in the name of God, first part of the Basmala phrase in the Qu'ran

Boishakh: the first month of the Bengali calendar, corresponding to April-May

Borhani: a yoghurt-based drink

Borof pani: playground game (literally ice-and-water)

Boroi: Indian jujube tree

Boroj: betel grove

Bouchi: team game consisting in rescuing or defending the 'bou' or bride

Bouma: address to one's daughter-in-law

Bubu: elder sister

Chhoa chhui: form of tag

Chika mara: subversive graffiti

Chil: vulture

Chochchori: shallow fry mix of vegetables with onions, mustard oil and spices

Choitro: the twelfth month of the Bengali calendar, corresponding to March-April

Chom chom: popular Bangladeshi sweets

Chota bhai: little brother or junior

Chutiya ka bheja ghas khane gaya hai: literally 'the idiot's brain has gone to eat grass,' to compare someone to a stupid ruminant animal

Ciburi: popular team tag-like game

Dal: lentils

Dangguli: boy's game, akin to cricket

Dariabandha: popular catch-me-as you-can team game

Deuya or dheu: monkey jack (*Artocarpus lacucha*), also known as lakoocha, badhal, dahe, lakuch

Devdaru: also known as asok and ashoka, the 'sorrow-less' sacred tree (*Saraca asoca*)

Dham: holy place in the Hindu religion (ashram)

Dheki: foot-operated rice grinder

Dhol: double-headed drum; someone who plays the dhol is known as dholi

Doel / doyel: oriental magpie robin (*Copsychus saularis*) and the national bird of Bangladesh

Dotara or dotar: a two or four or sometimes five stringed lute-like instrument (Persian doutar)

Dushto: naughty

Ekka dokka: hopscotch

Ektara: one-stringed instrument plucked with one finger

Falgun: the eleventh month of the Bengali calendar, corresponding to February-March

Gamcha: towel

Gaye holud: wedding celebration

Gila: turmeric

Ghotok: traditional matchmaker

Ghughu: spotted dove

Griho korta: custodian or head of the family

Gulab jamun: popular Bangladeshi sweets

Gulti: sling

Haor: extensive marshes

Hôrtal or hartal: form of mass protest in Southeast Asia involving a total shutdown of workplaces, offices, shops, courts of law as a form of civil disobedience

Hash: duck

Helencha: wetland plant species like watercress (*Enhydra flactuans*)

Hookah, hukkâ or huqqah: an oriental tobacco pipe with a long, flexible tube which draws smoke through water contained in a bowl.

Izzat: male-centred concept of honor prevalent in South-Asian culture

Jaggery: unrefined sugar made from palm sap

Jaldi: quick

Jamrool: wax apple tree / water apple tree (*Syzygium Samarangense*)

Jannat: paradise

Joi Bangla: Victory to Bengal, rallying cry of the resistance and freedom movement

Joishtho: the second month of the Bengali calendar, corresponding to May-June

Jook: leech

Kaak narua: scarecrow

Kabad(d)i: popular Asian sport akin to team tag or cops and robbers

Kachki or kechhki: yellowtail mullet (*Sicamugil cascasia*)

Kachon Punti: Bangladeshi rosy barb fish (*Puntius conchonius*)

Kaf(f)ir: infidel or non-believer

Kaka or chacha: Uncle

Kalo jam: popular Bangladeshi sweets

Kanamachhi: a kind of blindman's buff

Kaporer putul: traditional rag doll

Kartik: the seventh month of the Bengali calendar, corresponding to October-November

Katla or katol carp: Indian carp (*catla catla*)

Khaal: canal

Khala: auntie

Kantha: embroidered quilt

Khelna pheriwallah: ambulant vendor

Kharap: evil or bad

Kheer: traditional rice pudding offered to the bride and bridegroom

Kismet: Arabic term for fate, destiny

Kochuripana: water hyacinth (*Eichhornia crassipes*)

Koroi: silk tree (*albizia odoratissima*)

Kukur: dog

Kulkhani: Muslim funeral ceremony

Kumeer: crocodile

Kutkut: form of hopscotch

Kuttir baccha: son of a bitch

Kutum Paki: also known as harichacha, Indian rufous treepie, (*Dendrocitta vagabunda*)

Langta kuttar baccha: naked son of a dog

Latakan: lipstick tree (*Bixa orellana*)

Lungi: traditional tubular shaped garment worn by Bangladeshi men around the waist with a twist knot

Maa: mother

Maankochu: arum

Machranga: kingfisher

Magh: the tenth month of the Bengali calendar year, corresponding to January-February

Magoor: walking catfish (*Clarias batrachus* or *gariepinus*)

Makorsha: spider

Mashallah: Arabic phrase 'what God wills, happens' used to express amazement and the equivalent of 'wow'.

Maulana: mullah

Mehedi: henna

Mela: fair or festival

Moner manush: soulmate and ideal being of the Baul and Sufi mystics

Moori: puffed rice

Moyoor: peacock

Mrigel or mrigal: fish native to the Ganges and Brahmaputra (*Cirrhinus cirrhosus*)

Mukti Bahini: freedom fighters or Liberation Army, the Bengali guerillas operating from within East Pakistan and camps in India

Muktijuddho: the 1971 Liberation War

Nadi / Nodi: river (feminine)

Namaaz-e-Janaza: or Namaaz-e-Wahshat: the Islamic funeral ceremony

Nanee: Maternal grandmother

Neem or nim: Indian Lilac (*Azadirachta indica*), a Sacred Tree used in Ayurveda

Nikah: Muslim marriage contract

Ogrohayon: the eighth month of the Bengali calendar, corresponding to November-December

Pagol: fool or foolish

Paijam: (mota chal) coarse rice used for cooking

Pakistan Zindabad: 'Long Live Pakistan,' slogan of the Muslim League during Partition

Pati k(a)ak: house crow

Pati lebur sharbat: homemade lemonade

Patka machh: puffer fish, a poisonous balloon-shaped fish (*Chelonodon fluviatilis*)

Peyajkoli: spring onions

Poush: ninth month of the Bengali calendar year, corresponding to December-January

Pranchamkani: beautiful jungle babbler hiding in trees

Projapoti: butterfly

Pukur: pond

Puli pithe: dumplings with half-moon, crescent or sun shapes and date and coconut jaggery filling

Putul biye: game of dolls' wedding

Raka: prescribed movements and words followed by Muslims while offering prayers to Allah. It also refers to a single unit of Islamic prayers

Rani: queen

Razakar: collaborators of the Pakistani army from Jamaat-e-Islami, Islami Chhatro Sango and military outfits like Al-Badr and Al-Shams

Rôshogolla: popular Bangladeshi sweets

Rui or rohu: type of carp (*labeo rohita*).

Salaam alaykum: Arabic greeting used by Muslims meaning 'peace be upon you' (The response is 'Wa'alaykum assalaam')

Shabash: bravo

Shalik: Pied Myna or Asian Pied Starling (*Sturnus contra*)

Shapla: a pink or white water lily (*Nymphaea Nouchali*) and a national icon of Bangladesh

Shatchara: team game requiring a brick, a tennis ball and stones or small pieces of bricks

Shialmutha: plant used in folk medicine for its antiseptic and healing properties

Shimul Ful / Shimul Tular Gash: silk cotton tree (*Bombaxceiba*)

Shissay: disciple

Shokun: dragon-like bird

S(h)omeswari: major river in the Garo Hills of the Meghalaya and Netrakona Districts of Bangladesh

S(h)onali: golden eagle

Shondesh: popular Bangladeshi sweets; Pranaharaor (heart's thief) is a simple type of shôndesh sweet from the Dhaka area

Shorpu(n)ti: Bangladeshi olive barb (*Puntius sarana*)

Shoshurbaari: father-in-law's house

Sindoor: traditional red or vermilion powder, worn by Hindu married women along the parting of their hair

Singhi: airsac catfish (*Heteropneustes fossilis*)

Soi: term of endearment

Sojna, sojne or sajna: drumstick tree (*Moringa oleifera*)

Srabon: the fourth month of the Bengali calendar, corresponding to July-August

Subji or sabzi: vegetable curry

Sura: verse from the Qu'ran

Tabiz: amulets given by fakirs and shamans in rural Bangladesh, to ward off bhut or evil spirits

Taluqdars or talukdars: land holders and middlemen with tax collecting power and a high social status

Teer dhonuk: bows and arrows

Te(n)tool or te(n)tul: tamarind (*Tamarindus indica*)

Tora ke?: Who is it?

Tumio ekta manush, telapokao ekta pakhi: If you're a human being, then cockroaches are birds

Walima: festival celebrating the arrival of the bride into the groom's family

Wallah: Indian suffix indicating a person involved in some kind of activity, like chai-wallah, a boy or young man who serves tea

Yama: messenger sent by God to snatch away souls

Zamindari: system of feudal ownership

Acknowledgements

The epigraph by Rabindranath Tagore is taken from his poem 'Gift', translated by William Radice. Grateful acknowledgement is made to Penguin, for permission to quote from *Rabindranath Tagore Selected Poems* (1985).

I owe a debt of gratitude to many people for this book, a project that has travelled with me for a long while. I would like to thank Meenakshi Singh, Rights and Contracts Manager at Rupa for her enthusiastic support for the book from its inception. I would also like to thank the diligent team at Rupa, Dharini Bhaskar and Ishita Bal, who were instrumental in moving the book forward. A special thanks to Ishita for her perceptive edits and thought-provoking insights.

I am further obliged to Romesh Gunesekera whose feedback was highly valued.

Deep gratitude is expressed to Jackie Kabir, my translator and Dr Pascal Zinck, my editor, who shared the journey with me through winds and tides and helped me enrich the book without ever losing its essence.